A Taste for More

Other Books by Phyllis R. Dixon

Intermission

Down Home Blues

Forty Acres

A Taste for More

Phyllis R. Dixon

www.kensingtonbooks.com

DAFINA BOOKS are published by

Kensington Publishing Corp.
900 Third Avenue
New York, NY 10022

All Kensington titles, imprints, and distributed lines are available at special quantity discounts for bulk purchases for sales promotion, premiums, fund-raising, and educational or institutional use.

Special book excerpts or customized printings can also be created to fit specific needs. For details, write or phone the office of the Kensington Sales Manager: Kensington Publishing Corp., 900 Third Avenue, New York, NY 10022. Attn. Sales Department. Phone: 1-800-221-2647.

DAFINA and the DAFINA logo Reg US Pat. & TM Off.

ISBN: 978-1-4967-4313-8
First Trade Paperback Printing: July 2024

ISBN: 978-1-4967-4314-5 (e-book)

10 9 8 7 6 5 4 3 2 1

Printed in the United States of America

For my mother, the best person I know.

Acknowledgments

Writing a book and getting it published is a lot of work, but it doesn't feel like work because so many people have assisted and encouraged me. In the words of my favorite gospel singer, Daryl Coley, *I just can't tell it all.* I will name a few and start by thanking my Kensington team, particularly Michelle Addo and Leticia Gomez, for all their support. A special thanks to Nicole Baskin, Anita Bunkley, Janis Kearney, and my agent, Marlene Stringer, for their assistance.

I'm blessed to be surrounded by individuals who have cheered me on for many years: Tanya Beckley, Tujuana Britton, Sheryl Dean, Clarence Hale, Arlender Jones, Jackie Miller, Mary Randolph, Juel Richardson, my Elite Literary Book Club sisters, my sorors of Delta Sigma Theta Sorority, Inc. and my St. Andrew A.M.E. Church family. I don't take their support for granted. Thanks to Crystal Maddox and Sharon Williams, for being relentless boosters, and to Betty Washington and Patricia Montgomery for help with the recipes. I must acknowledge Michael Stewart for being a steady force in my life and for being a willing taste tester. I appreciate my children, Trey, Candace, and Lee who make me proud and inspire me. I'm not playing favorites, but I must express my gratitude to Candace. Who knew that the little girl I taught to read, would grow up to become one of my best editors?

As always, I am eternally grateful to my mother, Maggie Jackson Hale, for everything! And I thank you, the reader, for spending time with my characters. I hope you find it time well spent.

. . .forsake not the teachings of your mother.
—Proverbs 1:8

PROLOGUE

As Margo blew on her hands in a futile attempt to keep warm, she noticed the discolored indentation on her finger, where her wedding rings had been. She stuffed her hands under her armpits and shivered as cold, damp air gripped her bones. She was always cold. The doctors said it was a symptom of her anemia, one of the reasons she'd had trouble carrying babies to full term. Four pregnancies had yielded only one daughter—her precious Lana.

Less than a week ago, Lana and her fiancé, along with Margo and her husband, were basking in the radiant sun, celebrating Christmas in a Key West time-share, thankful they were missing record-breaking frigid temperatures back home in Milwaukee. Margo was loving the fresh seafood and had discovered meal ideas she could add to her restaurant's menu. Lana was embarrassed whenever her mother asked a restaurant manager if she could visit the kitchen, something she did when visiting an out-of-town restaurant. But it was those new ideas and recipes that kept people coming to her Fourth Street Café, sometimes in droves.

Margo tried to visualize herself sitting on the deck, enjoying a balmy ocean breeze, but that TV psychobabble wasn't working. She could visualize all she wanted; she was still cold. After two hours of shivering, Margo asked them to turn up the heat, but was told, "This isn't a hotel. You're in jail."

She checked her wrist for the time, but then remembered the guards had taken her watch, wedding rings, and the Cartier bracelet her husband had just given her for Christmas. She'd heard cheering a while ago and assumed it was past midnight. This wasn't how she had planned to spend the last moments of 1978. Some happy New Year this turned out to be.

She'd read articles and books that criticized solitary confinement as cruel and inhumane punishment. But right now, that seemed preferable to being packed in with three other women in a musty, six-by-eight-foot concrete box, designed for two. Margo's body betrayed her and even though she had vowed not to close her eyes in this germ-infested space that smelled like funk, urine, and saturated sanitary napkins, she'd leaned back on the hard surface that was supposed to be a bed and dozed off. She was startled awake when she heard the guard shouting her name. "Caldonia Margaret Dupree, are you deaf? I said, Come with me."

Margo threw off the scratchy blanket and followed the guard down a hall of packed cells, finally exhaling when she heard the heavy door slam behind them. The guard ushered her into a small room, where she was relieved to see George Parker, her lawyer.

"What in the world happened?" George asked, as he handed her an envelope stuffed with her belongings. "I thought you were going straight home when you left my office yesterday."

"I had some business to take care of."

"I told you to let me handle things."

"You can still handle things," Margo said.

"You're going to need more help than I can give. Meet Jill Shelton," he said, motioning to the woman standing next to him. "She's my new partner and she practices criminal law."

"Whatever you say. When can I get out of here? I need to find Lana."

"We're waiting for them to bring the release papers," George said.

"You told the police you killed your husband," Attorney Shelton said.

"I did and I'm not sorry," Margo replied, as she put on her watch and bracelet.

"As your attorney, I'm advising you not to make any more statements without representation present. This isn't a good situation."

"In the words of Moms Mabley, 'He's dead. That's good.'"

"And how does Lana fit into this?" George asked.

"She doesn't."

"The police questioned her," George said. "She told the police *she* killed your husband, then posted bail. That's how I got you released."

"That's ridiculous. She's trying to protect me."

"How do I know you're not trying to protect her?" George asked.

"Please tell us what happened," Attorney Shelton said as she pulled a tape recorder from her briefcase.

"Well, I closed the café early for New Year's Eve and was about to—"

"No, I mean start at the beginning."

PART I

AN ACQUIRED TASTE

CHAPTER I

Mama told me not to come here. But it was 1961 and I'd already had enough of Mississippi. Historians might say I was part of the Great Migration of Negroes who left the South fleeing racist violence, segregation, and poverty. *Migration* sounds natural and peaceful, but it doesn't reflect the appropriate level of desperation and persecution. *Great escape* is more like it.

I grew up just outside Price, Mississippi. I was the youngest of five, the first born in a hospital, and first to graduate high school. Segregation and discrimination were prevalent, but I stayed on our side of the tracks, oblivious, in the warm cocoon my parents provided.

The first crack in that cocoon occurred when I was fourteen. My beloved daddy died. He was a World War I veteran who had met Mama at a church social. They married, bought land, raised cotton and children. I was much younger than my siblings and was basically raised as an only child. My siblings tell stories of picking cotton, World War II ration books, and riding to town in Granddaddy's wagon. I never had to pick cotton or leave school during planting or harvest time.

When I turned thirteen, we moved into a four-bedroom

house Daddy was building, with indoor plumbing, electricity, and a wraparound porch. Mama complained the new citified stove didn't bake as well as her old woodstove. But I didn't miss toting firewood every day. I loved peering in the oven window to watch her biscuits and cakes rise. And, not having to go outside to the bathroom seemed life-changing. I remember getting a spanking for flushing and re-flushing the toilet. Unfortunately, Daddy didn't get to finish the house. Ten months after we moved in, he died in a car accident. Mama couldn't finish the house and didn't have money to pay farmworkers. My brothers lived in Memphis and offered to help. But Mama knew they weren't interested in farming and didn't want to return to Price. She reluctantly sold the farm, but after paying off the contract on the house, there wasn't much left. They say those white men cheated her out of the property, but there wasn't anything she could do about it. Even though she had never worked outside our home, she got a job as a domestic and we moved to a two-bedroom, shotgun house, closer to the railroad tracks in Price. At the time, I didn't realize how much Mama was struggling. I liked living closer to town and she brought home food we never had at home, like stuffed bell peppers, crepes, and store-bought bread.

My daddy was what some folks derisively called "blue-black." To him, this wasn't an insult. He said that meant our blood was pure and not spoiled by a white master. Daddy was black and proud before James Brown proclaimed it. He adoringly called me his Hershey's kiss, but in 1950s Mississippi, no one else complimented my mahogany brown skin, except Jesse, my first boyfriend. I was overjoyed that this popular boy with golden brown, cornbread-colored skin was interested in flat-chested, chocolate me.

Jesse Neal and I were high school sweethearts and my career goal was to be Mrs. Neal, have babies, and live happily ever after. He was a year ahead of me and we did everything together. He was on the track team and I was his biggest cheerleader. After he graduated, he started working at the paper mill, but within weeks, he was drafted. I was devastated, mostly because he wouldn't be home for my senior prom. But Mama was relieved. She didn't dislike Jesse, but she had plans for my life. "You got a letter from the colored college in Memphis, and with your grades, they'll offer you a scholarship. You can stay with one of your brothers. Nothing to do around here but have babies and keep house." I didn't say anything, but that was exactly what I wanted to do.

Mama gave me a beautiful, leather-inscribed Bible for graduation and a pair of white gloves. But the present I adored most was a sterling silver-plated engagement ring from Jesse. He surprised me and came home on leave for my graduation. We got married the next day, then had a two-day honeymoon in Jackson. He returned to Fort Benning and I stayed with Mama. I got a job at the dry cleaners, but only worked two months before I had to quit. I was pregnant and had begun to miss a lot of days at work because the cleaning chemicals made me nauseous. I had morning sickness the entire pregnancy and none of Mama's remedies worked.

Jesse scheduled leave to coincide with my due date, but I delivered six weeks early. Ultrasounds weren't routine back then, and I didn't know I was carrying twins until I delivered two babies. Lana slid out first, announcing her arrival with a demanding wail. My baby boy was breech and his delivery was more difficult. His umbilical cord was knotted, reducing oxygen flow and blood. He was much smaller than Lana and needed to be in an incubator.

Having a Negro hospital was a big deal for Price County, but it wasn't equipped for complications with premature newborns, and my doctor wasn't allowed to practice at Price County Memorial, the white hospital. This was déjà vu for Mama, since my daddy died because Memorial, the hospital nearest the accident site, didn't accept Negro patients.

This time, Mama wasn't taking "no" for an answer. After several frantic phone calls from my doctor, our pastor, and Miss Miller, the white lady Mama worked for, Memorial agreed to make an exception and care for my baby, but they wouldn't send an ambulance to pick him up. After thirty hours of life, my baby boy died.

Mama took care of the burial, me and Lana, because for weeks I couldn't function. Seeing other baby boys made me cry and I did something I had never done before—I began to tell my mother "no." I refused to go to church because my son was buried in the cemetery behind the church. I didn't emerge from my funk until Lana was almost four months old. Mama was outside hanging diapers on the line, and I was inside with Lana. She woke from a quick nap, crying, and I went to pick her up. She was dry and full, so I bounced her, walked her, and patted her. When Mama entered the room, Lana stretched out her arms and quieted as soon as Mama took her. Lana's rejection stung, but I could only blame myself. It was time to embrace my role as mother to my healthy, butterscotch-colored angel.

Mama kept telling me about families looking for help, hinting I should find a job. I told her, "I didn't graduate from high school just to work in some white woman's kitchen."

"You think you're too good to do what I do, what my mother and grandmother did?" she asked. "Your daddy took good care of us. But when he died, I had to take care of you, so I did what I know. Thanks to God, and me working in a white woman's kitchen, you never went without."

"I know, Mama, but isn't each generation supposed to do better than the one before? I believe I can do better than the lane white folks want me to stay in. I feel stagnant and I want something different."

"Different isn't always better."

"Yes, ma'am." I said yes, ma'am, but the only kitchen I planned to work in was my own. I saved the money Jesse sent and helped Mama make and sell her cakes, pies, and biscuits, while counting the days until my husband returned.

When he was discharged, I was ready to resume our path to happily ever after. I found a house, paid rent three months in advance, and Jesse was rehired at the paper mill. Things should've been on track, but Price didn't hold the same appeal. The fun-loving boyfriend who left for basic training wasn't the same man who returned from Okinawa. He had changed, or maybe I had. The Price that I had grown up in had felt safe and carefree. But I was outgrowing my youthful blinders. I clearly remember the first time I mentioned leaving.

"Jesse, is that you?" I said when I heard steps on the porch.

"Yeah. You got another man coming over here?"

"Of course not," I answered. "I didn't expect you home this early. Did they cut your hours again?"

"Yep. Cut 'em to zero," Jesse said as he grabbed a beer from the icebox.

"Not again. Did they say how long the layoff would be?"

"How does forever sound? They're closing and moving production to Mexico."

"Can they do that?" I asked.

"These white folks can do whatever they want."

"I read in the paper that A and P is hiring stockers. If you hurry, you can get there before their offices close."

"Damn. I haven't even been out of work an hour. Is it okay with you if I go tomorrow?"

"Everybody else who got laid off will be going over there. If you wait, you might miss—"

"I said I'll go tomorrow," Jesse said. "What's in these bags?"

"I went to McRae's and bought Lana new shoes, after I delivered peach pies to the American Legion."

"These bags look like more than a pair of shoes. Didn't

you just buy shoes? She's barely two, how many does she need?"

"Lana's growing so fast. It's important for her posture for her to wear proper fitting shoes."

"Your sister brought you boxes of baby clothes and shoes. None of those fit?" Jesse asked as he opened another beer bottle.

"Hand-me-down clothes are okay, but not shoes. Her bones are still forming and used shoes can damage her feet. One three-dollar pair of shoes won't break us. I did two wedding cakes last week and used that money."

"Rub it in that I don't make enough money."

"That's not what I meant."

"Then what did you mean?"

"I'm not arguing with you. Maybe if you weren't inhaling so many beers, you could make some extra money."

I may as well have been talking to the floor. Jesse grabbed his keys, another beer, and left. The next day, I applied for the A&P stocker job.

"This is a man's job," the manager told me.

"If I can do the job, what difference does it make?"

"You know this is a night job?"

"Yes, sir. That's why it's perfect. With a night job, I won't need a babysitter."

"I'll hire you, but I'm not going to make any special allowances," he said. Mama didn't like it. She said all that lifting would keep me from having more babies. But it didn't seem any more strenuous than lifting baskets of wet laundry or bringing in firewood. I was the first female stocker in Price County, but there were daily reminders that others didn't think I belonged.

The stockers entered through the back door. I thought that was because it was closest to the stockrooms. One day I worked past the end of my shift and exited through the store.

Judging by the customers' facial expressions, you would've thought I was Adolf Hitler. My manager rushed to my side as I crossed the parking lot and with his finger pointed in my face, said, "If you want to keep working here, don't ever use that door again. You know the colored door is in the back." He was standing so close spit was sprinkling my chin. Then in a lower voice he said, "I like you. I hope you aren't turning into a troublemaker."

I was just trying to hurry home. I had the car and Jesse needed it to get to work. I apologized and rushed home, more concerned about the trouble that would be waiting for me if I didn't get the car back, than some stupid whites-only rule.

Another day, I filled in when the bakery was short-handed. A customer saw me frosting a cake and told the manager, "I don't want that nigger handling my food." These were the daily slights that stung like paper cuts. But one benefit of working at the A&P was I could get bruised produce, dented cans, surplus bread, and the Green Stamps customers tossed aside. Their goods were fresher and more varied than the items sold in the A&P on our side of the tracks. Our pantry and Mama's chest freezer were full. Jesse claimed he only liked fresh vegetables and wasn't eating canned food. But by the time I doctored up those cans with onions, peppers, smoked meats, and celery, he didn't know the difference.

However, even with the extra groceries, Jesse still complained. "I don't like you working this late," he said one night, after I had put Lana to bed.

"I thought this was convenient so when you return to work, we won't have to make any adjustments. It's not like there are tons of jobs around here. And did you call the landlord about the roof?" I asked, as I emptied one of three buckets in the kitchen catching water from the leaking roof.

"He said he'll send someone over. I reminded him about the porch step too. We pay him good money. Maybe we should consider moving," Jesse said.

"Yes. Maybe we *should* consider moving, not just from this shack, but out of town. Aunt Lizzie said they're begging for workers in Milwaukee, and she's sure Uncle Max can get you on with him at Modern Metals. They're hiring colored welders now and paying good money."

"It's too cold up there. When I was stationed in Camp Drum in New York, I froze my behind off. They can have it."

"But there's much more opportunity. Nobody has a problem finding a job."

Mama's sister, Aunt Lizzie and her husband Max, had moved to Milwaukee two years ago, leaving Mama as the only member of her immediate family still in Mississippi. Their daughter Vanessa was my favorite cousin and she'd been despondent about the move right before her senior year. We wrote letters and I kept her up to date on the happenings at Pettus High. But it didn't take her long to get acclimated to her new home and shortly after they moved, she got pregnant. She didn't graduate, but she still found a job making more than she would have in Price. She said there weren't any white and colored signs. Negroes could try on clothes in the store and didn't ride in the back of the bus unless we wanted to.

"Northern white folks aren't any different than these crackers around here. At least here, you know where you stand," Jesse said. "You make more money up there, but everything costs more, and you're no better off. Three and four families are crammed into houses meant for one. And remember, everybody had a job during slavery too. We're staying here."

"There are boycotts, new civil rights laws, and everyone is excited about what President Kennedy has promised to do for Negroes, but it seems like times are getting harder instead of easier," I said. "They just found that man in Yazoo County, castrated and mutilated, tossed on the roadside, and they pulled Mack Parker's body from the Pearl River after he was arrested and jailed on some bogus charge. Those cases didn't get publicity like Emmett Till, but things aren't any better."

"I won't be run off. My family's blood and sweat is in this county and I have a right to stay here as much as any white man. I wasn't crazy about Eisenhower, but he did sign the Civil Rights Act. Somebody's got to stay and make them live up to it."

"You may be willing to sacrifice your daughter's future on the *possibility* things will improve, but I'm not. I thought we were a team. Don't I get a say?" I demanded.

"A team has one captain, and I say, we're staying here," Jesse replied while leaning back in the chair with his hands behind his head. "You've never been north of Memphis. You're gullible and naive and wouldn't last a week with those slick jokers."

I hadn't abandoned the idea of moving, but Mother Nature made the decision for me. That fall, I got pregnant. I could barely keep food down and I stayed tired. But I thought a baby would motivate Jesse to do better, especially if it was a boy. However, six weeks later, I miscarried. I was relieved, and that was when I realized I wanted out of the marriage. When I went to pick up Lana from Mama's, I told her my concerns.

"You're tired?" she asked with a chuckle. "You ain't seen tired yet. Wait until—"

"That's my point, Mama. Is this as good as it gets? I'm stocking at the store at night and baking all day, but we're always short of money. Jesse had a good job at the lumber-yard, but got into it with his boss and got fired. He knows you can't talk to these white folks any kind of way."

"Don't he babysit most nights?" Mama asked.

"It's not babysitting if it's your own child. And he was off work yesterday. Why did he even bring Lana over here?"

"Don't be too hard on him. Colored men have it hard."

"And colored women don't?"

"That's the way it is, honey."

"Jesse didn't stay at the house last night. I got off work early and he wasn't home. This isn't the first time either."

"Men got their ways is all I can tell you. Unless he beating on you or drinking too much, Jesse ain't no worse than the rest of them."

"Daddy always took care of us, and he didn't mistreat you."

"These young fellas ain't like they was in your daddy's day," she said, shaking her head. "Try being more under-standing and supportive."

"And who's supporting me?"

"Pray and lean on God, baby. He's all the support you need."

"I know Jesse is as miserable as I am. I've suggested we move and get a fresh start. Aunt Lizzie says lots of places are hiring up there. He won't even consider it."

"If your husband doesn't want to go, that's the end of it."

"Why should I struggle because he doesn't want to try something different? I'm moving, and I need you to keep Lana until I get situated and come get her."

"I thought you said Jesse don't want to go."

"I'm going, with or without him."

"It's a cold, fast life up there, and I'm not talking about the weather. Lizzie and Max work fifteen jobs just to survive. Your daddy instilled an independent streak in you, but the reality is, it's not easy for a woman on her own."

"It can't be harder than it is right now."

"You probably just need a change for a little while. Go visit your sisters in Detroit. Lizzie wasn't in Wisconsin three months before Vanessa got pregnant. She can't watch her own daughter, how is she going to keep up with you?"

"Nobody needs to watch me, and I want more than a *little* change. Aunt Lizzie said I can stay with her and Uncle Max until I get settled. But if things are like she says they are, it shouldn't take me long to get a job and my own place."

"You're still grieving the loss of your baby. Don't make no quick decisions."

This wasn't a quick decision. I'd been considering leaving for months. This wasn't the first time Jesse stayed out all night. When I got in from work, I could tell he'd just gotten in too. But other than him disrupting Lana's routine, I didn't care anymore. My pregnancy scare crystallized what I was afraid to admit. Another kid would've chained me to him and Price, and I was trying to break free.

For the next three months, I worked extra hours at the store. I aggressively sought bakery orders, and my house constantly smelled like vanilla, cinnamon, or nutmeg. But when a tornado came through town, the A&P closed. We had a few trees fall, but most damage was across the tracks. My white coworkers received unemployment checks, but when I went to apply, I was told I didn't qualify. With the rebuilding, Jesse found construction work, but I never knew when or if he was going to give me money. With my job on hold and my baking customers also rebuilding, I decided this was the time to leave. Otherwise, I was going to deplete my savings.

I'd written to Aunt Lizzie and told her when I was arriving. Vanessa's letters said she couldn't wait, and talked about the fun we were going to have. But I wasn't going there for fun. In the days leading up to my getaway, I took my things and Lana's little by little to Mama's house. Each time she tried to talk me out of moving, but eventually gave up and said, "It's a mistake, but every tub got to sit on its own bottom."

On the first Friday in January, Mama drove me to the Greenwood train station while Jesse was at work. Sitting in the colored section, we heard the announcement that the train was arriving. "It's not too late to change your mind," she said as the train approached.

"Don't worry. I know what I'm doing," I assured her.

"And you got your money pinned in your brassiere?"

"Yes, ma'am," I said with a smile.

We held hands while Mama prayed, then we moved toward the train. Mama hugged me and placed two rolled-up twenties in my hand. The blaring train horn and squeaky brakes startled Lana and she hugged my legs and began crying. I kissed the top of her head, then tightened the belt on my new coat, and turned my head so she wouldn't see my eyes watering.

"You take care of yourself," Mama said, as she picked Lana up.

"I will. And I'll be back for Lana in a couple months, September at the latest." Little did I know those months would turn into years.

CHAPTER 2

After riding for six hours, our third stop was Cairo, Illinois. Most of my fellow passengers were grabbing their suitcases. I assumed they were getting off, until someone told me we could now leave the Jim Crow car. I switched cars along with everyone else. I'd never been on a train and didn't know our car was inferior, until I entered the other one. Walking those twenty steps was like stepping into another world. The seats were upholstered and there was heat. There were luggage racks, and the bathrooms were larger and didn't smell bad. I reclined my seat, stretched out my legs and slept until dawn, when the train pulled into Chicago's Union Station.

I'd never been north of Memphis, and I was amazed by the tall buildings. The next amazing thing—when I switched to the Milwaukee train—was that black and white passengers stood in the same line and the white porter took my suitcase and helped me onto the train. I couldn't wait to write Mama and tell her about it.

The sun was up and I could see the snow-covered ground. Outside the city, the landscape looked like the fields back home when it was time to pick cotton. We finally pulled into the Milwaukee station, where there were more marvelous tall buildings. The train was delayed leaving Chicago, putting me in Milwaukee an hour later than scheduled. I found a pay phone and called Aunt Lizzie. She said she and Uncle Max had come to the station but couldn't wait once they found out the train would be late. Uncle Max had been called in to work and he didn't want to miss making time and a half. She was headed to work but recited explicit instructions on how to take the bus.

As soon as I stepped outside, I understood what Jesse had been talking about. It felt as though I had stepped onto another planet. The freezing weather didn't seem to be bothering anyone else, so I started walking, thinking movement would warm me up. It didn't. My eyes watered, my cheeks ached from the wind, and my suitcase got heavier with each step. The snow made a crunching sound as I walked between snowbanks that were nearly as tall as I was. And the air smelled like overripe fruit, an odor I'd later learn came from the breweries. My new twill jacket felt like a threadbare cotton bedsheet against the biting Lake Michigan wind, which whipped under my dress.

At the third corner, I saw the bus stop sign and waited. Standing still felt even worse than walking and I was relieved when I finally saw the Fourth Street bus. I sat in the front row since I wasn't required to go to the back. But every time the door opened an artic blast attacked my legs and I wished I'd sat in the back. These houses were so different, with blocks and blocks of huge structures, separated by narrow pathways. I didn't realize then that three or four families were living in each house. The ride was longer than Aunt Lizzie had said it would be, but I assumed the snow made the commute slower.

When we turned into a large parking lot, the bus driver said, "This is the last stop. I refuel, then pull back out in fifteen minutes."

I showed him the return address on my letter, and asked, "Sir, did I miss this address?"

"This isn't the right bus. You wanted the North Fourth Street bus. This is the South Fourth Street bus. I thought you were headed to work. You can stay on the bus."

Price had one set of numbered streets. I never considered there was a North and South Fourth Street. This time I went to the back of the bus, but it was still cold because the sun was setting. In about thirty minutes, we headed back downtown, then crossed to the north side. "You transfer here," he said, when we got to the corner of Fourth and Vine Street. "It's about ten minutes before your next bus comes."

I browsed a few minutes at the Sam's Shoes display window, then realized I had to use the restroom. I tried shifting from side to side, but I couldn't wait. Panda Palace was next to the shoe store, but it was closed. Then I saw the Fourth Street Café sign. I dashed into the café, as it was only a couple doors down.

"Hey, where are you going?"

I froze in my steps. I had heard places weren't segregated like they were down home, but maybe Jesse was right, and I had walked into a WHITES ONLY place. As I turned around, an older white man said, "Restrooms are only for customers."

"Sir, I'm in a hurry. What can I buy quickly?"

"You're from out of town?" he asked, looking at my suitcase. "Don't worry about it. Go ahead."

I rushed to the bathroom. As I washed my hands, I wanted to linger and let the warm water run over my stiff fingers, but I had no time to spare. I rushed back through the café dining room, just in time to see the bus pass by. *Now what was I going to do?*

I didn't realize I was hungry until I smelled the onions and coffee. A chunky white lady came toward me and said,

"It's Saturday. The next bus doesn't come for an hour. You might as well get something to eat. I'll seat you in a booth. Then you can put your suitcase in the empty seat. You want something hot to drink while you look at the menu?"

I was so shocked to have a white lady ask what I wanted, I barely mumbled my order. She brought me hot chocolate and I wrapped my hands around the cup until I could feel my fingers again. "I'm in a hurry. Can I get something quick, please?"

She brought me broccoli, a pork chop sandwich with fried potatoes and apple pie. It was a good thing I was hungry because the food was terrible. As I paid at the counter, the white man, who'd stopped me earlier, took my money and asked how I liked my meal. Since he asked, I told him. "Well, sir, the potatoes were on the greasy side; the broccoli must have been old because it had a strong smell, and the pork chop was dry and needed more seasoning. The apple pie was okay."

"You must be a cook," he said as he handed me my change.

"I *was* a cook. I just arrived from Mississippi."

"If you just arrived, you must be looking for a job. Gertie, my cook, is having a baby and can't work as many hours as she used to. I can use some help for a few months."

"No, thank you, sir, but if you have a pay phone, I'd like to use it."

"No pay phone, but you can use the phone next to the freezer."

I called Aunt Lizzie, but her line was busy. I grabbed my purse and suitcase, thanked the kind owner, and stepped back outside. Now that it was dark, the air was colder and the amber streetlight cast an odd glow on the street.

After about ten minutes, two young men joined me at the bus stop. I took this as a sign the bus was coming soon. One of them asked if I had change for a dollar for the bus.

When I opened my purse, he grabbed it and ran. The taller one grabbed my suitcase. He knocked me down and dragged me a few feet before the strap broke. I yelled, but the street seemed silent and deserted like an empty movie lot. My left heel broke, my right garter unsnapped, and my stocking fell to my ankles. My brand-new coat was also torn in the scuffle. I struggled to get up and then just stood there in a daze, too stunned to be scared and too cold to cry. Most of my money was in my bra, so I wasn't broke, but I did have a dilemma. Aunt Lizzie's address and phone number were in my purse. I didn't know either from memory, except that she lived on Ninth Street. I limped back to the Fourth Street Café, looking like Festus on *Gunsmoke*. Mama didn't have a phone and I refused to call Jesse. My plan was to call the long-distance operator and have them reach my brother in Memphis. He'd know Aunt Lizzie's address.

I made it back to the café, just as the white gentleman was turning off the OPEN sign. He unlocked the door and let me in.

"What happened? Are you all right?" he asked. "Where's your suitcase?"

"I was robbed. It happened so fast," I said, breathlessly.

"Should we call the police?"

"Unfortunately, a purse snatching won't elicit much of a police response. All they'll do is take a report, if that. Such a shame. I don't know what this city is coming to."

"I guess I was just introduced to the big city. Is that job still available?" I asked.

"Sure is."

"I'd like it."

"It's yours. I got a room upstairs you can rent too. Then you won't be standing on these dangerous bus stops alone."

"How much is it?"

"I'll let you stay the first month for free while you get yourself established. Then I'll take five dollars out of each paycheck, and you keep your tips. My name is Ben, by the way."

My mother named me Caldonia Margaret, but Caldonia sounded old-timey and Callie, which is what my family calls me, wasn't much better. I fell in love with the name Margo when I saw the movie *All About Eve*, and that's the name I selected for my new life.

"I'm Margo. When can I start, Mr. Ben?"

"Can you make biscuits?"

"Best you've ever tasted."

"Then you can start in the morning. We open at six o'clock, and there are extra aprons in the back. You can spend the night with my wife and I. She loves company."

"I hate to impose. If you don't mind me making a long-distance call, I can try to get my aunt's number."

"Nonsense. Nellie will be glad to talk to someone other than me, and she can tend to that nasty cut on your knee. Besides, it's hard to read addresses at night. We'll find your aunt tomorrow, after I taste those fantastic biscuits you've bragged about."

I followed him to the back door, amazed at the turn of events. In less than four hours, I had had a white person serve me, carry my bags, and invite me to their house. I had a new name, a job, and a place to stay.

I didn't come up north to be no cook, but I figured this would do until I found something better. His car was parked in a cobblestone alley that looked like a place for secret meetings in a gangster movie. I got in the passenger side, unaware this bleak alley would one day hold my secrets as well.

CHAPTER 3

What was supposed to be a temporary job became permanent when Gertie had to go on bedrest for the rest of her pregnancy and quit. Mr. Ben gave me her job and I officially became the first Negro to work on the block. The Fourth Street Café had a counter along the right side of the dining area with ten stools with battered red leather tops. The entire wall behind that counter was mirrored, so the café looked bigger than it actually was. There were seven booths situated along the left wall. Those seats were also covered with cracked red leather. Above the booths were framed, autographed pictures of celebrities and movie stars with local roots or who had eaten at the café, such as Liberace, Woody Herman, Golda Meir, Bart Starr, Les Paul, and Spencer Tracy, and a shelf of smaller pictures taken with his instant Polaroid camera. There was a table near the back door, where pinochle players met almost every morning. The floors were black-and-white checkerboard linoleum. Windows flanked the front door and were covered with red-and-white gingham patterned curtains. Two steps off the sidewalk led to a vestibule and the café entrance. A door with a sign that read Employees Only was opposite the front door. This door led to the restrooms, kitchen entrance, the alley door, and steps leading to upstairs rooms.

Business picked up as word spread about my cooking. I'm not bragging and I don't mean no harm against Gertie, but I don't know how she got hired as a cook in the first place. The kitchen was not equipped with any wooden utensils and the knives barely sliced butter. Cooking without the right tools is like building a house without a hammer. What really got me is that no paprika could be found anywhere in the kitchen. How anyone can cook and never use paprika is beyond me. I cut sandwiches diagonally to give the illusion that they looked bigger. I knew how to doctor up canned vegetables so they wouldn't taste so bland. And I missed drinking sweet tea. Up here they didn't serve iced tea in the winter, and it wasn't presweetened. I fixed a small batch, and Mr. Ben liked it so well he added it to the menu.

I couldn't believe the food Mr. Ben had been wasting. I showed him how to save chicken necks and backs to make bone broth for sauces and gravies. I shredded extra chicken breasts and made tortilla soup. Stale bread became bread pudding and French toast, and leftover cornbread became cornbread salad.

I learned a few things too. This was the dairy state and I was discovering why. There were cheeses I'd never heard of, and I quickly learned à la mode meant a scoop of custard, not ice cream. The Friday fish fry was a popular tradition and perch was the preferred catch of the day, instead of catfish, like at home. One of the most popular menu items was bratwurst, a grilled German sausage. They served it with German red cabbage. I'd seen red cabbage when I worked at the A&P, but had never eaten any. Steak tartare was the most expensive item on the menu. I thought that was because it was steak, but when Mr. Ben showed me how to prepare it, I learned it was raw ground beef and spices. He assured me it was safe to eat, but I declined to try it. We only offered it when he got a deal on sirloin, but I still wasn't interested. Another of his signature dishes was booyah stew. It was a slow-cooked chicken and beef stew with assorted vegetables, including rutabagas—a new vegetable to me. He would cook a huge kettle, then freeze in individual servings. Miss Nellie wasn't much of a cook, but she made a crab apple—also new to me—pie that was very tasty.

Mr. Ben said the steak tartare and booyah stew were "old country" recipes his grandfather brought from Germany. I was also quickly learning there were different types of white people. I had learned about Italians and Germans from my social studies and history classes. But in real life, white folks was white folks. Up here, there were Germans, Greeks, Irish, Italians, Polish, Russians, and people from countries I'd never heard of. They had their own neighborhoods and didn't always get along. But everyone was cordial to me. It took me a while to get used to white folks calling me "Miss" and having conversations with me. I got to know the regulars and sometimes, I didn't even have to take their order. I started cooking what I knew they wanted when I saw them come in. There was standing room only during brewery lunch hours and Mr. Ben had to hire another waitress.

But it wasn't just brewery traffic that picked up. I met Barbara and her husband at Aunt Lizzie's church and invited them to the café. Her husband Henry said he hadn't had sweet tea like mine since he'd left Alabama, and they too became regulars. Mr. Ben called him Hank and was as giddy as a schoolboy. It turns out Barbara's husband was the star player on the Braves baseball team, and he became the first Negro on Mr. Ben's wall of stars.

Soon the café served as many black customers as white and was busier than it had ever been. Mr. Ben added tables down the center aisle and even gave me a raise. And, since I lived upstairs Mr. Ben had me open the café, saying he was finally getting to sleep later.

Miss Yates, who owned the sewing shop next door, invited Mr. Ben to a meeting with some merchants on the block to discuss his increasing "colored" trade. I don't think he was a liberal or anything, but he said everybody's money was green.

Miss Yates wasn't the only person disturbed by my presence at the café. I overheard Bill Grabowski, one of Mr. Ben's roomers, complain to Mr. Ben that Fourth Street was going downhill and he didn't pay rent to live next to no "nigger." But Mr. Ben said he'd rent to whomever he pleased. The other roomer was a much nicer white man named Abe. He admitted that he liked me, and said I wasn't like most coloreds. I reciprocated by telling him I liked him too, and he wasn't like most white folks.

Someone else unhappy with my living arrangement was Mama. "You could've stayed here and done that," she said. "Thought you was too educated to be a cook. And Lizzie told me you were robbed. Lord have mercy! You could've been killed. What kind of neighborhood are you in?"

"This is temporary until I get settled. I have to learn my way around and see what's available," I explained to her. She left me alone when I told her what Mr. Ben was paying me.

"They pay you one dollar an hour? Miss Miller pays me a flat weekly rate, and I'm sure it's not close to one dollar an hour. That's a good law they got up there."

I didn't tell her it was a national law.

Mr. Ben let me use his phone a few minutes each week, so I called Mama on Tuesday afternoons when Miss Miller went to play bridge. If Miss Miller answered, I'd hang up. That was back in the day when it cost fifty-five cents a minute to talk long distance; therefore we didn't talk long.

But in those few minutes, Mama managed to tell me what new thing Lana was doing, what was going on at church, and who was cheating on who. She'd also inquire if I had met any nice young men, asked if I had joined a church, and if I'd found a new place to live yet.

Vanessa set me up on a few blind and double dates with her and her boyfriend Harper. The four of us went to see *West Side Story*. That was the first picture show (I mean *movie theater*; Vanessa told me *picture show* is country) I'd been to where we didn't have to sit upstairs. When I realized we could sit anywhere, I said to my date, "Let's sit on the front row." I had a crook in my neck for a week afterward and thought maybe the balcony had been the best seats after all.

Mama knew about my dates before I could even tell her. "I'm glad you're getting along up there, but you don't need to be living that close to no white men. It don't look right and Lizzie said there's no other colored working around there. I don't care how friendly they act or how much they pay you. It ain't safe for a single young lady. You can stay with Lizzie."

My attempts to assure her of my safety fell on deaf ears. I had a telephone installed in her house so she could call me whenever she wanted, and I could talk to Lana. But that didn't ease her worries. Mama was from a time when Jim Crow wasn't merely an inconvenience or an insult: it was life-threatening. And when I told her how nice everyone was, she said, "Those are the ones you got to watch out for."

Aunt Lizzie and Uncle Max came by the next day. "My sister will worry herself sick with you staying here. When you get off work today, we'll pick you up and move your stuff to our place. You can sleep in Vanessa's room." That evening, me, and my radio, two boxes of clothes, new sheets and chenille bedspread, were deposited in my new home at

Aunt Lizzie's. I wasn't happy about it, but at least I'd be able to save the money Mr. Ben was keeping out of my check. That meant I could get Lana even sooner.

Days were getting longer and the temperature was above freezing on most days, but it was still cold. The cold hadn't bothered me when I lived over the café, but now I had to catch the bus to work, and needed a heavier coat. Gertie had offered to give me one. She said it was practically new, but it had become snug on her before she got pregnant. It would definitely be too tight for her after she had the baby. Sometimes Mama brought home things "her lady" had given her to pass along to me. I was glad to receive them. But this wasn't Mississippi. I may have been a cook, but I was making more money than they were paying back home and now I could afford to buy new things. Instead of taking white folks' castoffs, I walked my proud self to Gimbels department store, not far from the café. The winter clothes were on sale because they already had Easter stuff on display. But even on sale, the price meant I would barely have enough left over for bus fare. I could've put the coat on layaway, but winter would be over by the time I finished paying on it. I had been wearing one of Aunt Lizzie's coats, but it was baggy on me. I wanted new clothes like those Aunt Lizzie and Vanessa had.

I selected a cobalt blue, double-breasted, cinch-waisted coat with a removable faux fur collar and took it to the register. The twenty-five-dollar price meant I'd have to stay with Aunt Lizzie longer, but I needed a coat. I also bought two pairs of pantyhose. Vanessa said garter belts were old-fashioned.

"Are these for you?" the salesclerk asked.

"Yes, ma'am," I said. (Some habits die hard.)

"Then you probably need a size ten. This looks too big for you. Here, try it on."

Another new experience for me—trying on clothes in

the department store! *Wait until I write Mama*, I thought. The salesclerk was right, I did need a smaller size. I had her put Aunt Lizzie's old coat in the bag and I wore my new coat out of the store. I was getting off my savings plan, but I looked good.

A few days later, I had another new experience—thunder snow. It began snowing around midnight. The bathroom light that Aunt Lizzie left on flickered a few times and we heard an occasional rumble of thunder. Lake Michigan did strange things to the weather, but I was glad to have an excuse to sleep in. I slept later than usual, enjoying the rarity of having the room to myself since Vanessa was gone.

"Ain't you working today?" Aunt Lizzie asked, as she knocked one time before entering.

"The snow is at least a foot deep," I said. "I'll miss the day in my paycheck, but I'm glad to have the time off."

"Child, these folks don't close down because of a little snow."

"A little snow?"

"Max sees money when he sees snow. He been out since midnight shoveling snow. If you hurry, you won't be too late."

Back home in Price, snow meant time off and we tried to gather enough to make ice cream. Up here, snow meant you left earlier for work. And sure enough, when I got to the café, Mr. Ben was taking orders and Donna, the new girl, was cooking orders one at a time. "I sure am glad to see you," Mr. Ben said. Turns out we were busier than usual in bad weather because people didn't have time to make their lunch. It amazed me how folks up here didn't let the weather stop them.

Then on Friday, Donna came to work wearing a cobalt blue, double-breasted, cinch-waisted coat with a removable faux fur collar.

"I must be overpaying you girls," Mr. Ben said. "You're both wearing new coats."

"Mine isn't new. I got this from Gertie," Donna said.

I was stunned. I didn't know white folks wore hand-me-downs. Her coat looked as nice as mine and she didn't part with twenty-five dollars to get it. I was learning that white and black people weren't as different as I'd been taught. But the main thing I was learning was that I had a lot to learn.

CHAPTER 4

The lingering dingy snow had melted and winter was finally releasing its grip. Aunt Lizzie worked part-time at a high school and was looking forward to spring break. I was counting the days too because we were going down home to Price, and Lana would be coming back with us. I was looking forward to getting my daughter, but I was also looking forward to seeing Jesse. I even had a slight hope that he'd come back with us. During the four months that I'd been gone, we were finding our way back to each other. We were a living example that absence did make the heart grow fonder, although it didn't start out that way.

When Jesse got home from work and realized I was gone, he went to Mama's house and wouldn't leave her porch. She said she tried to talk to him, but once he realized Lana was there, he stormed in and took her. He called me at Aunt Lizzie's and said, "You didn't have the decency to tell me in person? You had to sneak off?"

"I didn't sneak off. I told you I wanted to leave Mississippi."

"Wanting to leave and I'm leaving tomorrow isn't the same thing. And what kind of mother leaves her child behind? If you don't want to be with me, that's one thing. But to abandon your baby—"

"I didn't abandon her," I said. "She's in good hands with Mama and it's only temporary. As soon as I'm settled, I'll come get her."

"Not if I have anything to say about it. A mother who leaves her child isn't fit to have custody. You want to run off chasing rainbows, go ahead, but Lana and I are staying here. You'll never make it up there. You'll be back."

"She's my daughter too. I'm going to give her something better than—"

"Please deposit thirty more cents to continue the call," the operator interrupted.

"I'm not wasting another penny. I'm through talking," Jesse said, before the phone went dead.

I didn't hear from him again until six weeks later. I came in from work and there was a letter for me on the dresser. I took it into the bathroom, the only private space I had. Jesse had written a five-page letter, saying how much he missed me, that he still loved me, and wanted me to come home. I thought, *Why couldn't he have said these things when I was there?* I didn't reply until I received the third letter. In it, he continued to profess his love for me and seemed less opposed to moving. I told him having my family back together again would be the answer to my prayers.

We'd talked on the phone a few times since his first letter, and he continued to write the sweetest letters. Everyone in my family had gotten married and stayed that way. That's what I had expected to do, and even though I was the one who left, I missed my husband. I wasn't sure I'd be able to get off work and hadn't told Jesse I was coming home. When Mr. Ben agreed to change my schedule, I worked ten days straight in exchange for a four-day weekend.

Aunt Lizzie and Uncle Max had purchased a new adobe beige Chrysler New Yorker, just in time for our Easter road trip to Price. Vanessa had taken a second job, cleaning the auditorium after concerts at the Palladium. She claimed she couldn't get off work, so her baby Kendrick came with us. Aunt Lizzie said Vanessa wouldn't need a second job if she quit giving Harper money. I had learned not to waste my breath saying anything bad about Harper. He was good-looking and smooth-talking, and I could see why Vanessa's nose was open. I didn't care for the way he talked to her, but that was her life. I believe she was still embarrassed about getting pregnant—back then, there was a stigma attached to unwed mothers. She said Harper wasn't judgmental and he treated Kendrick as though he were his own son. Besides, her staying home meant there was more room in the back seat for Jesse.

The calendar said spring, but it was barely in the forties when we left Milwaukee. As we drove through small towns and farm fields heading toward Price, it was refreshing to be able to open the windows and feel the mild air. I fell asleep with Kendrick in my lap and awoke just before dawn. Even though it was dark, I could tell the dogwoods and sweet peas were blooming. *This is what spring is supposed to smell and feel like*, I thought, enjoying the light, sweet fragrance coming through the half-opened windows. However, the nostalgic mood dissipated as we crossed the county line and heard sirens following us.

"Damn," Uncle Max said as he pulled over.

"Were you speeding?" Aunt Lizzie whispered.

"No. My crime is being a colored man in a new car."

"What you folks doing around heah?" the officer asked when he approached our car.

"Heading home to see our folks," Uncle Max said, with both hands gripping the steering wheel.

"Who's your people?" the officer asked.

After we'd recited our genealogy, he ordered us out of the car. I had to wake Kendrick to take him out as well. I stood outside wearing one shoe because the officer said I was taking too long, and I couldn't find the other one. He searched the car, then went back to his patrol car and made some calls on his police radio. The crickets sounded louder than I remembered and the mosquitos seemed bigger as well. They appeared to be gathering to welcome us home. He came back, rifled through the glove compartment again, went through the cooler and snack basket. I had packed fried chicken, peanut butter and jelly sandwiches, chips, apples, and molasses cookies. He took the cookies, then let us go.

"Every time I come here, I swear I'm never coming back again," Uncle Max said, as we drove off. "Let our folks come visit us."

"He took our cookies," I complained. "I should have baked some with arsenic just for him."

Turns out NAACP officials were in Mississippi registering people to vote. Uncle Max's out-of-state license plate made us a target of suspicion and we were stopped two more times. "Once we get to Price, I'm not leaving the house until Sunday, when we leave this godforsaken place," he vowed.

I asked Uncle Max to drop me off at my old house. I hadn't told Jesse I was coming and planned to surprise him. I got my suitcase from the trunk, waved Uncle Max and Aunt Lizzie off, and walked up the porch, hoping to catch Jesse before he went to work. Most people didn't lock their doors back then, and I was surprised the door didn't open when I pushed it. I saw the curtain move, then heard a lady yell, "Jesseee, come to the door."

"You know I'm running late," he said as he opened the door. As our eyes met, he froze. "Callie, what are you doing here?" he asked.

"I wanted to surprise you."

Jesse stepped onto the porch and closed the door behind him. "How did you get here?" he asked, looking down the street.

"I rode with Aunt Lizzie and Uncle Max. They've gone to Mama's. But I couldn't wait to see you, and I came here first."

"Just a minute, wait here," Jesse said, as he went back inside.

I stood on that porch like a trained German shepherd. It hadn't occurred to me that Jesse was seeing someone. Mama usually told me all the gossip and she hadn't mentioned anything. But when I heard raised voices, I realized I was now the "other" woman.

"You told me you was getting divorced. Callie got a suitcase. That don't look like getting divorced to me," the lady yelled.

Jesse had another woman in the house I decorated. It was just a two-bedroom shotgun house. The bottom porch step still hadn't been fixed, the paint was peeling, and my rosebush needed trimming. But I'd lived there two years and still considered it our house. After a long two minutes, I lifted my head, picked up my suitcase, and walked to his car. I knew he kept the keys above the sun visor. I started the car and drove to my mother's house.

I didn't know if I was sad or mad. My biggest disappointment was for Lana. I wanted her to grow up with a mother and father. But if Jesse didn't want us, that was his loss. I made it my mission that she wouldn't suffer because of it. I thought about Jesse's letters and how I'd practically memorized each one. I'd been mailing my letters to his mother's house because he said he was looking for a new place and would be moving soon. I realized it was all a lie. I'd been so excited for this trip, and now I felt like a deflated balloon. His letters had rekindled feelings I had when we were in high school, and I didn't believe I'd ever love that intensely again.

I don't remember driving. I guess muscle memory brought me home. This was the longest I had ever gone without seeing

Mama. I'd barely turned the car off before she bounded down the porch steps and hugged me.

"How are you, baby? You feel a little thin," she said as she stepped back to examine me.

"I'm fine, Mama. I'm really happy to see you," I said, trying to discreetly wipe tears from my cheeks.

"I take it you've seen Jesse?" she asked.

"I've seen him and his woman," I said.

"Lizzie told me they dropped you off over there. I didn't know you and him was writing letters, or I would've said something. But you're the one who left. Men won't wait around, I don't care what they tell you," she said. "You're not too upset, are you?"

"It's just as well," I admitted, after taking a deep breath. "He's moved on. It's time for me to do the same. Is Lana still asleep? Do you have her things packed?"

"She can't go with you this trip," Mama said. "She's got pink eye and an ear infection. Her eyes are clearing up, but her ears are still bothering her. I made a doctor appointment for Monday."

I knew she must have been really sick for Mama to call a doctor. When I was coming up, she cured everything with Vicks VapoRub or castor oil.

Jesse came to Mama's and got his car while we were at Good Friday service. Mama and Aunt Lizzie prepared a big meal when we returned from church, while I spent time with Lana. She was cranky and kept pulling her ear. I read her stories and she took naps in my lap. Despite Uncle Max's vow to stay at the house, he and Aunt Lizzie went visiting both Friday and Saturday night. I stayed home with Mama. I'd forgotten how comforting it was to sit on Mama's porch and wave at neighbors and passersby. When I lived there, I thought it was boring. But I hadn't felt this relaxed since I'd left Price. Even though I was relaxed, it was like the feeling you have on vacation. It's a good feeling, but it's temporary and not your normal routine.

"You need to head out at night," Mama said. "I don't want Lana to see you leave and get agitated. Plus, the NAACP got the white folks stirred up. Best to get out of here when as few people as possible are watching."

Mama loaded us up with fried chicken, pork skins, boiled peanuts, canned tomatoes, plum and peach preserves, croker sacks full of peas and beans and three pound cakes. I packed okra, White Lily flour, MoonPies, and Nehi sodas, things I couldn't find in Milwaukee. We left before dawn. I peeked in on Lana, who was sleeping restlessly. I kissed her forehead and put the teddy bear I brought her, which she named Bubba Bear, in bed next to her. I was heartsick to be leaving my little girl, but I was glad to be leaving Price. It was clear that Jesse and I were over, and I needed to refocus on getting Lana. She was the only thing that mattered.

CHAPTER 5

Summer up north was different. It was noisy, people were everywhere, and the smell of barbeque always lurked in the air. Even the grass smelled differently. Then there were the children. They stayed in school a month longer than they did back home. But once they were out, they were everywhere. Children down home were kept busy weeding, picking, chopping, or babysitting. Their services were needed, and it also limited idle time. Up here, children were outside from sunup to sundown with no direction other than a vague warning to stay out of trouble.

My presence on Fourth Street was like a dam leak; the drip may be small, but there's a mighty force right behind it. I had been first, but as the weather got warmer, it was evident I was no longer "the only one." First National Bank hired a Negro parking lot attendant and Sam's Shoes hired a cleaning lady. Aunt Lizzie's sons got part-time jobs bagging groceries at Sunshine Foods, a few blocks over, and Gimbels hired a Negro elevator operator. Schlitz brewery began hiring black men, and First Lutheran Church in the next block, sold their building to Cornerstone Missionary Baptist Church, a black congregation. The pastor, Rev. White, came in every Sunday morning for breakfast. But the biggest news of all was a florist, photography studio, and furniture store opened for business—all owned by Negroes. We were moving on up!

In 1961, the finest man alive was Sam Cooke. Well, believe me when I tell you, Sam Cooke didn't have nothing on Thomas Reeves. He was just under six feet, with smooth, caramel-colored skin that didn't even look like he shaved. His teeth were cotton white and he had what we called "good" hair. (Of course, now I know we'd been brainwashed to think wavy hair like white folks was "good" hair.) Thomas drove a coal truck, and his employer had changed his route to include Fourth Street on Thursdays. He usually delivered around noon and picked up lunch while he was there.

The first time I noticed him, Mr. Ben was taking his order because I was tied up getting 7UP cakes out of the oven. Mr. Ben came over and cut him a slice, even though I raised a fuss about cutting the cake before it cooled. When I went to his table to give him the bill, Thomas said to me, "Tell me your name right now. But I only need to know your first name because I'm changing your last one. Nobody but my mama can bake cake this good. I can't marry her, so I guess I'll have to marry you. I could eat this cake every day."

I replied to him, "Any man who wants to marry me got to have more than a pretty face and slick tongue. If I wanted to bake cakes every day, I'd stay here and get paid for it."

He laughed and said, "Thanks for the compliment. Me and my pretty face will see you next week."

The next Wednesday evening, I put extra rollers in my hair to make my curls tighter. On Thursday, I wore earrings and my newest work shoes, even though they hurt my feet. When Thomas walked in, even the white ladies in the café turned to look at him. This time he sat at the counter. He ordered two cheeseburgers and I gave him an extra slice of cake. We made small talk about the weather and the Braves' season.

"A woman who can bake and knows baseball too. Now I know I'm in love," he teased. On his fourth Thursday visit, he told me the driver he had filled in for was returning to work and he was going back to his regular route. "I won't be coming in for lunch, but I'd still like to see you. Can I take you out?"

He picked me up from Aunt Lizzie's and we went to the movies a few times and out to dinner. Eating out was a new experience for me. There were restaurants that catered to blacks back home, but Mama didn't believe in spending money to eat someone else's cooking. A few times he asked me if I ever had the house to myself. I knew what was on his mind, but I played dumb. I told him the only time was on Monday mornings. I knew he had to work then. He said he lived with his mother and she was old-fashioned about women visiting men, so I couldn't come over. A handful of times I let him get a little too frisky in the back seat of his Impala. He was the first man I had been with after Jesse, who had been my first and only. But I was now a grown, divorced woman and he was the first man I'd dated who was actually interested in a relationship. He was good-looking, and I did like him a great deal.

One evening he came by when I was babysitting for Vanessa. We popped popcorn and watched *Perry Mason*. When Vanessa came in, Thomas was leaving, and they met at the door.

"Thomas, what a surprise to see you," she said.

"Yeah, hey there," he said and rushed down the stairs.

"Don't tell me he's an old boyfriend of yours," I said.

"No, but I do know something you won't want to hear.

He's dating Eva, who owns the beauty shop near the café. His sister works at the Palladium, and he picks her up from work all the time. Eva is usually with him."

"Are you sure?" I asked.

"Yes, I'm sure. Didn't you see the way he looked at me? He's worried I'll blow his cover. And he's right. These men up here think they're so slick."

I sat back on the couch and absentmindedly ate the last few kernels of popcorn.

"Well, what are you going to do?" Vanessa asked.

"I'm not fixing to confront him, if that's what you're suggesting."

"You've got to let him know you know. See what lie he tells. And stop saying 'fixing to'—that sounds country."

"We aren't an official couple," I replied.

"At least let him know he's not as slick as he thinks he is. You didn't give him any, did you?"

"Vanessa, thanks for the information, but you can mind your own business now."

"Well, I know you like him."

"I'm glad you told me. You shouldn't feel bad about telling the truth."

While I was still planning my next move, Thomas showed up at the café the next day.

"Aren't you worried your girlfriend will spot you?" I asked.

"Now what kind of greeting is that for a paying customer?"

"What will it be? We don't have 7UP cake today."

"What I want isn't on the menu."

"I know you're not trying to talk fresh to me. Folks tell me you're Eva's man."

"She and I went out a few times, and that was it. I'll prove it to you. Let's go over there right now."

"Fine. Let me get my purse," I said. I grabbed my purse from the cabinet, but when we got to the door, it started raining hard. I'd just gotten my hair done and didn't want to mess up a fresh press. The fact that he was willing was enough for me. I went back behind the counter, put my apron back on, and told Thomas to call me later. He blew me a kiss and left.

When I told Vanessa what happened, she said, "You should've called his bluff. I bet he's never been so relieved to see rain. Don't say I didn't warn you."

A few weeks later, when I was taking the garbage to the alley, I saw him and a lady, whom I presumed must be Eva, in a passionate embrace in his Impala. I marched over to the car and pounded on the hood. He jumped out, more concerned about me potentially damaging his car than seeing him kissing another woman.

"I'm not trying to get involved in any mess," Eva said, when she got out of the car. "You and him got something going on? Then you can have him."

"Lady, don't do me no favors," I said. "I don't want his two-timing behind."

"Both of you are crazy," he yelled.

I don't know what else he said. I left him and her arguing in the alley and returned to work.

Four days later, Thomas came in the café carrying a dozen red roses. I know, it sounds lame, but no man had ever given me flowers. He'd made his choice, and since Eva said she didn't want him, I gave him a second chance. Vanessa gave me a hard time about it, but who was she to give advice? Harper was trifling and none of us knew who Kendrick's father was. Thomas worked a lot, but we spent as much time together as we could. We went down to the blues clubs in Chicago. He took me to dinner in parts of the city I hadn't seen before. I had been in town almost a year, but I still hadn't gotten used to having whites wait on me. He came to a few family gatherings. Vanessa and I had a truce; if she didn't say anything negative about Thomas, I wouldn't say anything bad about Harper. Thomas and I went to a motel a few times. I felt embarrassed the first time, like everyone knew what we were getting ready to do, and it was obvious he'd done this before. He said this was temporary, and he was getting his own place so we could spend more time together.

Eva always ordered two 7UP cakes on Fridays for her beauty shop workers. One of her workers usually picked up the order, but on this day she came in herself. "Good morning, Margo," Eva said.

She and I hadn't spoken since our alley encounter.

"Hello," I said. "Just taking biscuits out of the oven. Your cakes will be ready shortly. I'll bring them to you when they cool off."

"My first customer canceled, so there's no rush. Sorry you and I got off on the wrong foot. There aren't many of us around here, we shouldn't be enemies."

"I agree," I said. "I haven't been up here long and I haven't met many people. These last few months with Thomas, I've been more places than I have the whole time I've been here."

"With Thomas?" she asked. "My Thomas?"

"Is Thomas Reeves supposed to be your Thomas? I thought you said you didn't want him?"

"I thought you said you were through with him?" Eva said.

"Well, like I said, I haven't met a lot of people and—"

"Wait a minute," Eva said, pacing around the table. "I think we're both getting played."

We compared dates and stories and confirmed her suspicions.

"I really am through with him this time," I said.

"Let's not let him off the hook that easy," Eva replied. "I've got an idea."

We both took off work early and Eva drove to the coal yard. His shift ended at 2:30, so we found his car and waited in the parking lot. When he came out, we followed him home. Neither of us had ever been to his house, since he said his mother didn't like him having company. We weren't concerned about his mother that day. We waited about fifteen minutes, then went to the door.

I would have been content to wipe my hands of him and move on. But Eva insisted on confronting him and I didn't want to look weak, so I agreed. We marched our bold selves up to his front door and rang the doorbell. He opened the door and stood there with his mouth open like a caught fish. He quickly stepped out onto the porch, pulled the door shut, and began stuttering and spitting excuses. He didn't speak long, because a very pregnant woman opened the door and said, "What the hell is going on out here? Who are these bitches?"

"I got your bitch," Eva snapped. "I see you're pregnant, but that won't keep me from kicking your ass if you can't respect me."

"How can you have the nerve to show up on my porch, talking about showing you respect? My husband and I—"

"Your husband!" Eva and I shouted in unison.

"I didn't know he was married," Eva said.

"You know it now. Please leave."

"But you gave me a pre-engagement ring," I shouted, flashing my ring finger.

"You gave her a ring?" Eva asked.

"That's *my* birthstone ring," his wife said. "I quit wearing it because my fingers are swollen."

"You told me it was turquoise because you would always

be true blue," I said. As soon as the words left my lips, I realized how stupid I sounded. Eva and I looked at each other and burst out laughing. Thomas's wife didn't see anything funny and was yelling so loud, neighbors had come onto their porches to watch.

"We'll leave you two lovebirds now. Let's get out of here," Eva said.

Eva got in the car and leaned over to unlock my door. She blew her horn, gave them the finger, then drove off. My laughter had turned to tears and at the red light, I rolled the window down. "I'm throwing this ring out. I never liked turquoise anyway."

"Girl, don't," she said while grabbing my arm. "Let's take it to the pawn shop and split the money. That's the least we can get for our wasted time and energy."

"Why would he lie?" I said between sniffles.

"Because he's a lying bastard and that's what lying bastards do. Don't waste your tears on him," Eva advised.

"But you were dating him too. Aren't you just a little crushed?"

"Nope. I'm mad at myself for believing his bullshit. I know these guys are full of game, especially the good-looking ones. I hope you made him wear a rubber."

I was so shocked at her statement I stopped in mid-sob.

She looked at me and shook her head. "Girl, you're going to need to wise up. This isn't your little country hometown where everybody couples up in the tenth grade and your male relatives protect your virtue with a shotgun if necessary. You got to look out for yourself."

We got five dollars for that ring. We went downtown to the Columbus Club and bought a bottle of cold duck (she drank most of it) and a large pepperoni pizza (my new favorite food) and spent the rest in the jukebox. I had a headache the next day, but we had a good time.

Eva was the first black adult I met who had been born in Milwaukee. I thought we had all moved from the South. She was a few years older than me, had been to college, but didn't finish. Her shop was across the alley from the café and for years we saw each other every day. I fried eggs and bacon and she fried hair. She was fun to be around and knew everyone.

Thanks to a two-timing man, I gained a lifelong friend. And, years later, she ended up saving my life, but I'll tell you about that later.

CHAPTER 6

Staying with Aunt Lizzie and Uncle Max was like living in a train station depot. I'd never been around people who partied so much. There was always someone's birthday or anniversary to celebrate. It was a constant flow of someone going away or returning, and Sundays were for watching the Packers, not church. An older couple lived downstairs, but they didn't complain, and often joined us. There was always a card game going on, with plenty of food and drinks. They had the latest records, including blue party records by Redd Foxx, Rudy Ray Moore, and LaWanda Page. It was hard to believe Aunt Lizzie and Mama were sisters. Mama didn't even have a record player, and even if she had, *those* records wouldn't have been allowed in our house. She believed playing cards was a sin and we rarely had company, other than my siblings when they came to town, or the pastor. If Mama had known this, she may have preferred I stay over at the café.

I shared a room with Vanessa and Kendrick. Aunt Lizzie's two youngest sons were in high school and shared a room. Max Jr. had been watching the baby since Vanessa worked second shift, but when I moved in, he found an after-school job and babysitting Kendrick became my responsibility. Watching Kendrick grow, learn, and change daily reminded me how much I missed Lana. But I was busy and didn't have much time to brood.

I had never lived in a house full of people, and I missed my privacy. I wasn't used to putting something in the icebox and finding it gone when I went back to get it. They loved the leftovers I brought home. But I seemed to be the only one washing dishes. I had to wake up earlier to get to work and the afternoon bus was always late. There was little privacy, I was babysitting for free, paying bus fare, and giving Aunt Lizzie rent money. She said I didn't have to give her anything, but Mama insisted I pay my own way.

However, there were benefits. Aunt Lizzie had gotten her own telephone line instead of a party line, and they had a new floor model television. She had *Ebony* and *Jet* magazine subscriptions, and I loved keeping up with movie stars, fashion trends, and national politics. She had a record player and stacks of 45s. Milwaukee had a black radio station, but it went off at sunset. It was a treat to pick what I wanted to hear, rather than having to wait for it to come on the radio.

I'd been back to Price twice since our Easter visit. I took the bus down for the Fourth of July weekend, and for a few days in September. Finding an apartment was harder than I anticipated. The location needed to be on a bus line and close to Aunt Lizzie and Vanessa so they could help me with Lana. Most places wouldn't rent to a single woman with a child. The available places were run-down or just rooms in a boarding house. I finally found a basement apartment over on Seventh Street. It wouldn't be ready until the first of the year, which turned out to be perfect timing. Aunt Lizzie had new living room furniture on layaway and said I could have her old set. Mama and Lana were coming for Christmas, and she was leaving Lana with me.

Aunt Lizzie and Vanessa were working a lot of overtime, and it looked like they were spending it all on presents. I had never seen that many wrapped boxes under a tree, except in a magazine. She bought a silver artificial tree with rainbow ornaments and shimmery icicles draped over the top. The bottom half was bare since Kendrick pulled anything not nailed down, but it was the prettiest tree I'd ever seen. We always had real evergreens down home and I missed the pine aroma, but having a sparkling new tree seemed perfect for the new life I was building.

The café would be closed the day before Christmas Eve, Christmas Eve, Christmas Day, and the day after Christmas, and I was looking forward to the time off. And since e business was good, Mr. Ben was paying me for two of those days. I only had two more payments on my bedroom set and still had almost two hundred dollars saved in a shoebox under the bed. I had been buying toys and clothes for Lana since October. I'd found the cutest red snowsuit and couldn't wait to see her in it. It was shaping up to be the best Christmas ever. Then the Grinch appeared.

During our after-breakfast lull, I was refilling ketchup bottles when Mr. Ben said I had a phone call. Whenever someone called me at work, I knew it was bad. Vanessa was calling from the corner store. The house next door had caught fire, and the houses were so close that ours caught on fire too. Mr. Ben left Donna in charge and drove me home, or to what was left of it. When we arrived, two fire trucks and a small crowd of neighbors stood in front of what was left of the house. The smoldering debris smelled like burning rubber and it made my eyes water. The house next door was burned to the sticks. The roof was gone on our house, the upstairs windows busted out, and the attic was exposed. Seeing our furniture strewn on the grass reminded me of the day Mama and I came home from church to find an eviction notice on the door and our belongings stacked at the edge of the yard.

Once I learned everyone had made it out, I thought of

my shoebox. I frantically asked a fireman when we could go inside to retrieve belongings. He said downstairs occupants could briefly go inside, but the stairs were unstable, and the second floor was a total loss. He suggested we file a renters' insurance claim. He may as well have told us to go to the moon. Most insurers didn't write policies in that neighborhood, and the ones who did charged twice what they charged in the white neighborhoods. There would be no Merry Christmas, Lana wasn't coming, and my money had gone up in smoke.

CHAPTER 7

I was away from home, broke, and homeless. Mr. Ben had rented his rooms, so I couldn't take refuge there. Aunt Lizzie, Uncle Max, and the boys moved in with his brother. Vanessa and Kendrick stayed with one of her coworkers. Aunt Lizzie's church members gave us clothes and Miss Nellie used her connections to get me a room at the YWCA. I was grateful and everyone was helpful, but I was still uncomfortable since I was the only black girl in the residence. I'm all for integration, but I hadn't planned on being such a pioneer.

Even though I was among women, Mama still didn't like me living around white folks. I told her everyone was nice and once Vanessa got her money together, we'd get our own place.

"You'll be all year, waiting on Vanessa," she said. "Why don't you come home?"

I dismissed her suggestion, as I always did. This was supposed to be the promised land. Everyone else was making their way. Surely I could too.

Aunt Lizzie had found a new place, but the rent was higher and it was smaller. With just two bedrooms, her sons shared a room, and Vanessa and Kendrick were on the couch. I was welcome, but I'd have to sleep on a pallet on the floor. Vanessa came to the café one evening and I was so glad to see her, I almost cried. I had talked to Mama and as usual, she urged me to come home. This time, I actually considered it. When I mentioned it to Vanessa, she said that might not be a bad idea. She hated winters up here and she wanted to get away from Harper. She gave me information on a free bus leaving in two days and suggested that we ride together.

Maybe living up north wasn't for me. Mississippi had its problems, but at least it wasn't freezing. I made less back home, but things also cost less. Plus, these Milwaukee men were full of jive and the females were contrary. I told Mr. Ben my plans and he said if I waited two months, I could have my room back. But why should I settle for a room when Mama had a whole house for me? I gave him my notice, and like the prodigal son, I was going home.

That Wednesday just before dawn, I took a taxi to the Brown Street Sinclair filling station. Since almost everything I owned burned in the fire, I only had three changes of clothing, my Gimbels department store coat, ten dollars, and my lunch of two meatloaf sandwiches, two slices of pound cake, and three apples. The bus was there, just as Vanessa said. I figured it was one of Aunt Lizzie's church group trips or Uncle Max's bowling league. But when I got on the bus, the passengers were about half black and half white, and I didn't see Vanessa. I went back up front to confirm with the driver, "Is this the bus to Mississippi?"

"Sure is. Welcome aboard," he said.

I searched again for Vanessa as I slowly walked down the aisle. Most seats were taken, so it didn't look like we'd be able to sit together. I found an aisle seat, stored my sparse belongings overhead and sat, figuring she'd arrive at the last minute as usual.

The driver gave us a ten-minute countdown for folks to take their last restroom breaks. I nervously checked my watch and wondered what to do. I figured Harper had probably sweet- talked Vanessa into staying, but I had given up my YWCA room and Aunt Lizzie's house was full, so I stayed on the bus. As promised, ten minutes later we were pulling out of the parking lot, and I was headed home to Mississippi.

The bus was quiet when we pulled off and I fell asleep. We were crawling through Chicago interstate construction when singing awakened me. Everyone was singing and clapping as though they were in a Sunday church service. When a young man stood, I realized this was not a regular bus—this was a group of Freedom Riders. I thought, *I done stepped in it now. I should have known Vanessa didn't know what she was talking about.*

Based on what I'd heard of the Freedom Riders, I expected unkempt, scary-looking beatnik, dope smokers. But this was just a bunch of young folks; most looked younger than me. They were laughing and singing like they were headed to a church picnic. I knew a bus had been bombed and riders had been beaten, but my riding companions were so confident and mild-mannered, I wasn't worried about anything happening on this trip. This group wasn't a bunch of troublemakers at all.

My seatmate was a college student from Iowa. Her small-town experience hadn't been much different from mine. She told me about the importance of voting, and I promised to vote in the next election. We stopped a few times and I bought candy bars, chips, and soda to supplement my bag lunch. She said my sandwich smelled heavenly, so I gave her half.

The driver had agreed to drop me off at Grenada's Greyhound bus stop, about sixty minutes from Price. When we pulled into the lot, my seatmate and I exchanged addresses and promised to write one another. A few got off to use the restroom and I went to the phone booth to call Mama collect. As I was waiting for the operator, there was a banging at the door. "Get your black ass out here!" the man yelled.

A crowd gathered around the bus, waving Confederate flags, chanting, and throwing rocks. As the driver was ushering us back into the bus, state troopers showed up. I was relieved, thinking they'd stop this crazy mob.

"We knew y'all were coming," an officer said, "and we got a special place ready for you. It's called Parchman prison." They arrested us for disturbing the peace, which was ridiculous. The only thing we were disturbing was their grip on black folks.

The officers loaded us into a paddy wagon. There were about thirty of us ladies crowded into the back of an old army-transport truck. The wagon had no springs and it felt like we hit every bump and pothole, throwing us against each other. We started out singing, but they ordered us to stop. By the time we arrived, I was in a cold sweat, with numb toes and aching knees.

Parchman Farm had a well-earned reputation for brutality. That's where death row and the execution chamber were, and some called it Little Alcatraz. I'd heard stories about Parchman and had imagined it as an imposing fortress, with tall brick walls, armed guards, and a barbed wire fence. I was surprised to see it was a long, one-story, cinder block building, surrounded by cotton and bean fields. There were houses on the grounds with neat yards. Other than the guard tower at the entrance, and a group of men in black-and-white–striped jumpsuits in the distant field, the property looked pastoral and serene.

As soon as we walked inside, matrons wearing rubber gloves strip-searched us and examined our lady parts by dipping their fingers into a Lysol-smelling concoction. I had gone from being scared to being humiliated, because they examined us in the same room.

After the strip search, we each got a rough denim skirt with black-and-white stripes and a T-shirt. Then we were taken to the cells. They put four of us in a six-by-eight-foot cell with bunk beds and a stainless steel toilet with a rusty sink. Blacks and whites were separated, and men and women were in separate wings.

Even though I hate to lie on a strange bed, I was exhausted and couldn't wait to get some rest. We laid two up and two down, on our sides, with one woman's feet at the other one's head. One of my cellmates said SNCC had been raising money to help Freedom Riders and we shouldn't be here too long. In my mind, it had already been too long, but I did drift off to sleep.

Later, an officer came to the cell, called my name and took me down a long hall. I thought they were going to interrogate me with a bright light on my face like I'd seen in the movies. But when I walked in the room, who was there but Mama. She signed some papers, the officer led us to the door, and I was a free woman again.

Turns out Mr. Ben called looking for me because he couldn't find the extra cash register key. Mama told him I wasn't there. She tracked down Aunt Lizzie, who tracked down Vanessa, and they retraced my steps to figure out I was with the Freedom Riders. Vanessa said when she found out it was Freedom Riders, not "free rides," she called the YWCA front desk and left me a message.

Mama shook her head and said, "I don't believe she left you no message. She was probably laying up with some man and forgot. That girl is as loose as ashes in the wind."

I felt bad about leaving the others behind, but Mama said

I could do them more good outside of jail than inside. She had packed me a lunch, which included a Royal Crown soda, two meatloaf sandwiches, and a peach. I devoured it all.

She fussed for fifty miles. "When they told me you was in Parchman, I cried and prayed loud enough for all of Price to hear. And I don't know who's the bigger fool," she said, more than once. "Vanessa, or you, for listening to her."

The next morning, I was awakened by Lana jumping on the bed. She had grown so much in the seven months since I'd last seen her. She could tie her shoes, count to twenty, and pour her own cereal.

The first week, I sat around the house, cooked, read Lana stories, and secretly collected donations to help the others get out of jail. Dick Gregory came to Jackson, and soon the others were released. It was amazing to see this on television and know I had been a part of it. That Sunday, the congregation gave me a standing ovation, and everyone wanted to shake my hand. Being a part of history was great, but if I was staying in Price, I needed a job.

I went to the A&P where I had previously worked. All the faces were new to me, and the manager said they weren't hiring. I went to the hospital, dry cleaner's, and florist and was told the same thing. Two places in Grenada had ads in the paper, but I needed a car to get there, and I couldn't get one without a job. Mama wasn't baking as much as she used to and didn't have many of her old customers. I did a few jobs, but that was pocket change. Mr. Ben had called several times to see how I was getting along. He said my job was still open. I politely thanked him, but I was going to stay in Price. The room over the café wasn't big enough for Lana and me and I didn't want to leave her again.

I finally found at job at Milton's Diner. I'd gone to the owner and told him about my experience practically running

Fourth Street Café. He seemed impressed and hired me as a dishwasher. I wanted to laugh in his face and walk out, but that was the only job offer I received. I couldn't believe this was happening, but at least I'd be making some money. Once I got a car, more jobs would be available to me. When I showed up for work the next day, the owner's wife was there and told me they didn't need any help.

I sighed heavily and left without saying goodbye. If it weren't for Lana, I would have caught the first thing headed north. Hanging around the house was depressing, but seeing Lana always brightened my spirits. She was inquisitive and a bundle of energy. I taught her to play hopscotch and jacks, and Mama even played Simon Says with us.

That Sunday after church, I was washing dishes when Mama said, "Dinner was real good, Callie. Your smothered chicken was almost as good as mine. I never added red peppers to my gravy. It adds just enough kick. I see why them folks liked you up at that café. You miss it, don't you?"

"I miss the feeling of making a way for myself, but I don't miss the cold and the snow. And now that I'm back with Lana, I couldn't imagine not seeing her every day. There's got to be someplace around here where I can get a job. Maybe I won't make enough to have my own place, but at least I can help you."

"I'll ask Pastor again if he knows someone," Mama said. "But don't worry about it. We'll be fine. The Lord will make a way."

The rest of the afternoon, Mama and I sat on the porch while Lana played catch next door with the neighbor, Mr. Sam and his grandson. We came inside at dusk and watched TV until bedtime. Lana and I shared my old room, which was hers now. She reminded me to say our prayers, then I read *Green Eggs and Ham* twice before she drifted off to sleep, snuggled next to me. She had me at the edge of the bed, but

I didn't want to disturb her by moving. It was amazing how someone so small could take up so much of the bed. I was uncomfortable, but it didn't matter. I loved watching her chest rise and fall while she slept peacefully. My job search was on my mind, and I couldn't fall asleep anyway. I finally dozed off to sleep, but was awakened around four o'clock in the morning when Mama came in.

"Callie, get up." She was whispering, but there was urgency in her voice.

I followed her to the front door, and there were two burning crosses in her yard.

CHAPTER 8

Mr. Sam was awakened when his dog kept barking. He told Mama he saw the truck drive away, then came and knocked on our door. He was hosing down the crosses, made from fence pickets, as we stood in the doorway. Thankfully, Lana slept through the commotion.

"I'm glad Mr. Sam saw the truck," I said, as we watched the smoldering pile in Mama's yard. "He can give that information to the sheriff and whoever's responsible can be arrested."

"Child, you've forgotten where you are. The sheriff won't do anything. He was probably in on it. And I wouldn't let Sam put himself in danger like that. Miss Miller told me folks around here believe you're involved with the Freedom Riders. They had planned to burn a cross on my yard weeks ago, but her husband talked them out of it. I guess he was overruled."

"This is ridiculous. It's been one hundred years. We can't let them—"

"Callie, this is how things are," Mama said, while patting my hand. "Seems like the more civil rights we get, the more threatened white folks feel. They aren't going to hire you and now I'm worried about your safety. Maybe you should return to Milwaukee. You can probably get your old job back."

"I can't leave you and Lana alone. Besides, you're the one who didn't want me to leave."

"Things are different now," Mama said.

"I'll leave if I want to leave, but I won't let anyone run me out of town," I said. "Why don't we both leave? I'll find us a place and you won't have to work. I don't like you down here with these racist fools."

"I'm too old to start over. I'll be all right. Payback is coming and those Philistines will reap what they sow."

"I'm not leaving Lana."

"What good are you to Lana, if they hurt you or arrest you on some made-up charges? Or if you disappear? When they were looking for Emmett Till's body, they found several bodies in the rivers around here. The more I think about it, you need to leave today. I'll buy your bus ticket and give you a few dollars to tide you over."

"But, Mama—"

"I can bring Lana once you're settled. Go pack."

CHAPTER 9

Once again, I packed my few belongings and a lunch for the ride north. Between Lana's whining and Mama spending her hard-earned money for my ticket, I felt horrible.

"Hold your head up. Everything will work out. This time, remember your Bible," Mama said, as she handed it to me. "This is your helper. Maybe you wouldn't have had so much trouble if you had kept it with you."

I put the Bible in my bag as she instructed. I wasn't taking any chances this time.

This time around, Milwaukee wasn't as intimidating. I knew how to dress in layers in the winter. I knew the bus routes, and the sweet-stinky brewery smells were familiar. I knew not to wave or nod to every black person I passed, like we did down home, and it was okay to look a white person in the eye. Aunt Lizzie and Uncle Max bought a three-bedroom bungalow on Twelfth Street. Their old house had been repaired and sold. The new house was smaller, but after the fire, they said they'd never live on the second floor again. Vanessa and Kendrick had a bedroom and the boys shared the third bedroom. Max Jr. had graduated, and he and Vanessa were moving into a duplex. I was on the couch, but when Vanessa and Max Jr. moved, I'd have her bedroom. Vanessa put in a good word for me and I got hired at the Kmart warehouse where she and Aunt Lizzie worked. There was plenty of overtime and I was rebuilding my Lana fund.

When I went to Eva's shop, we hollered, laughed, and hugged. I hadn't known her for very long, but she was now one of my best friends. I didn't fit in with the friends I once had in Price. If they were married, they were too busy or insecure to hang out with me. The others had moved away.

"It's good to see you, Miss Freedom Rider," she said when we sat. She filled me in on the Fourth Street happenings and said she hadn't been to the café since I left. "You must let me do something with your hair," Eva pleaded. "You look like a country gal from Mississippi with those pin curls in your hair."

"What's wrong with being from Mississippi?" I replied.

"Nothing, but you don't have to look like you just got off the bus," Eva said.

I let her talk me into getting a relaxer on my next off day. She smoothed the cool, creamy mixture over my head. It smelled like boiled eggs and bleach. But this wasn't the worse part. She hadn't warned me not to scratch my head the day before getting a relaxer. Within five minutes my scalp was on fire, and I yelled for her to come see about it. She was in the back, watching *Search for Tomorrow*, and came running up front to see what was going on. "Something is wrong," I cried. "This mess is burning my head!"

"That means it's working. Sit a few minutes longer."

"If this is how it feels, I'll stay a nappy-headed Mississippi gal." I rushed to the bathroom and started washing it out myself.

"Girl, get back in here. Let me rinse you properly then," she said with a sigh.

She rinsed me, then put another concoction on my head

that was supposed to ease the burning. It didn't. She rolled my hair and put me under a dryer—more misery. When she finally finished, my scalp felt raw and I had a headache, but I liked the result. I had the flip hairstyle like Mary Tyler Moore, and I did the white girl shake so much I lost an earring. Eva convinced me to wear bright red lipstick, and child, you couldn't tell me my kite wasn't flying high.

Since I was close to the café, I went to visit. "Well, don't you look fancy," Miss Nellie said. Mr. Ben came from behind the register and hugged me.

"Glad to see you," he said, vigorously shaking my hand. "I heard about your ordeal with those Freedom Riders."

"That was very brave," Miss Nellie said. "We're proud of you."

He gave me an update on what had been going on since I left. Donna was still working there and I had just missed her. He had to discontinue meatloaf Wednesdays—no one's tasted as good as mine. "You'll always have a job here, and I got a room open." I politely declined his offer. Working at the café had happened by accident. Now that I knew better, I planned to do better.

Since the holidays were Kmart's busiest season, I couldn't get off work for Thanksgiving or Christmas. I wanted Mama to bring Lana for a visit, but she said she didn't see the point since I was working all the time. We were scheduled to work six days a week with lots of overtime right up until Christmas Eve. We were looking forward to having three days off. The fire ruined the prior Christmas, and unfortunately this holiday was ruined too.

Four days before Christmas, Max Jr. received a draft notice. He was being inducted in three weeks. Aunt Lizzie was devastated, but Uncle Max urged her to see the bright side. "Vietnam is a small country and the fighting should be over soon. Plus the Army isn't segregated like it was when I was drafted. Veterans get a lot of benefits and he'll be able to attend college," he said. Despite the draft notice, we tried to enjoy the holidays. I fixed his favorite meals and we had a combined New Year's Eve and going-away party.

Vanessa asked me to move in with her, saying she'd paid the security deposit but couldn't afford the rent by herself. They say two grown women shouldn't live together, but Vanessa and I got along fine—most of the time. We worked opposite shifts, which meant I was babysitting again, but I didn't mind. Kendrick was potty-trained, and since I worked days, he was only up a few hours before bedtime. The three of us were our own little family. But there was another person in the equation, Harper. He practically lived at our place.

At times, our shifts overlapped, and Kendrick would spend the night at Aunt Lizzie's. I loved them both, but relished the times I was home alone. I could watch what I wanted on TV and not have many dishes to wash. On one of those rare occasions, I fell asleep on the couch and around midnight, I heard noises in the kitchen. I put on my housecoat and went to the kitchen, thinking maybe Vanessa wasn't feeling well and had left work early. I found Harper pulling pots out of the refrigerator. "I was hoping some meatloaf was left. Vanessa said you made it. I never knew a young lady who cooks as good as you."

"Vanessa won't be back until morning. She's working her second job at the Palladium tonight," I said, wrinkling my nose as his stale gin breath reached across the room.

"I know," he said, while grabbing bread from the bread box.

I went to my room and closed the door. It was bad enough with Harper hanging around when she was home, but him coming in and out when Vanessa was gone was unacceptable, and I planned to tell her so. Just after I dozed off, I was awakened when I felt the quilt being pulled back. I opened my eyes and there was Harper standing over me in his underwear.

"That meatloaf was good. Let's see what else you do good," he slurred.

"You'd better leave," I hissed.

"Don't be playing hard to get," he said. "I see the way you look at me."

"I don't know what you think you saw, but I do know you'd better get outta here," I said, scrambling to sit up.

"I won't tell nobody."

"Well, I will," I shouted. "I don't see why Vanessa puts up with you."

"I'm going to show you why she puts up with me. Now stop making so much noise," he said, and then he pushed me down. He was holding me down with one arm and trying to straddle me at the same time. I rolled toward the nightstand, but he was pulling me from behind. I grabbed my "helper" from the nightstand and whacked him in his jewels. He doubled over and wailed like a cat birthing kittens. I ran to the kitchen and grabbed a butcher knife and waited for him to come in. I gripped the knife handle and yelled for him to get out. After a few minutes, I tiptoed back to the bedroom. He was on his back, splayed across the bed, with his hands over his crotch, snoring. I turned on the light and radio. Harper stirred, then opened his bloodshot eyes.

"Get out," I said, still clutching the knife.

"This ain't over, you country bitch," he said, stumbling to put on his pants.

"It will be when I tell Vanessa."

"I don't think you want to do that," he said, while staggering to the door.

"Go to hell," I said and slammed the door behind him. I put the chain on the door and went to change the bedcovers. Mama had been right about the Bible being my helper.

The next day, Vanessa was asleep when I left for work. When I got off work, she told me, "I have good news and bad news. Which do you want to hear first?"

"Give me the good news," I replied.

"I'm pregnant," she said gaily. "Harper and I are getting married."

"I thought you said that was the good news," I said.

"I know you and Mama don't think much of Harper, but he makes me happy and we're good together. He's like a father to Kendrick and we're going to be a family. This is all I've ever wanted."

Seeing her so happy, I kept quiet about Harper. But I knew I needed to move. I figured I'd move back in with Aunt Lizzie and leave Vanessa and her trifling man to do whatever they wanted.

"What's the bad news?" I asked.

She showed me a yellow letter. Our warehouse was consolidating with the Texas office and everyone's hours were being cut for ninety days until they closed permanently. "You'll have one waiting for you when you go in," she said.

And she was right. My hours were cut in half. I had some money saved—this time I put it in the bank, but I didn't want to draw down my savings. Aunt Lizzie said she was going to ride it out until they laid her off, then take a break and collect unemployment. With Uncle Max working two jobs, they'd be able to cover their bills. Vanessa and I didn't have that luxury, and we began looking for new jobs.

Vanessa found us jobs at Quality Pork Processing, paying even more than we were making at Kmart. I worked on the main line, with an endless stream of pig carcasses speeding by. My job was to debone, trim, and keep the line moving. The stench made me nauseous and it lingered in my nostrils even after I was off work. I was raised in the country and was familiar with animal smells. But this place smelled like a combination of rotten meat, blood, ammonia, and manure, and I couldn't seem to get it off me. I bathed as soon as I got home every day and washed my hair every day—at least I had my perm and didn't have my hair all over my head.

Going to the bathroom was an ordeal. We couldn't just step away from the line—we had to raise our hand, like we were in grammar school. A "floater" was supposed to come take our place. But there weren't enough of them and one day I waited almost an hour. My coworkers said they limited their liquid intake so they wouldn't need to step away from the line. The lunch breaks felt like those in a prison movie scene, with managers watching to make sure we didn't exceed thirty minutes. The plant was loud, cold, damp, and slimy. I stood in the same spot doing repetitive motions all day and my shoulders ached at the end of my shift. I kept my work shoes in my locker because they had blood and guts splattered on them and smelled awful, no matter how much I scrubbed them. That was the longest five days of my life, and I spent my weekend searching the classifieds for another job.

When Monday came, I couldn't make myself go back. The money was good, but I hated it. I threw those shoes away and it was a long time before I ate bacon again.

This time, finding a job was more difficult. The good jobs were moving farther out of the city where the buses didn't run. I could've gone to the café and asked Mr. Ben for my old job, but that seemed like moving backward.

That Saturday, Vanessa and Harper cooked breakfast, wasted grits on the floor and didn't sweep, wash dishes, or offer me any food, although I didn't want any. It was just the principle of it. As soon as he left, I knocked on her bedroom door. "We need to talk. I am not the maid. I'm tired of cleaning up behind everyone."

"And I'm tired of you walking around here like you're the Queen of Sheba. You should be grateful after all we've done for you," Vanessa said.

"I don't know where you get 'we' from," I replied. "I

wash and clean around here like your house slave and I pay
half the rent when I should pay a third since Harper is here
all the time. I babysit for you for free, and since you're
always with Harper, I probably spend more time with Kendrick than you do."

"Sounds like you have a problem with me and my man.
If you don't want to be bothered with Kendrick, just say so."

"I didn't say I didn't want to be bothered with Kendrick.
But I do have a problem with Harper. I know you're
engaged, but I'm still here, and I don't like him hanging
around so much," I said.

"What business is it of yours?"

"A few weeks ago, he tried to get in bed with me while
you were at work."

Vanessa was quiet for a few minutes, then said, "Wow.
I knew you were jealous, but I never thought you'd stoop
this low."

"Why would I make this up?"

"You're jealous. You've never liked him. And now that
we're getting married, you're afraid you won't have a place
to stay."

"That's the craziest thing I've ever heard. I never liked
him because he's a liar and he's using you."

"For your information, Harper told me how you seduced
him. I was mad, but he begged me not to say anything
to you."

"You have got to be kidding. Harper came on to me!"

"That's not what he said."

"What do you expect him to say? He lies as good as he
looks."

"Then why didn't you tell me? Seems like you would've
said something if he was bothering you."

"I didn't want to hurt your feelings. You should know I
wouldn't do that to you. We're like sisters," I said, holding
back tears.

"Save those fake tears. I'm hip to your little Miss Innocent act. Not to mention that you're not even working. I'm about tired of carrying you."

I didn't know what to say, but I was so hurt, I grabbed my purse and walked out. One guess where I ended up—the Fourth Street Café. "Mr. Ben, is that job still open?"

"Yep."

"And what about the room?"

"It's available."

"When can I start?"

"How about today? If you start now, we can have your Wednesday meatloaf."

I was back on Fourth Street.

CHAPTER 10

Vanessa had a girl and named her Harleen. She and Harper didn't get married after all. They broke up a few weeks after the baby was born. She and her kids moved back with her mother. I had managed to time my visits so we wouldn't run into each other, but on this day, Aunt Lizzie invited me over on the pretext of giving me something my mother had sent, and Vanessa was home.

Before I could ring the doorbell, Aunt Lizzie opened the door and ushered me inside. "Vanessa, come here," she said. Vanessa came in, with Harleen on her hip. The baby was plump, with a head full of curls and reminded me of Lana at that age. "You two have been close since you were in diapers. Now you're not speaking because of some no-good Negro. He could be gone tomorrow, but the two of you will always be family. Work this mess out."

Within seconds, Vanessa was crying and apologizing. She admitted she was wrong and she was through with Harper. I resisted the urge to tell her "I told you so" and we picked up as though nothing had happened.

Since we were on speaking terms again, Aunt Lizzie asked when I was moving back to her house. But other than now having to go to the washateria, (I forgot Vanessa said it's called a laundromat), I preferred living over the café. Plus, I had easy access to the café kitchen, and was building my cake clientele and Lana fund.

Lana was starting kindergarten and had grown into a real daddy's girl. She was glad to see me when I visited, but Jesse's house was home. I still wanted her with me, but Price offered more stability. Between Mama, Jesse's mother and Jesse, Lana was well cared for. Even if I had a place, I'd still need a babysitter, and Aunt Lizzie and Vanessa had their own responsibilities. Jesse was working steadily with the railroad. He'd remarried, had two small sons, and an older stepson. Lana shared a room with her younger brothers and loved bossing them around. Sometimes I thought maybe I should've stayed with him, but I also wondered if his expanded family responsibilities had triggered his evolution. Maybe I didn't love him enough to wait, or maybe when I lost our babies, I lost him too. All I knew was he had the life I had wanted for us, and most importantly, he had Lana. But rather than wallow in could-have-beens, I focused on working and saving money, and visited as often as I could.

Dating was not on my to-do list, but as with most things in life, they happen when you're not looking. Winston worked for Larsen's Meat Market. He was a butcher, but sometimes he made deliveries for the owner. One Thursday, which was smothered chicken day at the café, he delivered our beef and poultry order and ordered a chicken dinner to go. After that, he came every Thursday and ordered a smothered chicken dinner. On his fourth visit, his truck wouldn't start and he was in and out, trying to get it going. It was freezing outside, and I offered him soup to warm up. I was waiting on another customer when I noticed he was coughing. I couldn't finish taking the order because he kept coughing, then wheezing.

"Are you okay?" Mr. Ben asked.

I went back to the counter and refilled his water glass. "You don't look well."

"The soup," he said in a tortured whisper. "What's in the soup?"

"It's tortilla soup. Maybe it was too spicy. I used cayenne pepper instead of chili powder. There's chicken, beans, corn, ground cashews—"

"Cashews," he mumbled. "Allergic to nuts. Call doctor."

"He's allergic to nuts. He needs a doctor!" I yelled.

Mr. Ben called an ambulance, and Mr. Carter, who had integrated the pinochle players, ran to Dr. Brown's office.

I had never seen anyone so distressed. I tried to pat his back, but he waved me away. His forehead was sweaty and his eyes were brownish red and watery. Dr. Brown rushed in, asked several questions, then took a long needle from his bag and injected it into Winston's arm. The ambulance arrived with sirens blaring. Onlookers had gathered at our door, while the attendants put him on their cot, then left.

Mr. Ben called Larsen's to update them and to let them know to come move their truck. The next Thursday, Winston came in, looking no worse for the wear.

"Well, here's the little lady who tried to take me out," he teased, as he lit a cigarette with a monogrammed lighter.

"I'm truly sorry. How was I supposed to know you were allergic to nuts?"

"No apology needed. I usually keep an Ana-Kit with syringes so I can inject myself in an emergency, but I forgot it when I switched trucks. I do know how you can make it up to me," he said, while taking a seat at the counter. "How about going to see *A Raisin in the Sun* with me?"

I hadn't considered him as a potential date, but now gave him another look. He was trim, slightly taller than me, light-skinned, with smoky hazel eyes, the color of weak tea. His process was slick and glistened like his hair was wet. "Okay. I get off early tomorrow."

When he picked me up, I did a double take. I had only seen him in his Larsen's uniform. He had on shiny Nunn Bush shoes, slacks with creases sharp enough to cut yourself, a double-knit zippered shirt, and a camel fedora. I only knew the Larsen's truck, but his personal car was a Pontiac Catalina, the first car I rode in with electric windows and locks. He owned four duplexes and lived downstairs in one. His place looked like an *Ebony* magazine layout. He had a white leather, sectional couch, Mediterranean-style coffee tables, and color televisions in the living room and his main bedroom. There were custom-made curtains and valances throughout the house, and new avocado-green appliances in the kitchen. There was a waterbed in the second bedroom and a poker table in the third. His place was the size of Aunt Lizzie's and she had six people living there.

He was always working, but not at a regular job, other than Larsen's. He drove a cab and was managing a couple of singing groups while trying to get them record deals. He carried a wad of cash and people were always bringing him money, or he was paying someone. He told me, "I don't plan to work at Larsen's the rest of my life. Nine-to-five is another form of slavery."

"You make a regular job sound dreadful. Most men would be glad to drive for Larsen's. You have regular first-shift hours and don't have a boss watching your every move."

"I'm not a regular cat. I want to make money while I sleep like the white boys do."

He took me to Zeppoli's Italian restaurant, one of our favorite places. You'd think by me working in a café, the last thing I would want to do was eat out. But I liked trying new foods. Other than pizza, the only Italian food I was familiar with was spaghetti and Chef Boyardee. Many places Winston took me were integrated, and if they tried to seat us in the back, he'd request another seat, or we'd leave. Usually, the food wasn't even good. It seemed a shame that people were marching and losing their lives for the right to pay to eat this crummy food. But I did like getting dressed up and going to dinner, like in the movies. We drove to clubs across the Midwest to watch his groups perform. They were small clubs, but I felt like a VIP. He always got a good table and drinks were always on the house.

He also took me to the racetracks in Chicago. Winston sat in the same spot each time we went, and all the guys seemed to know each other. I couldn't believe the money he spent. He'd bet fifty or one hundred dollars on a race without blinking. I had never been wined and dined like this before. Most men I met wanted to go to a neighborhood tavern, buy me a drink and two pieces of chicken, then expect me to go to bed with them. Vanessa said I was too picky, but I wasn't having relations with everybody who spent two dollars on me. I didn't need a man. I was content spending time with family and focusing on rebuilding my Lana fund. Winston came along when I least expected it. He was romantic, generous, and fun.

After we'd been dating about three months, I began spending most weekends at Winston's place. Every time I went, he had something new for me: earrings, a necklace, and a transistor radio. I told him he was spending too much money on me, but he said he enjoyed it. Who was I to stop his fun? Since he worked at Larsen's, he had a freezer full of choice steaks and thick pork chops. I loved cooking these expensive cuts and Winston loved my cooking. A few times he mentioned he didn't like me living over the café, but I wasn't ready to give that up. After my incident with Vanessa, I liked having my own place, even if it was only a room—it was mine.

One Saturday morning, I came in from Winston's place. I rarely worked weekends anymore, so before I headed upstairs to my room, I peeked into the café and waved to Mr. Ben. He was on the phone and he beckoned me over. When he hung up, he said, "I know you're supposed to be off, but can you close tonight and tomorrow? Nellie hasn't been feeling well and I need to get home."

"No problem. I miss seeing the weekend customers," I said.

"I thought you didn't want to work weekends."

"What made you think that?" I asked. "I like weekends off, but I'm flexible."

"That Winston fellow said you didn't want to work weekends."

"Winston said?"

"Yes. He came in and asked me if I could make sure you had weekends off."

"Mr. Ben, have you ever known me to have a problem speaking my mind?"

"No, can't say that I have."

"From now on, if you don't hear it from me, it don't count."

When Winston came in for his usual lunch, I told him to sit in a booth instead of at the counter. When I brought his pork chops, I slid across from him and said, "You told Mr. Ben to limit my weekend hours. I didn't ask you to do that and please don't interfere again."

"What are you talking about?" he said. "You said you liked sleeping in on weekends."

"I mentioned it, but not for you to run and tell Mr. Ben. Do you see me running over to Larsen's repeating your complaints?"

"I'm only looking out for you. Most women would be glad to have a man look after them."

"You make me sound like a puppy. I don't need nobody to look after me."

"That's what's wrong with you modern women, trying to be the man." He put a five-dollar bill on the table and left.

I didn't call him and he didn't call me, but the next Thursday, he came in. He sat in a booth, which meant he wasn't getting his order to-go. I fixed him a plate of smothered chicken, peas, rice, and German red cabbage—a new dish I'd learned since moving to Milwaukee. I took the plate to him and sat across from him. He begged my pardon and said he was only looking out for my best interest. I assured him, I could look out for myself, but maybe I overreacted. He grabbed my hand and kissed it, then ate like someone who hadn't eaten in days.

"I know your birthday is coming. I made reservations to go to Idlewild—that is, if it's okay with you," he said.

I had to smile at his compromise attempt. "Sure, is that some new club?"

"Girl, Idlewild is Negro heaven. You'll love it. Everything is first-class and the golf course is as good as any PGA course." He described the western Michigan resort as though he were a tour guide. I was from the country, therefore swimming, boating, and horseback riding didn't sound like something to get excited about. And I'd never known a black man who golfed, so having a golf course didn't impress me. But I didn't have the heart to hurt his feelings.

I went to Eva's to get my hair done for the trip. "Hello, stranger," she said. "Some people get a man and forget about their friends. I should tell you I'm closed and to make an appointment, but looks like this is the only way I get to see you."

"I'm sorry," I said. "Between working and Winston—"

"I know. I know. No need to explain. He doesn't seem like your type, but I'm happy if you're happy."

"You know Winston?" I asked, which was a dumb

question. The black community in Milwaukee was a small place in the 1960s, and there were at best two degrees of separation between most Negroes.

"Everybody knows Winston. You know he does policy sales," she said, while setting her cup on her styling station.

"Yeah, he's always working. The butcher shop is his full-time job, but he seems to spend as much time with his insurance policy business."

"Insurance policy business?" Eva said, as she squeezed shampoo on my hair. "He ain't no insurance salesman. Haven't you ever heard of a numbers runner?" Eva went on to give me a lesson on the policy business. "Folks pick any three numbers. Winston jots down the numbers, the person's name and their bet, usually a nickel or a dime, but some bet more. The winner is determined from that day's horse race at Maywood or Sportsman's Park. Winston drops off the bets, pays the winners, and he gets a cut."

"Drops off the bets to who?"

"To one of those Mob guys."

"You mean it's illegal?" I asked.

"Girl, you are so green," Eva said, shaking her head.

"How can it be illegal?" I asked. "He's right out in the open and the police don't bother him."

"The police take their cut. Winston pays on time and everybody's happy."

"That explains why he carries lots of cash," I said.

"One of my operators used to do his ex-wife's hair," Eva said, then took a sip from her cup. "She always paid her five-dollar charge with a fifty-dollar bill, and we had to scrounge for change. I think she just wanted to show off that Winston gave her money. They say she ran off with one of his tenants."

"I can't believe he's a criminal and interacts with gangsters. He seems so nice."

"Child, please. Politicians and big business owners—

those are the real criminals. This is not the movies, where the bad guys wear black hats and have a scar on their face. Don't go acting all flaky. He's not hurting anyone and can show you a good time."

"He is generous," I said, thinking about the crisp fifty-dollar bill in my purse he'd given me. *It would be a big boost to my Lana fund.*

"It's only a weekend. Every man you date doesn't have to be *the* one. Just enjoy it while it lasts."

Winston had a new Thunderbird, and he was picking specks of dirt from the hood when I came outside. "Two suitcases? You know this is a weekend trip, right?" he asked.

"I wasn't sure what to pack," I said. "I'd rather have too much than not enough."

"And why do you have all this food for a six-hour drive? We can stop if we get hungry. Sometimes you are so country," he said with a smile.

I'd been living up north for three years, but still had some of my Price County habits. Whenever we traveled, I packed food and drinks in case we passed through sundown towns. About an hour into the trip, Winston said, "Since you brought groceries, let's see what you got in those bags."

"Are you sure you want one of these 'country' sand-wiches?" I asked, waving it under his nose. I gave him a ham sandwich and ten minutes later, he asked for another one. I'd ridden on this highway several times, but the Chicago skyline still fascinated me. I couldn't imagine working in a skyscraper or walking on sidewalks so crowded you couldn't see the concrete. We got stuck in traffic, but Winston's car had air-conditioning, a first for me, and we weren't bothered at all. We finally made it through traffic and rode through small towns that looked like carbon copies of each other. But when we got to Idlewild, we entered another world.

The town looked like a postcard, except with black people. When we got to our hotel, I couldn't believe I was walking the same grounds where Madam C.J. Walker, W.E.B. Du Bois and my daddy's favorite, Joe Louis, had lived and vacationed. There was horseback riding, swimming, boating, and a skating rink. But these weren't dingy afterthoughts like the facilities down home. Everything was first class. Winston golfed every morning and won third place in the tournament. I told Winston I'd never heard of a colored golfer, and he excitedly told me about the United Golf Association and that the Professional Golf Association had just opened to Negro golfers. Nancy Wilson and Billy Eckstine were the nighttime headliners, and we had a table up front. My new shoes wouldn't let me dance much, but I enjoyed watching everyone else. I ate food I'd never heard of, like chicken marsala (Winston ordered it for me and I liked it so much, I ordered it every day), quiche, and square pizza. The room and service were excellent and the weekend had been magical. When we got back to Milwaukee, Winston drove to his place.

"Aren't you taking me home?" I asked.

"You tired of me already?" Winston said.

"Not at all. I can't remember when I've had a better time," I said as he parked. I followed him inside and turned on the television while he brought in our suitcases.

"You look natural sitting there," he said. "You should move in with me."

"And get married?" I asked.

"Oooooo, slow down, slow down," Winston said, then coughed. "I always said I'd never marry again."

"And I always said I wouldn't be shacking up with nobody."

"Why do we need a piece of paper? I want to be with you. We make a good team."

"Well, if I did marry you, we'd need a bigger place," I

said. "Unless you plan to move that table from the back bedroom."

"That table is for my poker games."

"Use the dining room table or a folding card table like Aunt Lizzie does."

"I run real games, girl. That back room is a money-maker."

"Then where is Lana supposed to sleep? I wouldn't want her on the waterbed."

"Your daughter? I thought she lived with her father."

"She does, but it's always been my goal to have her live with me."

"If she's doing fine where she is and you're doing okay, why change?" he asked.

"Because this arrangement was supposed to be tem-porary. Lana and I are a package deal. That's why I live in a little room, so I can save money and get us a decent place. I thought you understood."

"And I thought you understood I'm not into the daddy scene, especially with another man's kid. I like us being able to take off whenever we want, like going to Idlewild," he said. "Sounds like we have some things to work out before we take the next step."

I nodded, but I knew there was nothing to work out and no next step. Lana and I were a package deal, and there was no need wasting time with a man who didn't understand that.

CHAPTER 11

A phone call after midnight is rarely good news. I was still living over the café and didn't have my own phone. When I heard the phone ringing downstairs, I hurriedly put on my housecoat and slippers and went to answer it. My heart was pounding by the time I reached the telephone.

"Hey girl," Vanessa said.

"Is something wrong?" I asked, short-winded from dashing down the stairs. "The baby's not sick, is she?"

"No, nothing like that," Vanessa said calmly. "What are you doing?"

"What do you think I'm doing? It's almost midnight. What's going—"

"Listen to me," she interrupted. "Get dressed and fire up that grill. You'll never guess who I'm bringing to the café."

"I don't have to guess. You're not bringing anybody at this time of night."

"It's barely midnight. Since you and Winston broke up, you've become such an old fuddy-duddy," Vanessa said. "What if I told you I'm looking at Marvin Gaye, Mary Wells, Smokey Robinson and the Miracles, the Marvelettes, Supremes, Temptations, and four fine Tops? And what if I told you they're hungry, and they're loading up their buses right now, and they're coming to the café?"

"I'd say you need to quit eating pork late at night, it's giving you strange dreams."

"I'm serious. You know I'm working part-time at the Palladium. Well, I was emptying ashtrays backstage and overheard some of the artists talking about how hungry they were and where could they get something decent to eat this late. I told them about the café and by the time I finished describing your buttery biscuits, crispy fried chicken and smothered potatoes, they were begging me to bring them over. Their driver will follow me. See you in a few minutes."

"Vanessa, wait—" I heard a dial tone and stood with the receiver in my hand until I heard the operator's voice. I vaguely remembered radio ads promoting the Motown Revue coming to the Palladium. I also remembered the time Vanessa said we could get a free bus ride home to Mississippi, only to find out it was the bus for Freedom Riders. I let her set me up on a blind date, only to find out the guy was married when his angry wife chased us out of the movie theater. And, she still owed me money for buying the Avon inventory that "we" were going to sell, which ended up in the back of her closet.

However, since there was always the possibility of a kernel of legitimacy in her conversations, I decided to get dressed. No sooner had I brushed my teeth, slipped on a dress and taken the rollers out of my hair, did I hear banging on the door. I looked out the window and there were two buses with what looked like a parade of folks getting off. Eddie Kendricks was holding the ladies' hands as they got off the bus.

I squealed as I ran downstairs. I unlocked the front door and they filed in, thanking me for opening up for them. They didn't seem like big stars without their gowns, wigs, and suits. They were just down-to-earth folks. Some played cards and others sat and talked as I pulled a menu together. Vanessa helped me prepare chicken, waffles, eggs, green beans, cornbread, corn, and anything else I could pull from the freezer. We spread everything out on the counter, combined breakfast foods with dinner foods, and let folks fix their plates buffet-style.

We used Mr. Ben's Polaroid to take pictures, and I posed for pictures with all of them. My favorite picture was of Marvin Gaye kissing me on the cheek. The nicest person, and I know this may surprise you, was Diana Ross. She was very polite and the only one who offered to help me clear the tables. And she ate her fair share too. Hard to believe she was that skinny, seeing the way she ate. They came in like a whirlwind and by five o'clock, they were gone. The bus driver gave me three fifty-dollar bills to cover their tab and asked me for Vanessa's phone number.

When Mr. Ben came in, he handed me one of the fifties. He said the publicity and the pictures were worth ten times that.

Mr. Ben added their pictures to his wall of stars and a few pictures ended up in *Jet* magazine. The café became a go-to spot for out-of-towners. Etta James came the next month, and when Chuck Berry arrived in town for the state fair, he had his driver bring a dinner from the café to his hotel room. A few Cowboys ate at the café after a preseason football game against the Packers. Even vice presidential candidate Hubert Humphrey stopped by (he asked for a second helping of meatloaf).

However, those magazine pictures had an unintended consequence. Six months after the Motown stars visited the café, I received a certified letter. Jesse was suing me for child support. When I called him, he said, "You hanging out with those rich people, I'm sure you can afford it." Other than a tip every now and then, cooking and serving those "rich people" didn't translate into higher pay for me. And to hear Mr. Ben complain, the café was always one step away from going under. If Jesse had asked for more money for Lana, I would've sent whatever he asked—within reason, of course—but to drag me through the courts was trifling, particularly since Lana was with Mama half the time. That letter was the wake-up call I needed. Living over the café was cheap, but it was time for me to move to a place where Lana could be with me.

CHAPTER 12

Since I was living on my own, with no Aunt Lizzie monitoring my comings and goings, and no baby Kendrick to worry about, I went out more often. Folks passing through probably got the impression the north side was full of alcoholics, because there was a tavern on every other corner. These were small gathering places with a bar, a jukebox, and a four-square-foot space that served as the dance floor. Nothing fancy, but compared to the hole-in-the-wall juke joints down home, these clubs seemed like palaces to me.

Eva and I made the rounds because she had connections everywhere. There were clubs for folks from Arkansas, Georgia, Alabama, Memphis, and several from Mississippi. Everybody knew your name. The bartender knew your payday, and he'd advance drinks on credit because he knew where you worked and that you'd be back.

Big Jim's was one of our favorites. It was considered a little upscale because the tavern had waitresses and food, not just snacks. The first time Eva took me there, the waitress asked me what I was drinking. I didn't know what to order, so I got what Eva ordered, a rum and Coke. "Tastes like spoiled molasses," I said, coughing.

"Give it to me," Eva said. "No sense in letting a good

drink go to waste. I know what you'll like." She ordered me a sloe gin fizz which was much better. However, I felt myself getting woozy, and made my way to the small buffet to put something in my stomach. The chicken tasted like it had been fried two weeks ago and the spaghetti was runny, with meatballs that had more mystery ingredients than meat. The corn and the pork and beans tasted like someone just dumped them out of the can.

A friend of Eva's asked her to dance. I pushed my plate to the side and people-watched until Eva and her partner returned to the table. Pointing to my full plate, he said, "That's probably cold by now. Would you like me to get you another plate?"

"Please don't," I replied. "I guess that's why they serve strong drinks, so folks won't notice how bad the food is."

Eva cleared her throat, then said, "Margo, this is Jim, as in Big Jim, the owner. Jim, meet Margo, the food critic."

I didn't know which tasted worse, the food, or my foot in my mouth. As I stammered for something to say, a man with a fancy camera around his neck rescued me. "Hey Jim, why are you hogging all the pretty women? My name's Clark Gibson. Would you like to dance?" he asked, reaching for my hand. I followed him to the dance floor, and we hitchhiked to two Marvin Gaye records, then he delivered me back to my table.

"Girl, I have made you the deal of a lifetime. You can thank me later," Eva stated, excitedly. "I told Jim that you cook for the Fourth Street Café and could prepare something better and probably for less than he paid for that slop."

"Who said I was looking for a new job?" I asked, as I dabbed the sweat around my temples.

"This would be something you do on the side," Eva said.

Folks worked such long hours down home, there wasn't much time to do side jobs. But up here, many had a side hustle. Soon, I began working some of Big Jim's parties. I paid Mr. Ben to let me use the café kitchen after hours, and he helped me buy products wholesale. Big Jim wanted fried chicken, spaghetti, baked beans, and green beans. I baked cakes that he sold by the slice. He also asked for roasted peanuts, fried okra, and pork skins. Big Jim said salty foods made people thirsty, making then buy more drinks.

I was working one Thursday night after the café was closed. There was a knock at the alley door, and I went to answer it as I wiped my hands on my apron. Big Jim usually came by or sent someone to pick up his weekend order around midnight.

I cracked the door and saw a familiar face. "Hey Margo, I'm here to pick up Big Jim's order."

I remembered dancing with him and said, "You're Clark, right? Come in and lock the door behind you. Big Jim's order is in the refrigerator," I said, as I placed the last fried apple pie on a rack.

"Those smell good. They may not make it to Big Jim's."

"I had extra dough, so I made a batch for the café. You can have a couple of these, but they're very hot."

"How about you put a couple to the side for me, and I'll come by later and get them?"

And that's how we started dating. Mama and Aunt Lizzie were glad I had a "steady." Vanessa said he seemed boring, but after Thomas and Winston, and witnessing her Harper drama—who, by the way, was pregnant again—boring suited me fine.

Clark was average height, average build, with a slightly receding hairline and skin the color of russet potatoes. He wouldn't turn your head if you passed him on the street. But he had twinkling eyes and a playful smile that made him look like he was getting ready to share a funny story with you. His smile was the hook that drew me in. He was a few years older than me and had fought in Korea. He was divorced with two sons.

Clark was a foreman at Phillips Foundry, not far from the café. Once we started dating, he began coming to the café for lunch. Vanessa, Eva, and Winston had shown me how to party in Milwaukee, but Clark showed me another perspective. A sunflower field, a historic downtown building, or vivid sunset were reasons for him to pull over and take a picture. And he couldn't believe that I liked to fish. I hadn't been since my daddy died, but it was one of my favorite pastimes, and Clark and I squeezed in visits to Quarry Lake as often as we could. We were spending a lot of time together, although we almost didn't make it to the second date.

We'd gone to see *Robin and the 7 Hoods* and had stopped for a burger before he dropped me off. "It's hard to believe it's almost September," Clark said, while dousing his French fries with ketchup. "My oldest boy will be starting middle school."

"And Lana will be starting kindergarten. Seems like yesterday, she was a baby."

"I guess she'll be coming home soon. I can't wait to meet her," Clark said.

"She won't be back up here until Christmas."

"Oh. I assumed she'd be coming back for school. Doesn't she live here?" Clark asked.

"No, she lives in Price with her father."

"Why?"

"Why do your sons live with their mother?" I replied.

"Uhhh, I always thought children stayed with their mothers. I mean, that's just the way it is unless—"

"Unless something was wrong, or she was unfit?"

"I didn't mean to imply that," Clark said.

"Are you unfit? Do you love your sons?"

"Of course I love my sons. I'd give anything to be with them. When their mother and I divorced, she left Milwaukee and went back to St. Louis to live near her mother."

"You could've found another job. Why didn't you move too? You said you'd give anything to be with them."

"Look, I wasn't trying to pick a fight with you. Just seems like a mother should be with her child."

"And just seems like you should mind your own business. I see the bus at the corner. I can catch it if I hurry. Good night," I said and rushed out the door. I sat near the front, still fascinated by being able to sit at the front of the bus. It was a short ride and when I got off the bus, a car horn startled me. It was Clark. He parked in a no parking spot, then ran up behind me.

"Look, I didn't mean to upset you. And I certainly didn't want you taking the bus alone at this time of night."

"I'm fine. I take the bus all the time. You'd better move your car before you get a ticket."

He got back in his car and drove slowly as I walked the remaining two blocks to the café. I tried not to look over my shoulder, but I knew he was trailing me. When I got to the café, he parked and said, "I wanted to make sure you arrived safely."

"I'm here. You can go now," I said. And he did. I didn't see him for about three weeks, until he came by to pick up Big Jim's order.

When I answered the back door, I said, "Oh, it's you."

"Wow. Is that a way to greet a paying customer?"

"You're picking up Big Jim's order, so you're not a paying customer. You're the paying customer's driver."

"What a low blow," Clark said, and then he simulated a boxing punch. "Now I know how Floyd Patterson felt."

I rolled my eyes and went to pull the pans out of the refrigerator.

"No samples today?" Clark asked. "If I apologize, can I get a couple fried pies?"

"Why would you want fried pies from such an unfit mother?" I asked.

"Margo, I didn't say that, but maybe I insinuated it and I apologize. I should extend the same understanding to you that I expect to receive. Who am I to judge?"

"Apology accepted," I said, in a shaky voice. "I guess I got mad because you were saying what I know others have said, and probably what I thought but wouldn't admit. Barely a minute passes that I don't think about my daughter. My plan was to come here, get established, then send for her. But she seems so settled, I thought maybe she's better off in a more traditional family setting. My ex, Jesse, has had more children and they seem like the perfect little family. I feel like I've failed her and I've missed my chance." I hadn't meant to divulge all that, and I hadn't meant to start crying.

"Do you see what time it is? You're working here almost twenty-four hours. I know you like to cook, but I'm sure that's not why you're here. Lana is lucky to have you working this hard for her and when the time is right, your hard work will pay off," Clark said as he passed napkins to me. "Can we call a truce?"

I sniffled, smiled and nodded.

"Now can I get a couple of those fried pies?" he said, flashing his playful smile.

And that's how we became a couple. He was easy to be with. He made me laugh. He made me feel pretty. He loved everything I cooked, and as far as loving, let's just say I could've written Aretha's song, "Dr. Feelgood."

I should've stayed with him. But I'm getting ahead of my story . . .

CHAPTER 13

It was hard to believe I was spending my third Christmas in Milwaukee. Back home we rose early and exchanged gifts, had a hearty breakfast, then went to church. Christmas in Price was more reverent, but Christmas in Milwaukee (and I hope the Lord forgives me for saying this) was more fun. In Milwaukee, it was easy to forget Christmas is a religious holiday.

Aunt Lizzie had a house full of company on the Saturday before Christmas, then again on Christmas Eve. She played Christmas music I'd never heard, like "Please Come Home for Christmas" by Charles Brown, "Santa Baby" by Eartha Kitt, and "Merry Christmas, Baby" by Chuck Berry. I felt guilty dancing to Christmas music, like God would strike us down, but Vanessa told me to sip a cup of Ripple and loosen up. At midnight, the couples exchanged kisses. Clark had gone to St. Louis to spend the holiday with his boys, but he called at midnight, as he'd promised. We only talked a few minutes, but that made my night. I excused myself from the party and went to bed, where, despite the noise, I quickly fell asleep.

At daybreak, Aunt Lizzie woke me up to help her with dinner. Not much later, Kendrick invaded the living room to claim his gifts. I called Lana around nine, and her perky voice was my gift. She had gotten the clothes, Slinky, Play-Doh, and Chatty Cathy doll I'd sent. She was having me listen to everything the doll said, but Jesse was rushing her off the phone. Mama was coming to take her to church.

I was supposed to be *helping* Aunt Lizzie with dinner, but I think it was the other way around. I prepared the fried chicken, turkey, dressing, pinto beans, two cakes, two pies, and Mama's ambrosia salad. Vanessa made greens and macaroni and cheese. Aunt Lizzie made candied yams, deer steaks, and opened the cranberry sauce. After dinner, some played cards and some snoozed. By five o'clock, the kids had tired of their toys and were fighting over an alleged offense. They were sent to bed and by seven we were eating again. After, we gathered around Aunt Lizzie's new color television to watch Sammy Davis, Jr. on *The Ed Sullivan Show*. The weather cooperated with enough of a dusting to say we had a white Christmas, but not enough to get in the way.

I was sitting on the couch, nodding despite the loud music, when Vanessa poked me in my side. "Wake up, party pooper."

"I have to get up early for work tomorrow," I said. "Don't mean to be rude, but I'm going to bed."

"As much work as you do at the café, that white man should let you off whenever you want. I don't know why you stay there. It's time for you to get a real job, Vanessa said.

"I had a so-called real job chopping up Porky Pig and his cousins. I didn't like smelling like rotten meat and doo-doo every day. No, thank you."

"The post office, Spiegel catalog, and U.S. Can Company are hiring. You're not working with dead animals and they pay at least two dollars an hour," Aunt Lizzie said. "What do you make at the café?"

That was none of her business, but my high school math

told me two dollars times forty hours a week was twice what I was making at the café. Mr. Ben and his wife were spending six weeks in Arizona. He left Ben Jr. in charge, and I didn't like the changes he was making. I made fresh biscuits every morning, and peeled potatoes to cook around lunchtime. Ben Jr. had me double the batch and make biscuits every other morning. He said this used less electricity and it was more efficient to make biscuits, mashed potatoes, and cornbread every other day. I told him Mr. Ben wasn't fond of serving leftovers. Ben Jr. said these weren't leftovers. We were doing the same thing the big restaurants did, and they kept freezers full of precooked foods. *Precooked* sounded like another word for "leftover" to me. Then he asked me to write down my cake recipes. He said others could help and my workload would be lighter. Whenever he asked about it, I told him, I forgot, but I was stalling until Mr. Ben came back. Asking a cook for their recipe was like asking a magician to reveal their secrets. The latest irritant came when he put a large pickle jar at the register for tips and split them at the end of each day. He said this was fair to everyone. Didn't seem fair to me. Why should I hustle and grin, just so everyone could share my tips? Especially the new girl, Sylvia, who was slow and mixed up the orders.

The longer I listened to Vanessa and Aunt Lizzie, and the more Ripple I drank, the more I became convinced it was time to make a move. Up north wasn't like down home, where you found a job and kept it until you died. Up here, Negroes had options. It was time for me to explore my options and move on.

Two days after Christmas, Vanessa took me to three places. I was hired on the spot at U.S. Can Company, and started the next day on second shift. My job title was production wrap feeder. That's a fancy name for feeding can labels into the machine. I remember the *I Love Lucy* episode where she and Ethel couldn't keep up with the conveyor belt at the candy factory. U.S. Can was the same way. I shadowed someone on my first day and after that, I was on my own. I quickly learned to pace myself, since the faster I worked, the faster the line moved.

The work was intense and every day I considered quitting. Our lunch break was a strict thirty minutes, something I hated. At the café, if we were busy, I wouldn't take an official break. I'd eat and sit whenever I could. But if I needed to get my hair done or stop at the store, I could squeeze in errands when we weren't busy. At U.S. Can, we hustled to the cafeteria and spent ten of our thirty minutes in line, before gulping down bland, overpriced food.

However, sitting for those twenty minutes was the shift highlight. While working, we stood all day and I developed corns for the first time. The only solace was knowing I was making more money. I'd be able to get my own place sooner and send for Lana. I planned to send half of my first paycheck to Mama. The last time we had spoken she complained that her washing machine was broken and the hardware store in town said they couldn't get replacement parts for at least three weeks. She had a wringer washer as old as I was, and I wanted to surprise her with a new top loading machine. I calculated that by my third paycheck, I'd have enough to get my own place. Then I could send for Lana.

The fifteenth came and my paycheck was only thirteen dollars. I learned about something called "holding back." I didn't understand the purpose. If I had worked, why wasn't I getting paid? The lady in the personnel office said I was paid in arrears, and I only worked one day in that pay period. To me it sounded like a slick way to get you to work for no pay. But Vanessa and Aunt Lizzie said that was standard practice now. I hadn't planned on no holdback and had to dip into my savings to make it to the end of January.

I had been at U.S. Can three months and was very disciplined about not dipping into my Lana fund. But Mama and Lana were coming for Easter, and I was going to make an exception. They arrived on Good Friday, and our first stop was Gimbels department store. Spring snow caught Mama off guard, as she and Lana had only brought thin jackets. I bought them both new coats and Easter dresses. I treated them to lunch at Marco's, and pizza became Lana's favorite food. We took the bus and Mama made sure we sat up front. When we got home, Lana recited her Easter speech for me. Mama had made her learn one, even though they wouldn't be at the program. We prepared our Sunday dinner on Saturday so we could eat as soon as we got home from church. This time, I wasn't the leader in the kitchen. Mama was directing the cooking. We congregated around her in the kitchen, while Lana and Vanessa's kids played in the back bedroom.

Monday morning, I called my supervisor and told him my mother was in town and I wasn't coming in. He spoke to me in an ugly manner and made a comment about "you people." Vanessa shook her head when I told her about it.

"You can't take off work because you feel like it. You should've told him you were sick," she said.

"But I'm not sick."

"Tell him you have bad cramps. Men don't like to hear about that stuff."

"I'm not talking to that man about my period."

"Then tell him your mother is sick."

"I'm not going to tell that lie. Besides, I'd already told him she was coming to town. I can't believe he won't let me off work. I told him I'd work extra."

"It doesn't work like that. U.S. Can is not the café, and this isn't Price. It's hundreds of people working there. That man probably doesn't even remember what you look like."

I was making more money but had less time to visit with Mama and Lana. Each day when I got in from work, I heard about the fun they'd had at the lake, the zoo, shopping, and going to the movies. Mama was as excited as Lana, but for a different reason. "Everywhere we went, black and whites were sitting together. I never took you to the zoo when we went to Memphis, because colored day was Thursday, and I had to work. Lord have mercy, it's like being in another country," she said.

I was glad Mama was enjoying herself since I'd been trying to convince her to move up here. But she and Lana were spending more time with Aunt Lizzie than with me.

They left Thursday afternoon. This time I took Vanessa's advice and called in sick in order to spend the last two days with them before they left. I was heartsick, so technically, I was telling the truth.

I had dipped into my savings while Mama and Lana were in town, so to rebuild my stash, I began bringing my lunch. Plus, I wanted to get away from my new line partner. She was a whiner, and gossipy. I don't know which was worse, the droning machines or her. I always had too much, and ended up giving some away. A couple of my coworkers said they'd pay me to bring extra for them. Soon I was taking orders and making as much from my lunch side business as from the job itself.

There are always a few crabs in the barrel that don't like to see folks get ahead. The next thing I knew, I was written up for soliciting on company property. "But they asked me," I protested. "I was minding my own business and folks wanted to know where my lunch came from."

But as Mama would say, there's more than one way to peel the onion, so on weekends, Vanessa and I prepared sandwiches, tamales, and cake slices. We took them to the parking lot edge to sell during the first shift and Uncle Max sold for us during my shift. We always sold out. This lasted for a few months, until a police officer gave me a citation for selling without a permit, *after* he ordered a ham and cheese sandwich. After the citation, the solicitation write-up, and taking off during Easter week, I was fired, since I was still in my one-year probation period.

I wasn't sorry. Chopping cotton would've been better than working at U.S. Can. At least you could feel a breeze, hear a bird and see the sky. Imprisoned in the windowless factory, you couldn't tell if it was day or night. The din of the machines gave me a headache and the goggles strap wore down my hairline edges. I missed talking to people, and I like putting my touch on things. One week's chili may have kidney beans and next week I might make it with pinto beans. Bell peppers could be stuffed with rice or orzo pasta. But in the factory, you must perform each movement just like the one before, just like you did it last week.

I lost my job and had to pay a fifty dollar fine, further denting my Lana fund. I investigated getting a permit, but it cost three hundred dollars. I decided to ask if Mr. Ben would be interested in a partnership in my sandwich business. Since he had a permit, I could pay him a portion of the proceeds.

It felt strange going to the café in regular street clothes. I had given away my aprons and smocks when I quit. The bus ride seemed shorter than I remembered and the Fourth Street bus stop now had a three-sided shelter and a bench. I stuck my head into Eva's shop, but she wasn't there. I also stopped and spoke to my friends in Dr. Brown's office, Lawson's Photo Studio, and Panda Palace on my way to the café.

"How nice of you to visit us common folks," Mr. Ben said with a mock bow when I came in. The savory smell of fried onions met me at the door. Sylvia greeted me with a hug and the men in the pinochle corner waved. Marvin Gaye was on the jukebox and the sun shone through the gingham curtains. "I'm glad to see you. I called a few times and left a message with your aunt."

Aunt Lizzie hadn't passed on those messages. She and Mama thought all white men wanted one thing from black women. "I guess she forgot to tell me," I said.

"I figured you were doing so well, you weren't interested in the café anymore. But I'd be lying if I didn't say I wish you were still here. The biscuits haven't tasted right since you left, and we had to take the ambrosia salad off the menu, since no one else could make it like you."

"I'm not working at U.S. Can anymore. I'm starting my own business." I explained my sandwich concept and asked if he was interested.

"You need a food peddler license. I have a food dealer license, which is different. Plus, there are new requirements, even for a food dealer license. Mine is grandfathered in, but if I make changes, I have to make updates. Unfortunately, I can't help you."

"You can still help me. I need a job," I said.

"I was hoping you'd say that. When can you start? And you can have your room back too, at your old rate."

I was back at the café, and thankful to be there. But I felt like I was going in circles. I'd never get Lana at this rate.

CHAPTER 14

I had a standing hair appointment every other Tuesday, but I had missed my last couple appointments; either Eva wasn't feeling well, or I was doing something with Clark at the last minute. My waitress bonnet no longer hid how rough my hair looked, so even though it was Thursday, I asked Eva to squeeze me in and she said she'd call when she was ready. It was six o'clock and she hadn't called yet, so I guessed she was busy and I'd try again in a few days. I watched the evening news, ironed my clothes for the rest of the week, and was writing a letter to Mama when she called.

"It's so late," I said, out of breath from rushing down the stairs, a little disappointed that it wasn't Clark. "I'll touch up my edges and wear a ponytail for another week," I told Eva.

"Get your tail over here before you burn your hair out with that kitchen hot comb. Besides, I have juicy news."

I put my letter aside and went across the alley to Eva's. Fourth Street after work hours was slow and quiet. Anybody on the street was a business owner, an employee, or someone's regular customer. It felt like a neighborhood rather than a business district, and I felt at home in this close-knit community.

"Sorry I didn't call earlier," she said, when I walked in.

"A state board inspector showed up as we were about to close. We got another excellent score, but that picky lady wore me out. I'm tired."

"You've been on your feet all day. We can do my hair another time."

"Okay, but I still want us to do something. Let's go out," she suggested.

"Didn't you just say you're tired?"

"I'm tired of working. Let's do something fun. We haven't been out in a while."

"Now?" I asked.

"Yes. Now. I'm not taking *no* for an answer," she said. "Big Jim's has a nice crowd on Thursdays. I'll press your new growth right quick, then we'll go. We won't stay late."

"Okay. What is this juicy news you have for me?" I asked.

"Remember me telling you I met a guy?" she asked.

"You know I can't keep up with your love life. As soon as I meet and like one of your guys, you've broken up."

"That's because I'm selective," she said.

"Well, tell me about him."

"He's a bartender at Big Jim's. That's where we met. But he's just working there until he graduates from law school. His name is George. Can you imagine a more homely name? I hope he doesn't want a George Jr. I am not naming my baby George."

"Baby? Are you pregnant?"

"Yes," she answered with a big grin.

"Congratulations," I said. "No wonder you're tired. How far along are you?"

"Seven weeks. We got married last month, but we haven't told anyone. That's my news."

"How could you go this long without telling me?" I asked.

"I liked him right away, but as you said, my track record isn't too good, and I didn't want to get my hopes up. That's why I kept things to myself. Plus, you've been rather busy yourself," she said with a smile.

"Will I get to meet him tonight?"

"He's not working tonight. He's studying for finals."

"Then it will be just us girls. We'll toast to your good news—nonalcoholic drinks, of course."

I was happy for Eva, but her pregnancy news triggered thoughts of my miscarriages. They say time heals grief, but I don't think *heal* is the right word. It's like having a broken leg. It heals, looks fine from the outside, and you learn to use it without a limp. But when the weather gets cold, you're reminded of the break. Eva's news put a chill in the air.

The parking lot was surprisingly full for a weeknight. "I'll go speak to the bartender," Eva said as we entered. "You find us a seat."

I stood near the door and as my eyes adjusted to the dim light, I noticed Vanessa and Harper sitting close to the dance floor. She waved before I could avert my glance. I still didn't see how she could stand him, but since she'd had two kids by him, I guess she wanted to make it work. I took a deep breath, then headed her way. "Hey cuz," she said. "Sit with us."

"I'll go get you ladies a drink," Harper said. "What would you like?"

"Nothing, thank you," I replied, wondering what was taking Eva so long. I didn't trust that man and wouldn't eat or drink anything he touched. As Vanessa and I were catching up, she stopped mid-sentence and nodded her head toward the door.

"Girl, ain't that Clark coming in the door?" Vanessa asked.

"It sure is," I said, waving to get his attention. He still had on his work clothes and was standing in the doorway, looking around.

"Put your arm down," Vanessa said, grabbing my hand. "Wait and see if he's with someone. Didn't you say he was working?"

Before I could answer, Clark and I made eye contact and he came to our table. "Hey Vanessa," he said, without even looking at her. "Margo, I thought you were getting your hair done."

"We were tired. Eva and I decided to go out instead."

"Well, I changed my mind about working and got off early. Let's go."

Vanessa grabbed my arm as I rose. "He don't own you and he ain't your daddy. Tell him you don't appreciate him coming in here, ordering you around."

"Well, I don't appreciate you sitting up in no club, lapping up liquor, while I'm out working overtime so we can get married," Clark said.

"Girl, don't fall for that line. If he had wanted to get married, he would've said something before now. Do what you want. I'm going to find Harper."

Clark sat in Vanessa's seat, then asked, "How long you been sneaking out?"

"I didn't sneak out. Eva and I wanted to come out for a little while. That's all."

"I guess I was just surprised to see you. I came here to pick up money Big Jim owes me. I'm sorry if I came on a little strong. I worked a double three days in a row and I'm dog-tired."

"Apology accepted. Now what was that about working overtime? This is the first I've heard you say anything about us getting married."

"I've been looking for a bigger place so Lana can stay with us whenever she wants. I put a ring on layaway and planned to surprise you and propose properly at Christmas."

As if on cue, "How Sweet It Is" by Marvin Gaye, came

on the jukebox. "Mr. Gibson, I'll leave with you on one condition. Let's dance."

"I'm still wearing my work clothes," he said.

"Not for long. Let's dance, then get out of here."

"Can I take that as a 'yes' to my proposal?"

"That would be a yes."

We planned to get married at the courthouse, then have a get-together at our new place. Eva wouldn't hear of it. Since she and George didn't have a formal wedding, she said I should have one for both of us. Rev. White officiated at his church. I rarely wore heels and everyone complimented my gold, three-inch pumps, and white, sateen, off-the-shoulder, hip-hugging, knee-length dress, which I wore with white evening gloves. During the ceremony, Clark's mother did make a crack about me wearing white. Although, the gloves didn't stay white. I kept dabbing my tear-streaked face, forgetting that I was wearing makeup. Eva and Vanessa were my bridesmaids, and Clark's sons were his groomsmen. Uncle Max gave me away, but the sweetest part of the day— Eva and Clark arranged for Lana to be my flower girl. She and Mama arrived on the train that morning and surprised me. It sounds corny, but I was marrying my best friend, and having Lana there made it perfect.

We had a respectable reception in the church basement and Mr. Ben paid for the food. Later, we took the leftovers to the café and had a real party. We moved the center tables. Eva spiked the punch and Mr. Ben set the jukebox to free play. James Brown, the Marvelettes, and Stevie Wonder were in heavy rotation. We were barefootin' and doing the hitchhike. But Mr. Ben and his wife were the life of the party. He played Frankie Yankovic records, and they showed off their polka moves. I never knew I could be so happy and a good time was had by all.

Too bad it didn't last.

CHAPTER 15

Clark and I found a two-bedroom downstairs unit. The area was racially mixed, with the whites leaving as fast as they could. Our new place was a block away from a bus stop and my first time cooking on an electric stove.

Clark saw his mother more often after we got married than he did before. Seems like she always needed a ride somewhere, he needed to do her yardwork, or something needed fixing, or had to be moved. My mother-in-law and I didn't have a bad relationship. We had no relationship. Our paths rarely crossed, since I never went to her house. It hadn't bothered me and Clark didn't seem to care. My family was more lively and hearing them call me Callie was the funniest thing to him. Clark and Uncle Max acted like they'd known each other their whole lives. Aunt Lizzie always claimed him as her bid whist partner and Mama said since he was older, he should be stable and finished chasing women. His mother never said she didn't like me, but she didn't have to. We'd been married four months and she'd never come to visit. She didn't come to our housewarming party, and when I invited her to a get-together I had when Lana was visiting, she said she had another engagement.

I learned she was hosting her annual family dinner for Clark's birthday. While we were dating, I didn't feel compelled to go. But his sisters were coming from Chicago, and he insisted I come. This would be my first time at his mother's house since we'd gotten married.

To help me prepare for the party, Eva came by to refresh my curls. "Girl, if you don't relax, you'll sweat out your hair. Quit worrying. You already got the man, you don't need to impress his mother."

"I'm not trying to impress her. I just want us to have a better relationship. I never had to get to know family before. In Price, everybody already knew everybody."

"Forget about her. She'll love you when you present her with a grandbaby. When are you going to tell Clark?"

I was pregnant. I'd missed two periods and certain smells, especially onions and garlic made me nauseous. But I was waiting until I went to the doctor before I told Clark.

"I'm about to burst, keeping this secret," Eva said, whose due date was just weeks away. "By the time you start showing, I'll be rocking this baby, and you can have my maternity clothes."

"Right now, I need to concentrate on what I'm wearing today," I said. "What do you think about these new paisley bell-bottoms with a ruffled white blouse?"

"Where did you buy those? That's bad," Eva said.

"Really? It's a bolder pattern than I usually wear, but the salesgirl was very complimentary. I should've known she was just trying to get a sale."

"*Bad* means *good*. Keep up, Daisy Mae," Eva teased.

"Why didn't you just say that?" I replied.

"Somebody's got to keep you up-to-date. Just because we're almost thirty, doesn't mean we have to be lame."

"And I suppose *lame* has nothing to do with a broken leg or foot?" I asked.

"Help her, Lord," Eva said, as she grabbed her purse and the 7UP cake she'd been craving. "I'll talk to you on the flip side—that means tomorrow."

"Girl, get out of here," I said, checking my watch. As usual, time flew when we got together, and I was running behind. I still had to frost the carrot cake I made to take to Clark's mother's house, iron and change purses.

I was ironing my blouse when the doorbell rang. Clark had forgotten his keys before, so I thought it was him. To my surprise it was Vanessa and her kids.. "What are you doing here?" I asked. When she stepped inside, I knew why. Her left eye was black, her bottom lip was busted, and she and Kendrick were wearing house slippers. Harleen was sucking her thumb, something she'd quit doing, and Junior was only wearing a t-shirt and diaper. "Give me the baby," I said, and stood to the side for them to come in.

"You look dressed up," Vanessa said. "Are you going out?"

"We're going to my mother-in-law's house. Today is Clark's birthday."

"I know this is inconvenient, but I need a favor. We need a place to stay—just for tonight. I promise we won't get in your way."

"You're always welcome," I said, leading them to our bedroom. I didn't ask any questions and she offered no explanations. Back then, we didn't get in folks' business.

When we were kids, Vanessa got in fights all the time, and I couldn't understand why she was so docile now. I didn't think Harper was worth two teaspoons of spit, but whenever I said something about him, she got mad at me. All I could do was help her until she woke up from his spell. I made sure she had a change of clothes, showed her where everything was in the kitchen, then hurriedly finished dressing.

When Clark came in, I met him at the door, with my

index finger over my lips. I pointed to our bedroom and led him to the kitchen.

"What's up?" he asked.

"Vanessa and the kids are in our room. She's beat up pretty bad," I said in a low tone. "Maybe this time she'll leave Harper for good."

"I thought we'd have time for a quickie before we leave," he said, and tapped my behind. "Looks like no birthday nookie for me. I just hope that fool don't come over here starting no mess."

Clark changed his shirt and I made sure Vanessa had my mother-in-law's number in case she needed to contact us. Walking through her house, it was hard to believe this was the same place my husband grew up. Obviously, he hadn't inherited her neat gene. Everything was in its place down to the perfectly placed doilies on her coffee tables. She had wall-to-wall cream- colored shag carpet, an orange and peach–flowered couch, healthy ferns hanging in the window, and a huge grandfather clock. She declined my offer to help in the kitchen, which was good, since my stomach was a little queasy. Sitting on the plastic-covered couch reminded me of days my mother took me to work with her and told me to sit and not touch anything. Pictures of Clark and his siblings in their graduation caps adorned the piano, along with Clark in his basic training Army pictures. I'd never seen his hair cut so low.

"Is this you?" I asked when I picked up a black-and-white picture of a little boy wearing a sailor suit and short pants. His sisters and mother were in the kitchen, and they called him to come help with something. I browsed through the photo album on the coffee table. There were several smiling photos of Clark, his boys, and who I assumed was his ex-wife. Despite Clark's version of his marriage, apparently there had been happy times. Hopefully by year-end, there would be new baby pictures in this book.

I had dozed off in the living room when Clark called me to come eat. His mother was serving sweet peas, corn, broccoli, meatloaf, and ham. "All my son's favorites," his mother said.

"Try the meatloaf," Clark said, as he heaped a serving on my plate. "No one makes it like my mother."

Thank goodness, I thought. I've never been a fan of meatloaf with brown gravy and her gravy was runny and garlicky. I tried to be polite and sample the meatloaf, but it was full of onions and I could barely tolerate the smell. We discussed the weather, Lt. Uhura on the new *Star Trek* show, and Dr. King's upcoming march. His older sister said my greens had too much pepper and his mother said she already had a cake, and she left mine in the kitchen.

She put candles on her store-bought cake, and we sang "Happy Birthday." Then his sister asked, "So are you still a cook down on Fourth Street?"

"She sure is," Clark interjected before I could answer. "I get to eat her delicious cooking every day. It's a wonder I haven't gained fifty pounds."

"I haven't been down there in ages," his mother said. "Once the new Gimbels department store opened out in Capitol Square, the quality of merchandise at their Fourth Street store declined. I wasn't surprised when it closed."

"But if everyone abandons the original locations for the new one, what happens to the original location and neighborhood?" I asked.

"It's called progress," Clark's mother said. "I'm sure something else has moved into their old location."

Businesses on the first floor of the old Gimbels now included a pawn shop, a thirty-member church, a psychic, and a convenience store whose primary products were malt liquor and Zig-Zag rolling papers. The second floor was vacant, and there was a farmer's market in the parking lot in the summer. Hardly an equal swap for Gimbels, but Clark caught my gaze and jumped in before I could speak.

"That store had the best toy department," Clark said. "But I hated those babyish suits you used to buy. I was the only boy in third grade wearing short pants."

"I loved shopping at Gimbels," his younger sister said. "We'd get shoes at Sam's, an ice cream float at Woolworth's counter, and fried rice from Panda Palace to take home for dinner."

"Yes, Fourth Street was better before all these new people moved up here," Clark's mother said. "I'm all for integration, but some of those people…"

The corn his mother had prepared had been bathed in butter, and it wasn't sitting well on my stomach. Or maybe her condescending attitude was making me sick. Mama would've said she was so stuck up she'd drown in a rainstorm. I excused myself from the table and went back to the living room.

As they strolled down memory lane, I thought about her question. I *was* still a cook. I'd been up here almost six years and had a decent job, made way more than I ever would've made down home, and my regular customers were like family. I'd ignored Clark's mother and his sister's snide, uppity remarks, but they had a point. Was I going to scramble eggs and wait tables the rest of my life? I'd married a good man. We had a nice place and were starting our family. But I realized I hadn't done what I came north to do— make a home for my daughter. As bitchy as Clark's mother and sisters were, they seemed to enjoy each other's company and shared memories. What memories of me would Lana have? I was a holiday visitor and a vacation stop where she could get pizza. I was delighted to be pregnant, but was I neglecting the child I already had? Even Vanessa, barefoot and bloody, had her babies with her. It was time for me to get my baby girl and have the family I'd envisioned. Clark's mother began clearing the table and I offered to help.

"No, thank you, dear. You're in a kitchen all week. I'm sure you're enjoying the break."

I was about to assure her I didn't mind, but first I rushed to the bathroom to throw up. I almost made it.

PART II

The Main Ingredient

CHAPTER 16

I lost the baby, but I never told Clark. To explain the two days I spent in bed, I said I was having extra bad cramps. My recovery from this miscarriage was slower than it had been after my previous one, and thankfully Vanessa was still at our place. While Clark was at work, she took me to the doctor for the D&C procedure, where they scraped remaining tissue from my defective womb. She kept urging me to tell Clark, but I'd never told him about my previous miscarriage. I decided there was no need informing him of something that wasn't happening.

Clark thought Vanessa was just helping, unaware I had any medical issues. She cooked, cleaned, and washed, but one thing she couldn't do was keep her kids quiet. Hearing them reminded me of what I'd lost and could never have. And when Eva came to the house to do my hair, seeing her swollen stomach reminded me of my loss. Four weeks later, when she had George Jr., I sent her a card but didn't visit. I told her I had a cold and didn't want to pass it to the baby. Then on Mother's Day, Lana sent me the sweetest handmade card. I felt foolish. Here I was grieving a loss when I already had a precious daughter. I resolved to take more aggressive steps to get Lana, and Clark said he'd do whatever I needed.

The time Vanessa and her kids spent with us showed me our apartment was sufficient for newlyweds, but it wasn't family friendly. Also, while the house we were renting wasn't in the freeway's path, the surrounding neighborhood was, and every day we drove past more empty, bulldozed blocks. Rather than renew our lease, we decided to move.

We had saved a modest down payment for a home, and I'd been looking through the classified section for weeks. Now that we were ready to begin house hunting, I asked Ben Jr., who was a Realtor, to help us. The city's unofficial black boundaries were spreading, so in addition to looking at houses in the café's vicinity, I selected houses in newly integrated areas and surrounding suburbs. Ben Jr. and I toured houses, then I took Clark to those I thought we should consider buying. Some suburban and newer houses that I selected miraculously became unavailable after our walk-through. Ben Jr. said it was bad luck.

"Bad luck, my eye," Clark said. "I bet if you showed up with a white couple, you wouldn't have this so-called bad luck."

"Wow. I never thought of that. I can't believe people are that prejudiced," Ben Jr. said.

"Welcome to our world," I said. After looking at a *Leave It to Beaver* style house on Johnson Lane four times, we put in an offer. I jumped every time the phone rang, hoping it was Ben Jr., telling us we had the house.

"Yes, this is Mr. Gibson," Clark said, in his speaking-to-white-people voice, when he answered the phone during dinner. "That's right. We made an offer." He remained quiet for what seemed like hours, and I tried to lean next to him and listen, but he kept shooing me away. "No, we won't be able to do that. It wasn't our first choice anyway. Good night."

"Sounds like we didn't get the house."

"We don't want the house. White folks..." he said, shaking his head. "That was a Johnson Lane Neighborhood Association officer. He's representing a group offering to pay us to withdraw our bid."

"Like in the movie, *Raisin in the Sun*?"

"I don't know about a movie, but if those are the type of people living there, we don't want to move there," he said.

"These northern bigots are no different than the ones down home," I said. "How much were they offering?"

"What difference does it make?"

"I'm curious. We don't want to move there—right? They don't know that. Why not take their money?" I asked.

"All money ain't good money. I don't know why you want to move around white people."

"It's not that I want to be around white people. I like the houses and if we can afford it, why let some backward racists stop us?"

Clark answered the phone when the first representative called, but I answered their second call. The man on the line said it was his understanding from speaking with my husband that we weren't interested in the house, but it still had a *sold* sign in the yard. I told them I really liked the house. Before I completed my sentence, he said they'd double their offer. That was the easiest thousand dollars I ever made. I told Ben Jr. I wanted to look at houses in Germantown, an all-white suburb. I got the same response and made another thousand dollars. I then started attending open houses by myself. Within two months, I made eight thousand dollars.

I could have continued longer, but I visited a new subdivision in Brookdale and after I toured the model, I was sold. The new harvest gold kitchen appliances sparkled. The bathroom grout was spotless, and there was plush carpet throughout the house. We'd get to pick paint colors, cabinet hardware, and floor coverings.

"This house is even farther out than the last one," Clark said when I took him to the subdivision. "And there's no grass or trees."

"We get to plant our own trees. Grass doesn't take long to grow, and the yard is big enough for a small garden and a swing set for Lana."

"Don't try to make it as though this is about Lana. This is about you. I don't see why you're intent on living around white folks," Clark said.

"Show me new subdivisions full of Negroes and I'll consider it."

"I prefer an established neighborhood," Clark said. "Besides, this is way past our price range."

"Ben Jr. already called the bank officer. We only need five thousand more in a down payment, and we'll still qualify."

"Where is this five thousand supposed to come from?"

"Remember when I told you I had a surprise—well, here it is," I said, handing him our bank passbook.

"This is our account?"

"Yep," I proudly said.

"Where did this money come from?"

"I found a way to make the system work for us. I had Ben Jr. show me houses in lily-white neighborhoods that I knew we weren't interested in. A few homeowners took the bait and offered money for me to withdraw our offer."

"It wasn't *our* offer, since I knew nothing about it. I thought I said we weren't interested in making deals with any racist bastards."

"I thought you meant on that one house."

"Don't play with me, Margo. You know what I meant, or you wouldn't have been sneaking around."

"I didn't sneak. I didn't steal it, and no one got hurt. We have enough for the down payment, new furniture, and your pool table."

"Mrs. Gibson, I don't know if the NAACP would approve of your tactics, but it looks like we're integrating Brookdale."

As I leaned over to hug him, he stepped back and said, "I'm going along with this because it's already done, but you're out of the real estate business, okay? We had the last laugh, but those honkies don't know that, and still believe they're better than us."

"Okay, baby. My goal was to get us in a nice house, and it's done," I said.

Selecting the lot, the ranch floor plan, colors, and finishes was fun. We drove out to the lot every other day and photographed every stage of the build, from pouring the foundation to framing the structure. I even got a library card, so I could check out decorating magazines for ideas. The process was supposed to take six months, with completion coinciding with Lana's move date at the end of her school year. But our rainy spring delayed completion several weeks.

Then Lana called one night in April. I usually called her, or Jesse dialed, then gave her the phone, or she'd call from my mother's house. "Mommy, I want to come live with you," she said in a voice that told me she'd been crying.

"As soon as school is out, I'll be there to get you," I said. "Is something wrong?"

Then Jesse took the phone and told her to go to her room. "What's going on?" I asked.

"It's not a good time," he said. "She'll call you later."

I called back several times, but got no answer. Then I called Mama and asked her to find out what was going on. Turns out Lana and her stepbrother got into a fight, and both were being punished.

"Is that all?" Clark said when I told him.

"I want to go get her," I said. "She's never called me crying before."

"My siblings and I fought all the time. Once my sister

was babysitting and tied me to a chair, then went outside to play. Kids do that," Clark said.

"This is different. Jesse's at work. He doesn't know what's going on and of course his wife will favor her child. I'm going to go get her." I got the Yellow Pages and began searching for the Greyhound Bus phone number.

"I think you're overreacting."

"And what if I'm not?"

"Your mother won't let anything happen. I wish you wouldn't do this," Clark said.

"And I wish you would support me," I said.

"It's not that I don't support you, but there's just a few weeks until semester's end. If things are that bad, Lana could stay with your mother."

"If you don't want her here—"

"You know that's not it. But I don't like her playing you and her father against each other."

You don't believe her side of the story?" I asked.

"When we were coming up, kids didn't have a side."

"And a lot of things happened that shouldn't have. I'm going to get my baby," I said as I thumbed through the Yellow Pages.

"But she's not a baby. She's a girl who's learned to manipulate the situation when she doesn't get her way. Will she call your ex when something happens here that she doesn't like?"

"We'll never have that problem."

"Baby, it's just a few more weeks," Clark said. "Then we'll drive down and get her."

I reluctantly agreed, but two weeks later Mama called the café, something she rarely did.

"Callie, I'm sorry to bother you at your job, but—"

"Is Lana okay?"

"No. I mean, she's not sick or anything—"

"Mama, what is it?"

"She's in the Price County Juvenile Detention Center."

"What happened?" I asked, pulling the long phone cord into the hall.

"Lana said Eric has been messing with her—"

"Isn't that Jesse's stepson? And what do you mean, messing with her?" I asked.

"As far as I can make out, he's been touching her and grabbing her, and—"

"That boy is in high school. How could Jesse let this happen?"

"She said she kept telling him to quit and he wouldn't, so she stabbed him with a fork. A neighbor heard the commotion, called the police, and they took her to juvenile. They won't release her to me since I'm not her legal guardian."

"That nasty boy molests an eight-year-old girl. She protects herself, yet she's the one who gets locked up? Oh, hell no! I'll be there as soon as I can."

I told Clark what happened and I was going to get my child. I called Mr. Ben and told him I had a family emergency, then packed a bag, and caught the last flight of the day. It was my first time flying, but I was so upset, I forgot to be scared. I flew into Jackson and Mama picked me up. The detention center was closed to visitors until the next morning. By daybreak, I'd found an attorney, called Jesse's house, and cursed him and his wife out three times.

"Callie, you should know I wouldn't let anything happen to Lana," he said, when I went to his house.

"Then how did this happen?" I asked.

"You know how kids are. They fight one minute and they're playing together the next," Jesse said. "Eric is a good kid."

"You believe him over your own daughter? Why would you leave them home alone? Young girls are violated every day because no one thinks it'll happen in their family."

"Now you're supermom and you're going to swoop down here and tell me what to do in my house?"

"I could care less what you do in your house. I've gotten a lawyer, and all I want is for you to sign over custody to me, or I will call Price County Protective Services."

"Lana is fine, but she misses you. She thinks you hung the moon, so it would be good for her to be with her mother awhile," Jesse said.

He brought four bags to Mama's house, signed the papers, and three days later, Lana and I landed in Milwaukee.

Clark had done his best to spruce up the second bedroom for her arrival, but everything had happened so fast, and some of Vanessa's and her kids' things were still there. Lana seemed pleased, even with all the boxes. She played school and pretended they were her students' desks.

The next day, she and I went shopping, and got pizza, then I took Lana to Eva's to get her hair done. Two days later, I enrolled her in the neighborhood school. When we rented the duplex, schools weren't one of our considerations. I was concerned about her adjusting to her new school, so I drove by the playground at recess to see if I could spot her. She wasn't hard to pick out. She had on the prettiest dress and she was jumping rope while two white girls turned the rope.

That evening during dinner (pizza—our third time that week), I asked how her first day at school had gone. "It was fun," she said. "I had a desk to myself and our books were so new, they cracked when I opened them. I've never had a new book before." She went on to fill me in on the rest of her day while I combed her hair and put a roller in her bangs. As I wrapped the scarf tight to protect her style, she reached up and hugged me. "I love it here, Mommy. I miss Daddy, but I never had my own room before, and I get to eat pizza. If I had known living here would be this cool, I would've made something up about Eric a long time ago."

I removed her arms from around my neck and asked her, "What did you say?"

"I said I like living here."

"I mean about making something up," I said, and slowly stood.

"I wanted to come live with you," she said with a whiny tone.

"You made it up?" I said, with my voice rising. "I wanted you to come here, but you can't say untrue things about people. Eric's in a lot of trouble because of what you said."

"You're mad at me," she said with tears filling her eyes.

"I'm not mad at you, but what you did was wrong. Now everyone thinks badly of Eric. You wouldn't like someone to do that to you, would you?"

"I guess not. Please don't send me back," she said and flung her arms around my waist.

"You'll always be with me," I said, as I sat on her bed. "But you can't make up things just to get what you want. You're old enough to know better."

I'm sorry," she said between sobs.

"I'm not the one you owe an apology. I'm going to call your father and you need to tell him what you've told me." I made Lana follow me to the kitchen wall phone. I dialed Jesse's number, but the line was busy. "It's late. Go to bed and we'll call your father in the morning."

The next morning when I went to her room, she was sleeping soundly with Bubba Bear snug under her arm. I closed the door and we never spoke on it again.

I probably should have handled it differently, but how could I punish her for wanting to be with me? As I look back, I wonder if things would have turned out differently if I had.

CHAPTER 17

The delay in our house construction had an unplanned benefit. Lana helped us pack, got to pick her wall colors and her bedroom curtains, and selected the bedspreads for her twin beds. She wasn't moving into our house; we were starting a new chapter together. We were pleasantly surprised that our move seemed to be well accepted. We got a few stares but no one was overtly rude. One neighbor brought us a pie, but Clark said not to eat it. He was mistaken for the gardener a few times and asked what he'd charge to do their yard. But overall things went smoothly. We planted two aspen tree seedlings, and even though it was already June, I tilled a small garden. Lana helped plant tomatoes, collards, bell peppers, carrots, and a border of petunias. She loved the neighborhood park. There were swings, a slide, a seesaw, and a baseball field. How different from the park in our old neighborhood, which had a raggedy slide and concrete where the basketball court had been.

Two weeks after we moved into the house, I began looking for private schools. I came home with several brochures and showed them to Clark. "You're a native, how would you rank these schools?" I asked.

"I'd rank them all high," he said. "As in high cost. Sometimes the Catholic schools have tuition scholarships, but those are for low-income families, and we probably don't qualify. Why are you looking at private schools? I thought the whole point of moving into this neighborhood was so Lana could attend a white school."

"I don't care if the school is white or blue, I just want the best," I said. "I didn't think you'd be opposed."

"I'm opposed to you starting this without discussing it with me. These schools aren't cheap, and we just moved into this house. We're going to be broke as the Ten Commandments."

"We'll figure something out," I said, while I changed clothes.

"That's not a reliable budgeting strategy. I had planned to take you and Lana to the matinee tomorrow. I guess all we can afford is TV and Jiffy Pop," he said, then walked out and slammed the door.

I didn't understand why he was irritated. Now that we were in the house, the money we had been putting aside for the down payment could go toward Lana's tuition, plus we still had some of my *Raisin in the Sun* money. Problem solved.

After attending several open houses, I selected Parkview Academy. Class sizes were small, standardized test scores were high, and they had other Negro children, as the counselor was quick to tell me. I only worked half days during Lana's first few weeks of school. She adjusted well and made friends right away.

For our anniversary, Clark drove me to a Buick car lot and said, "We're going to finally get you a car. My car is almost paid for, so it shouldn't be a strain for us. If you'd prefer something different, we can go somewhere else."

I reached over and hugged him. "How thoughtful." We had been a one-car family. The duplex had been on the bus route to the café, so having one car hadn't been an issue. But our new house was three miles from the closest bus stop, and the buses ran less frequently. Now that Lana was with me, I was always running late. I couldn't sleep until the last minute anymore. I usually ate breakfast at the café, but now I had to make sure she ate breakfast. And the biggest task was combing her hair. I tried combing her hair the night before and wrapping it in a scarf, but Lana slept all over the bed, and her hair still looked raggedy the next morning. And invariably, even though she was wearing school uniforms, she'd want to change a part of the outfit I had picked, and it usually required ironing, adding another ten minutes. But with the new car, my morning routine became more manageable.

Life was good. Then Clark got laid off from the foundry. He made up some of the difference by working concessions at Braves games and at the airport with Uncle Max. He worked all day on weekends, but his weekday hours were erratic because he timed his airport schedule to coincide with incoming flights from either coast. He said those passengers were the biggest tippers. Then, Clark's transmission went out and we were back to a one-car family. The one benefit to his reduced work schedule—he was getting through my "honey do" list.

"Glad I brought dinner home," I said when I came in and saw Clark working under the sink.

"I thought I'd have the kitchen cleaned up, but this is taking longer than I expected," Clark said. "We'll have to eat in the dining room."

"All right. I'll go get Lana."

"She's in her room."

I went to her room and saw she was asleep, which was unusual.

"She still has on her school uniform. I hope she's not coming down with something," I told Clark.

"She's pouting."

"What's she pouting about?" I asked.

"I popped her little legs and told her to go to her room. I guess she fell asleep."

"What do you mean, popped her legs?"

"When I came in, I told her to clean the dishes from the sink so I could install this new faucet. I had my mother's car, and I went outside to wash it. When I came in she hadn't washed the dishes. I reminded her to do the dishes. She said you told her to do her homework when she got in, then left the room.

"I followed her and nicely asked her to wash dishes. She sat her mouthy behind down, crossed her legs, and said I wasn't her daddy, and she didn't have to do anything I said. I took off my belt and tapped her legs a couple times. I haven't mentioned it, but this isn't the first time she's sassed me."

"Really?"

"You say 'really' like you don't believe me. I'm not going to be arguing with a child."

"She was wrong, but I thought we understood you'd leave the discipline to me," I said.

"That's fine when you're around. But some things must be handled immediately. What I look like telling her, 'Wait till I tell your mama'? She'll have zero respect for me."

"You'll have to find another way to make your point."

"We can't let her play us against each other," Clark said, as he turned the faucet on and off.

"You are not to touch her."

"The only thing I hurt was her feelings. You act like I beat her. I know you're protective, but I'll be damned if I'm going to have a child in my house disrespect me."

"She was speaking her mind, something I encourage her to do."

"Speaking her mind is one thing, disobeying me is another. And if you believe that's okay, then we have an even bigger problem."

"She's spent most of her life away from me. I don't want her to hate being here."

"We should've set boundaries from the beginning. I was trying to do it your way, but it's not working. You're trying to be her friend, not her parent," Clark said, and dried his hands.

"How can you be such an expert? I'll bet you'd feel differently if your sons told you their mother let some man hit them."

"I wouldn't let my sons manipulate me and neither will a third-grade girl. And I thought I was more than *some man* to you."

"Of course you are," I said. "I'm sorry—"

"I'm going to make this easy for you," Clark said as he went to the closet and grabbed his coat.

"Wait," I said and grabbed his arm. "I shouldn't have said that. You're a great father. And I want you to be a father to Lana."

"I'm not treating her any different than if she was my biological daughter. You want her to like you. But I don't need any eight-year-old friends. I'm gonna let you and your friend hang out as much as you want," Clark said as he put his toothbrush in his pocket.

"Like I said, this isn't the first time this has happened, and you need to decide if you want a husband or a babysitter."

I went to the bathroom and slammed the door. I couldn't believe this was happening. Many times I had wished Lana was here, to complete our family. I finally had my daughter, but I was losing my husband.

A week later, Clark and I were still in a cold war over his spanking Lana. But time only strengthened my resolve. I'd never seen him strike his children, and didn't see why he thought he should put a hand on mine. He spent a lot of time at his mother's, said he was painting. I think that was his way of getting away from the house, since she'd been asking him to paint for over a year. By the time he got home, I'd spent the evening weeding the garden and ironing before going to bed. We didn't speak when he got in the bed. I worked at the café every other Sunday, and usually left Lana at home on the Sundays I worked. But under the circumstances, I didn't think it was a good idea to leave her with him, so I woke her up and told her to get dressed. I felt bad since it was dark and she was still groggy.

"Why are you making Lana get up? Don't tell me you're afraid to leave her with me," Clark said, as he looked in her room.

"I figured you didn't want to be bothered."

"Did I ever say that?" he asked. "I knew you had a daughter when I married you. I just want what's best for her. We don't agree on everything, but I think we can both agree it's not in her best interest to get up before daybreak and go sit at the café. Let the child sleep."

"All right. Thank you," I said.

"Don't thank me, like I'm an outsider doing you a favor. Are we a family or not?"

I nodded my head because I was near tears and didn't want to start crying. Clark went back to bed. I got my purse and went to the kitchen. After about three minutes, I returned to the bedroom and got back in bed. "I thought you were leaving," Clark said.

"Then you better work quick," I said, as I unbuttoned my blouse. "But not too quick."

Clark put a finger under my chin, lifted my face, and kissed me. I put my arms around his neck and held on like he was a life preserver. This was our first argument about Lana. Unfortunately, it wouldn't be our last.

CHAPTER 18

Some years fold into others and memories are a blur. However, 1967 wasn't such a year. The year started with frozen pipes that burst and flooded the café basement, and we were closed for three weeks. One night, we were awakened by a loud noise. Turns out the house had extensive gutter damage from the snow and ice. Then Lana and Clark both caught the flu. Then our refrigerator quit working, and the glow of home ownership was fading like the new car smell.

There was one troubling headline after another. The Vietnam War was escalating, with many local young men among the casualties. Clark was anxious because his oldest son had been deployed to the Mekong delta in Vietnam. He wouldn't discuss it much, and whenever newscasters mentioned the war, he left the room or changed the station. They stripped Muhammad Ali's title. Women were burning bras, students were sitting in and protesting on college campuses, and riots were erupting in black neighborhoods across the country.

A malaise was in the air, and it trickled down to Fourth Street. However, this mood wasn't caused by riots, integration, or drugs. It was the interstate freeway. Freeways are supposed to mean progress and growth, but for our neighborhood it meant displacement and disenfranchisement. Those who lived between Fifth and Tenth Street south of North Avenue were in the freeway's path and forced to move. Their migration pushed black neighborhood boundaries—or I guess we were still Negroes then—further north. But as we moved north, neighborhoods didn't stay integrated long. White folks moved further north, faster than roaches flee from light. Jobs and services followed them, in a game of leapfrog, hollowing out once vibrant areas like the Fourth Street I encountered when I moved to town.

At the time, we weren't concerned with these socio-logical issues. A few business owners complained the freeway would cut Fourth Street off from its customer base. Others accused those in power of creating a reservation for Negroes—I mean, black people. But thanks to the freeway construction workers, the café stayed busy. I didn't see anything wrong with the freeway. That is, until the freeway's path ran close to home.

Aunt Lizzie came to the café on a Thursday, so I knew it was either real good or real bad. She and Vanessa never came on Thursdays. They knew Mr. Ben would be there, and I couldn't give them extra servings or let them play the jukebox for free.

"Callie, where's Mr. Ben?" she asked as she burst through the door. "I need him to call Ben Jr."

"What's the matter, Lizzie?" Mr. Ben asked, peeking his head out of the storage room.

"This letter came today. It says they're going to take my house."

"Who is *they*?" I asked.

"Are you behind in your payments?" Mr. Ben asked.

Aunt Lizzie lived at 886 Twelfth Street, the house she and Uncle Max bought after the fire. Since buying the house, they had replaced the roof, created a rec room in the basement, and installed a fence with a kennel sectioned off for Vanessa's dog, Goldie. It was supposed to be their forever home.

"Can the government do this?" Aunt Lizzie asked.

"It's called *eminent domain,*" Mr. Ben said. "I can call Ben Jr., but it won't do any good. This was one of Eisenhower's big projects, and the plan was set years ago."

The freeway's path ran through the center of the black neighborhood. It was as though someone had taken a marker and drawn a line on a map through these areas. We now know someone did draw these lines through so-called "less desirable" areas. City leaders called it "urban renewal." The same thing was happening everywhere...from Tulsa to Newark to Minneapolis to Los Angeles. But like Mr. Ben said, the plan was set years earlier. We just weren't invited to the planning.

Fourth Street wasn't in the new freeway's path, but the surrounding neighborhoods were. Our customer base, property values—and most importantly, our spirits—were adversely impacted. Dr. Brown, Woolworth's, the post office, and the Texaco station moved. Even Mt. Zion Baptist Church, the largest black church in town, was torn down and had to move.

Then, with little notice, the president of Modern Metals announced the factory was closing and after working there ten years, Uncle Max was laid off. Modern was joining the parade of jobs heading out of town.

Aunt Lizzie and Uncle Max received two thousand dollars for their house and were given four months to move. They had paid three hundred dollars down on a five-thousand-dollar contract for deed, and took over the payments on the Twelfth Street house. However, the mortgage remained in the seller's name, so they didn't have a payment history and couldn't get financing for a new house.

Since they couldn't get financing, they settled for a rental over on Twenty-third Street. It was a two-bedroom upstairs unit, and they could use the garage and the basement. But no children or pets were allowed. Vanessa was on the waiting list for an apartment in Imperial Village, so Aunt Lizzie announced since I had a big new house, Vanessa, her three kids, and their dog, Goldie, were moving in with me. I could've refused, but they had opened their home to me when I came to town, and I was expected to do the same.

Vanessa and I had lived together before, so we already knew our housekeeping styles were different. When I lived with Aunt Lizzie, it was liberating not to have to clean the refrigerator every week and mop daily. She left clean dishes in the dish drainer rack overnight, something unheard of in my mother's house. They sometimes ate on TV trays in the living room, another no-no in my mother's house. And Mama didn't believe in sitting on the bed in your outside clothes. Aunt Lizzie's rules were more relaxed and I was told to "make myself at home," but I still did most things my mother taught me.

To my chagrin, that worked in reverse. Vanessa made herself at home and brought her no-dishwashing, crumb-leaving self to my house. And no matter how many times I explained the "good" towels in the bathroom and the couch throw pillows were for decoration, her children kept using them. Even Goldie disobeyed rules and kept digging up my tomatoes and petunias.

Vanessa and Junior slept in the third bedroom, with Kendrick on the living room couch, and Harleen shared Lana's room. However, Vanessa didn't mention that Kendrick still had night "accidents." We moved the dining room table against the wall and squeezed a twin bed in there for him. We were cozy, but didn't mind being inconvenienced for a few months.

Lana initially liked having kids around to play with. They played school (she was always the teacher), had Hula-Hoop contests, and skated up and down the block. But the novelty soon wore off and she and her cousins argued as much as they played. She complained when Junior tangled up her Slinky, and when she stepped in Goldie's dog poop in the yard, you would've thought the world was coming to an end. Harleen combed the hair out of Lana's dolls, used up the Easy-Bake Oven cake mixes and left half colored pages in Lana's coloring books—all major offenses. "But it's mine," she would say when I told her to let her cousins play with a toy she had long since forgotten. Usually the toy ended up broken, escalating Lana's resentment.

"Why is she in my room?" Lana whined. "When are they going home? They drink up all the Kool-Aid and that stupid dog chewed up Bubba Bear."

"You must share," I told her repeatedly. "Family helps each other."

"How is letting her tear up my stuff helping family?"

But within a few hours they'd be playing as though nothing had happened, as Vanessa and I had done. I gave Lana the responsible adult response, but I was also ready for them to move. Their two-month sojourn had turned into four months, and our spacious 1600-square-foot house now felt crowded with seven people and a dog calling it home. Our utilities doubled, the bathroom was always occupied, our phone stayed tied up, and Goldie's fur shed over everything. Vanessa inched closer to my last nerve as the weeks passed.

In addition to Vanessa, her kids and Goldie, Joel, her latest boyfriend was always around. He belonged to the Commandos, Milwaukee's version of the Black Panthers. Vanessa now kept her hair cornrowed and wore dashikis. He was always marching for some cause. Clark didn't care for him and said anyone wearing sunglasses inside was up to no good. I didn't appreciate Vanessa and Joel keeping my phone line tied up, but if he could get her to forget Harper, he was okay with me.

And there was a benefit: I didn't have to rush home to get Lana. Vanessa made sure Lana changed from her school clothes and finished her homework before dinner. I no longer had to worry about Lana being a latchkey kid, but there was new drama.

One evening I drove up to a crowd standing in my yard. Vanessa was consoling a crying Harleen, and both sets of neighbors were outside, looking serious. I took a deep breath, then walked over to Vanessa, who explained that Goldie was missing. No one knew how she got out of the yard. When the kids got in from school, she was gone. Lana and Kendrick were walking the neighborhood, looking for her. When the streetlights came on and they hadn't returned, Vanessa and I were going to ride through the neighborhood to search for them. Just as I was pulling out of the driveway, they came around the corner. Kendrick was crying and carrying Goldie in his arms. They found her several blocks away. She'd been hit by a car and someone had pulled over and put her on the curb. Harleen cried herself to sleep for several days and Kendrick barely talked. I'd never had a pet, but it did feel like someone had died.

A few weeks later, I arrived home to find a police car in my driveway, Joel in handcuffs, and Vanessa shouting like a drill sergeant.

"What's the problem?" I asked when I exited the car.

"Here's the owner," Vanessa said, waving her hand toward me. "Please tell these honkies I live here."

"Are you the owner of this house?" the officer asked me.

"Yes. What is the problem?"

"We had a call about suspicious individuals."

"Don't you mean black people?" Vanessa asked. "Lana and I both forgot our keys, so we climbed in through the bedroom window."

"It's a misunderstanding, officer," I said.

"I tried to tell them that," Vanessa said. "He patted us

down like we were murderers. I believe he just wanted to feel my legs."

"Do you have identification?" the officer asked me.

As I was looking through my purse for my wallet, my neighbor drove up and said, "Hey, Margo. Is everything okay?"

"Just a misunderstanding," I said.

She waved and went in her house. Then the officer walked back to his car, saying, "Ladies, I'll be leaving now. But your friend must come with me."

Turns out, Joel had two joints in his pocket and was arrested. I didn't know who I was madder at—the police, Vanessa, or Joel. I stood in the yard with a plastic smile, but once the police car was out of sight, I spun around and said, "What were you thinking? You were antagonizing the police on purpose."

"Them pigs started it."

"The police are supposed to respond to a call about a stranger climbing through a neighbor's window. I don't appreciate them asking me for identification, like they didn't believe me, but it's over now," I said. "Where's Lana?"

"When the Commando meeting ended, she wanted to—"

"You took her to a Commando meeting?"

"It was the last planning meeting before the march this weekend. Neither you nor Clark were here, and I didn't want to leave her here alone."

"You should have waited until one of us returned or called me at the café." I saw my neighbor across the street pulling back her curtains. "This is so ghetto. Let's go inside."

"You afraid what your neighbors will think? I could care less. Let them look," Vanessa said and stuck out her tongue.

I shook my head and went inside.

"Like I was saying, my kids were going. I didn't think you'd mind," Vanessa said, as she plopped on the couch.

"That's the problem. You don't think."

"Who appointed you Queen High and Mighty? I can think enough to know not to be busting my behind for no white man. You need to be marching with us. You're just a cook—making money for Mr. Ben. If it weren't for you, most customers wouldn't even patronize that run-down café anymore. You have the apron; all you need is an Aunt Jemima head wrap. And I didn't know my rent included babysitting duties."

"What rent?"

"I give you my food stamps. You want rent too?"

"I want you to respect me and my house. Lana is a child," I said.

"That girl isn't as naive as you think. Just hang loose. There were lots of kids there."

"Not my kid, and not without me knowing about it. Don't they have guns there?"

"They say that stuff on TV to scare people. Everything was fine," Vanessa said. "She was helping paint signs for the march this Saturday. Lana is very artistic, by the way. No wonder she's so protective of her crayons."

"This could've been serious. You had her in a car with drugs, and you're talking about crayons."

"When did you become so bougie? You act like Joel had kilos of heroin. Thank goodness my housing voucher finally came through. We'll be moving the first of the month."

"That's great news," I said. "It took them long enough."

"We moved to a shorter waiting list since we no longer have Goldie. And speaking of Goldie, Harleen said Lana let the dog out on purpose. I never saw such a selfish kid. She didn't even want to share with a dog. I miss Goldie, but I'll be glad to move."

Not as glad as I will, I thought, but I didn't even respond to her ludicrous accusation. Imperial Village was a public housing development built during the Depression, first to house white working families and was now low-income housing for blacks. Vanessa had always had a job or two, but with three children, she qualified for low-income housing and had registered for on-site GED classes.

Vanessa was a beneficiary of President Johnson's War on Poverty. Housing subsidies, food stamps, and education grants were implemented to help alleviate poverty and economic inequities. But what the subsidies couldn't alleviate was the growing mood of despair and desperation.

The Commandos led protests against racial profiling, excessive police force, and harassment. The police arrested young black men for minor infractions like jaywalking and those encounters often escalated. Open housing was a hot-button issue, as the city council repeatedly failed to pass laws prohibiting restrictive covenants and other discriminatory practices. Even the weather was instigating unrest, with unusually high temperatures adding kindling to smoldering discontent.

Between the war, job loss, police mistrust, and urban re-newal and displacement, people were on edge. Aretha was telling us to demand respect. The Impressions were telling us "We're a Winner," and we may have to leave here "to show the world we have no fear." These young folks weren't like we were. I wasn't much older than many protestors, but I seemed to be from another generation. Most black people my age had moved to Milwaukee from the South. We knew things here were unfair. We also knew they could be worse. But these young people expected more. I'm not condoning what happened next, but I understood.

CHAPTER 19

I loved my cousin, but we were glad to have our house back. Even Lana commented that she was glad she didn't have to watch out for dog poop in the yard anymore. I steam cleaned the carpet and bought new living room throw pillows. And Clark surprised Lana with a canopy bed. She had been wanting one, but he said they cost too much. Lana and I had gone to a mother-daughter tea at Aunt Lizzie's church. When we returned, the new bedroom set was in her room, and the twin beds were in the third bedroom. He'd hauled Kendrick's pee-stained mattress away.

"Thank you so much," Lana gushed. "It looks just like a princess bed."

"You're welcome. Your mama can thank me later," he said with a wink.

Lana stayed in her room the rest of the day and we spent a quiet evening with no television or children fighting. "If I'd known I would get such good loving, I would've gotten her a bed a long time ago," Clark teased, after our third round of lovemaking. I slept so well, I overslept. Even though Saturday mornings were usually slow at the café, I didn't like to be late. I had to stop and get gas, and when the attendant finished filling the car, he said, "Thank you and be safe. I'm not trying to scare you, but you know most places are closed today. I see you have on white. I suppose hospitals never close."

"Is this some government holiday?" I asked.

"No holiday. Just a lot of trouble last night," the white attendant said.

"What kind of trouble?" I asked.

"The police shot a couple Negro boys last night. It's been all over the news. Some witnesses say the boys were unarmed, but I say, why were they running if they hadn't done anything? Now the Negroes over there are upset and threatening to riot. Be careful, miss."

I didn't know what "Negroes" he was referring to, since I was a Negro and I wasn't planning to riot. Besides, Mr. Ben would be the one rioting if he knew I hadn't opened yet. The gas station attendant's report didn't concern me. I wanted to get to work, finish my shift, and go home.

The sun was rising as I parked in the alley. There was no breeze and the heavy, humid air suggested another sweltering day. The phone was ringing as I walked in the door. It was Mr. Ben. He and Miss Nellie had gone to their upstate cabin for the week, but he said the news made the city sound like a war zone, and he was cutting their vacation short. I told him not to worry, but he said they were coming back anyway. I called Clark to tell him about my conversation at the gas station, but the line was busy. I turned on the radio and searched for a news station. Then I completed my usual tasks of starting a pot of coffee, rolling out my biscuit dough, and sweeping away the discarded forty-ounce malt liquor cans, potato chip bags, and candy wrappers the vestibule attracted like a magnet.

Business was heavier than usual and everyone had their own version of the story. Eva had the most details. She said some teenagers started fighting at the skating rink over on Brown Street. The police were overly aggressive when they came to break up the fight and shot an unarmed young black man. The crowd turned on the police, rocking police cars and throwing stones. The story got distorted the more times it was told, and according to whose version you believed, there were hundreds of violent teens roaming the streets or there were hundreds of armed police threatening to shoot on sight.

Milwaukee was becoming a tale of two cities. Everyone knew what had happened a few weeks earlier in Detroit, Tulsa, Tampa, and Newark. Those cities had seen days of rioting and looting, with arrests in the hundreds and loss of life. Milwaukee's black population was smaller and supposedly less militant than in those cities. City leaders kept saying Milwaukee's problems weren't that bad and riots wouldn't happen here.

The morning sun had disappeared behind ashen gray clouds. The window air unit was noisy and not doing much cooling. Clark called around ten o'clock, concerned about what he'd read in the paper. I told him people were talking but things were okay. He showed up an hour later, after taking Lana to Aunt Lizzie's. Turns out civil unrest rumors are good for business, because the café was extra-busy. There was a nervous energy in the air. Mr. Carter came in and turned the pinochle corner into the dominoes corner and we put the jukebox on free play. Sylvia called in, so Clark ended up waiting tables. To keep up, I shortened the menu to burgers, chili dogs, grilled cheese, and fries. We ran out of ground beef, fries, and bread and finally put the *closed* sign up at six o'clock.

While we were cleaning, the turmoil arrived on our street. Clark rushed in from taking out the garbage, saying it smelled like smoke outside. We began hearing continuous sirens and sporadic gunshots. We quickly finished cleaning and locked up. We left, but were only able to drive three blocks before running into a roadblock. Streets surrounding the café were closed to traffic. The officer stated, "The mayor has declared a state of emergency and a dusk-to-dawn curfew."

"But we're going home," I said as a fire truck whizzed by.

"You'll be safer going back where you were," the officer stated. "We'll send a squad car to escort you as soon as one is available."

We returned to the café, called Aunt Lizzie and gave her an update. Mr. Ben called for the twentieth time. I assured him we were fine and he didn't need to come to the café, and probably couldn't get through the roadblock anyway. Clark and I sat in the last booth and ate the dinners we had planned to take home, feeling like hostages.

I had lived and worked on Fourth Street for years and never been scared. But this was different. After eating, we went upstairs to my old room. Mr. Ben hadn't rented it out. We took the café radio and listened to the news reports in disbelief. Then we heard glass shatter and ran downstairs. Someone had thrown a brick through the front window. The riot was no longer just talk, or something on television or the radio. Clark sent me back upstairs and took up guard in the last booth. He left the door unlocked, saying "no use in allowing them to break the lock." About an hour later, two young men tried the door and came in. They were met with the cocking of a Remington semiautomatic shotgun, something I didn't even know Clark had.

"Peace, man, peace," they said as they raised their hands and walked backward. "We didn't know you were a brother. You need to identify yourself on your window." Black business owners were spray-painting the words *soul brother* on their windows and doors as a notice to looters. Looters claimed to be targeting white-owned businesses, but their rage was pretty random. They took cameras from Lawson's studio, ravaged the florist shop, and cleared out Mr. Peterson's furniture store—all black-owned businesses. Looters took televisions, radios, and entire bedroom sets. A couch and recliner sat at the bus stop a few blocks away for weeks. Even street signs were torn down.

Around midnight, a police officer came to get us. The drive home was surreal. Police cars, vans, and paddy wagons lined the smoke-filled, glass-littered streets. However, as soon as we passed Thirty-fifth Street, nothing looked amiss. It then became apparent that we were burning our own neighborhoods. I understood the frustration, but I didn't see how this was making anything better. I blamed it on the freeway. People didn't destroy things they owned.

The curfew remained in place for four days and folks gradually emerged to pick up the pieces. Mr. Ben was hurt and didn't understand why the café had been attacked. "My family has been in this spot for decades and we've always been fair to your people. When other businesses wouldn't serve colored, we did. I know many things in America aren't right, but how does attacking your friends help? I don't get it," he said, shaking his head.

"You call it progress, but to us it's slow. I'm grateful to work here, but what good is it if I still can't live where I want? You wouldn't believe what we had to go through to get our house. Or how many younger white guys Clark has trained, so they can become his boss. We don't just want to be workers—last hired, first fired. We want to be managers and owners. We can shop in stores now, but they follow us around. Laws are changing, but it's been one hundred years and sometimes it's a small straw that breaks the camel's back," I said as I patted his shoulder. "Everyone around here knows you're a fair man. Don't take it personally."

"It feels personal when I have to spend money to replace windows and pay higher insurance premiums. It's a damn shame. And Nellie is a nervous wreck. She doesn't even want me to come down here. Most old-timers aren't reopening. Maybe I'm out of place here."

After the riot, Mr. Peterson never reopened his furniture store, two bank branches closed, and many buildings stayed boarded up. I tried to talk her out of it, but Eva moved her shop too. She said her clients didn't feel comfortable, and her insurance almost doubled. Sunshine Foods, which took up a half block, closed, and its boarded-up windows were covered in graffiti. As established businesses closed, a thrift resale shop, two pawnshops, four barbershops, three liquor stores, and six storefront churches opened within a five-block radius. Mighty Sounds, a new record shop, opened across the street. But their customers were primarily teens spending their allowance on the latest 45s, not potential café customers. Our business fell dramatically and Mr. Ben cut café hours.

To commemorate the ninety-day riot anniversary, a TV news reporter was doing an eyewitness report. She stopped in front of the café as Mr. Ben was painting the new door. They spoke outside a few minutes, then he brought her inside. "Talk to my new restaurant manager, if you'd like additional information," he said, pointing to me with his liver-spotted hand. "I'll be retiring soon and Mrs. Gibson runs everything around here."

In less than ten years, I'd gone from stocking shelves for sixty-five cents an hour to managing a restaurant. My promotion was due to regrettable circumstances, but Mama always said God works in mysterious ways. I was proud of my new position, but couldn't help wondering if I had been promoted to captain of the *Titanic*.

CHAPTER 20

Being a manager had its privileges. I made the schedule and ended my shift at three o'clock so I could pick Lana up from school every day. I got rid of those tacky aprons that made the café workers look like cooks in the big house. I changed the uniform to black pants or skirt and any white top as long as the name tag was visible. The post-riot rebound we expected never came, so we closed on Sundays and at three o'clock on Saturdays. And even though Mr. Ben gave me a twenty-cents an hour raise, with the cut in hours, my check was almost the same as it had been before I was promoted. But since I got home earlier, I began baking wedding cakes again.

Clark found a part-time job at a Sears warehouse shortly after the riot. It was seasonal, with full-time hours and a lot of overtime during the three months before Christmas, then he'd return to part-time.

After the riot, the buses ran less frequently on Saturdays. Clark would drop me off, take Lana to Aunt Lizzie's, then visit his mother and come back and hang out with me until closing time. I was usually alone in the café since Sylvia quit after the riots. She said her family felt the area was too dangerous. Business was slow, so I didn't replace her. If we had a little rush, Clark would come help me. He could balance four plates as well as I could, was a quick dishwasher, and didn't mind clearing tables. I've heard people say they couldn't work with their spouse, but it was actually kind of fun working together.

We still had an occasional argument, mostly about Lana. But our roles had reversed. He was usually the good cop and I was the bad one. Especially since she was experiencing a growth spurt. Her breasts were budding. The dirt that I thought was in her armpits, was sprouting hairs, and I was now "Mother" instead of "Mommy." I tried to keep a tight rein on her free time, but Clark said girls from the strictest homes were usually the wildest ones, and to give her some space.

As difficult as 1967 had been, 1968 was just as bad. Vince Lombardi resigned, signaling the end of the Packers dynasty. The assassination of Dr. King and Robert Kennedy sent shock waves coast-to-coast. Near Fourth Street, there were marches to oppose the closing of three schools near the café, marches for open housing, and marches to protest the war, which culminated in a bonfire of young men burning draft cards. There were rumors that Diana Ross was leaving the Supremes, then Nixon was elected.

The only place to go was up, and the 1970s brought positive changes. The city had professional baseball again and our NBA team won a championship. A black-owned bank opened, the first black woman was elected judge, and suburban neighborhoods were integrating. Business picked up and I got a few raises, which was a good thing, since Lana needed braces and her tastes and activities were becoming more expensive.

By 1972, Fourth Street was bustling again. The community was now black and proud, and Fourth Street became the center of all things cool. The small neighborhood taverns were for "older folks," a demographic I now belonged to, since I was over thirty. The younger, hip crowd went to nightclubs in and around Fourth Street, with disco balls and lighted dance floors. Sam's Shoes' biggest sellers were platforms. Soul Man Style opened in the old dry cleaner's. The store featured bell-bottoms, velour jackets and vests, silk shirts with butterfly collars, and wide-brimmed hats, so everyone could walk around looking like Sweet Sweetback or Priest from *Super Fly*.

Mighty Sounds carried the latest records and 8-track tapes. WISE radio station broadcasted live from the store on Saturday afternoons and whenever they had live interviews, business boomed, since fans often hung out in the café. I had met Al Green, Betty Wright, B.B. King, and Linda Ronstadt. Aretha Franklin raved about my sweet potato pie. Millie Jackson was my favorite. She asked for extra banana pudding to take home, and when she teased Mr. Ben, I'd never seen him turn so red. Even Lana didn't protest having to come to the café the day Jermaine Jackson was scheduled to come to Mighty Sounds. He was promoting his first solo album and the owner had agreed to let Lana come in the back door to meet him. I took Lana to the record shop to wait for Jermaine's appearance. Of all people, I saw Winston behind the counter. I walked up behind him and tapped his shoulder. "Don't tell me you're a Jermaine fan?" I asked.

"Margo, it's good to see you. And this must be lovely Lana," he said as he shook her hand. "Your mother has told me so much about you, but she didn't tell me how pretty you are." His slick hair was gone and in its place he had a three-inch Afro. He was wearing a Nehru jacket and large medallion chain.

"Honey, this is an old friend of mine, Mr. Dupree. He's—What are you doing here?"

"One of my groups signed with Motown. They're opening for Jermaine on a few dates, and they're taking publicity shots today. He should be here in an hour or so. Would you and Lana like to hang around?"

"Can we, Mother? Please?"

"I can't leave the café that long, dear. We'll come back when Jermaine arrives."

"It'll be too crowded to try to get in then," Winston said. "Why don't you let her stay? I'll keep an eye on her, and I'll walk her back across the street when we're done."

I'd never seen Lana that excited about anything, so I agreed. I rushed back to the café, where the Jermaine Jackson excitement was translating into a busy day for us. The radio broadcast went on longer than scheduled and we had one of our busiest days ever. Winston delivered Lana as promised. She had albums, signed pictures, and stars in her eyes. She ate, then went to the back room and called everyone she knew to tell them she'd met Jermaine Jackson.

After we'd closed and were cleaning, Mr. Ben said, "I'm tired."

"Take a break," Clark said. "Me and Margo can finish up."

"Not that kind of tired," he stated. "I've been in this business almost fifty years. I looked forward to coming in, talking with, and serving customers. It never felt like work. Today was one of the most profitable days we've ever had, but I'm not enjoying it anymore. Everyone seems so young and I feel out of place. Maybe it's time for me to retire."

Clark and I made eye contact, but we didn't speak. Mr. Ben would get in melancholy moods and reminisce about the good old days, but within an hour, all was forgotten. This time he surprised us.

"I guess I was holding on because I wanted to keep the café in the family. I was proud to continue my grandfather's legacy. He came to this country with nothing and built this business. It may not be much to some, but I've taken care of my family and tried to do right by customers and staff.

Maybe I should have sold out to Miss Yates when she offered. I wanted to pass the café to my children. But Ben Jr. isn't interested and has been urging me to sell ever since the riots. My daughter's been bugging me to retire and move near my grandkids in Arizona. These winters are getting harder and harder on Nellie."

The phone rang and while Mr. Ben explained why he wasn't home yet, Clark and I finished cleaning, double-checked the locks, and sat in a booth to wait for him. We always walked out together and followed Mr. Ben to the bank to make the deposit before going our separate ways. As Mr. Ben grabbed his keys, he said, "You two are practically running this place. Why don't you buy me out?"

"I never thought about owning a restaurant," I said.

"We don't have that kind of money," Clark said. "We had to practically give blood to get a home mortgage."

"You're a veteran," Mr. Ben said. "The Small Business Administration has programs to help veterans. And there's plenty of money for minority businesses. I can get Ben Jr. to investigate it. That is, if you're interested."

"We'll discuss it and get back to you," Clark said.

"Great. Nellie and the kids will be thrilled."

"This is great," Clark said on the way home. "How many people get to take over an established business? It's about time Uncle Sam repaid me for freezing my behind off in Korea. Well, what do you think?"

"Sounds like a great opportunity, but what happens when your seasonal Sears hours kick in?" I asked.

"What if they do? I'll tell them I have a job and the best boss ever: me. I can think of several things we can do to wring more money out of that place. Other than more paperwork, I don't see how it will be much different from what we've already been doing. Except we'll be in charge—for real."

"What should we call it?" I asked.

"Let's keep the same name. We don't need to broadcast the ownership change or do a grand opening. Folks will be thinking we got lots of money and either want to borrow money or rob us. Do you want to do it?" he asked.

"I do, if you do."

We reviewed everything from bank statements to roof repair receipts with Mr. Ben and worked out a deal.

All that money for minorities never materialized. Turns out the SBA doesn't lend. They guarantee bank loans. We went downtown to First Bank, the largest bank in town. We assumed our eighty-five-thousand-dollar loan would be chicken feed for them. We completed mountains of paperwork and waited three weeks before we got a denial letter. We went to Fidelity Bank, but they wouldn't even give us an application. They explained that since we would be new business owners, we wouldn't qualify. New businesses were considered risky. That seemed dumb to me. How do you become an old business if you couldn't get started as a new business? Ben Jr. suggested we go to his bank. He said his father had banked there for thirty years, so they couldn't claim they were worried about financing a new business. But when we met with the loan officer, he said they didn't make loans on property in that census tract anymore, but they would consider it if Mr. Ben or Ben Jr. cosigned.

"You won't loan to us unless we get massa to sign. That affirmative action crap is just noise to get votes. Let's go," Clark said and stormed out.

When I told Ben Jr. what happened, he asked us to meet him in his office. "I know you're disgusted with this whole process, but I hope you won't give up," he said. "My father wants to cash out and will lower his price."

Clark and I mentioned the incident to Rev. White, an officer in the local NAACP. The NAACP had received other complaints, and called a press conference to bring attention to redlining practices and announced they were demanding action from state officials and bank regulators. Banks had the safety of a government guarantee, but weren't serving all citizens and when they did lend, the interest rate was significantly higher than rates offered to white borrowers. Within hours, the loan officer called. Our SBA loan had miraculously been approved. We had our loan, at a lower purchase price and interest rate.

We held a small retirement party for Mr. Ben and opened the next day as usual. Aunt Lizzie agreed to pick Lana up from school. Clark and I stayed at the café after closing on our first full day as owners. I saved and framed the first dollar bill we took in to commemorate the day. I showed it to Clark as I was counting out the register.

"There's something else we should do to commemorate this occasion," he said. He went to the jukebox, found Marvin Gaye and Tammi Terrell's "Your Precious Love," set it to repeat, then with an outstretched hand reached for me. We danced across the room like Fred Astaire and Ginger Rogers. When we ended up next to the back booth, we kissed like we used to—before bills, layoffs, and Lana. "I've been wanting to do that all day," Clark said as he caressed my butt.

"Then let's hurry up and get home, and finish what we started," I whispered in his ear.

"Why do we need to stop?" Clark asked. He sat on the bench with his feet in the aisle and unzipped his pants. "I know the owners. They won't mind."

"Here? Now?" I said.

Clark nodded his head and pulled me into his lap, and we had our own grand opening.

CHAPTER 21

The first change we made was to paint the dull, greasy, pea-green walls a crisp white. We reupholstered the booths that had been patched and repatched and installed new light fixtures. Mr. Carter helped with the renovations and Clark said it would be cheaper to put him on payroll. He was our first hire. He reminded me of my daddy, and our staff was beginning to feel like family.

I also revamped the menu. Breakfast was now available only until noon. I cut the number of soups down to home-made chicken-noodle and soup of the day. I deleted steak tartare and booyah stew, since those were Mr. Ben's specialties, and milkshakes, since the machine was always broken. Fried fish was a favorite, so I changed it from Fridays only to a regular menu item. I added a daily chef's special, which would be whatever we had too much of, could get on sale, or from my garden.

We'd spent months planning and preparing, but it didn't sink in until the first pay period, that I was a business owner now. Making the schedule and calculating employees' hours had been my responsibility. Now I was preparing check stubs and putting cash in payroll envelopes too. I was definitely more than a cook.

We spent a great deal of time those first weeks, running between the bank and suppliers. When we made our first loan payment, the teller suggested writing checks would be simpler. We could mail it and wouldn't have to stand in line. Neither of us had ever had a checking account and learned about overdrafts the hard way. We eventually worked out a system where I kept the checkbook and balanced it weekly. Clark carried one check in his wallet and only used it when he had to. He'd call and let me know and I'd record it in the check-register.

Something always needed to be done and I missed carrying on long conversations with customers. I usually acknowledged regulars and old-timers with a wave and a smile, or a free soda. However, when Eva waddled in, pregnant with her second child, she disregarded my wave and followed me into the storage room. "I just came from my doctor appointment and decided to pick up the cakes myself," she said, rubbing her protruding belly. "Some people become big-time entrepreneurs and forget about their friends."

"Try big-time busy," I said. "There aren't enough hours in the day. I'll drop the cakes off on my way home."

"Don't worry about the cakes, but even bosses need their hair done. You're past due for a retouch," Eva said. "I'll be at the shop late today. Come on over when you close."

"Close?" I asked. "What's that? The café has become a twenty-four-hour job with no days off. When I leave here, there's still work to be done at home: bills to pay, supplies to order, scheduling, payroll, and taxes. Even buying toilet paper is my responsibility."

"Why don't you take a business class at Milwaukee Technical College? The business courses helped me, especially the accounting courses, and the business center helped me find my new location."

"Number one, I don't have time. And number two, I

can't afford to spend any extra money. Lana's tuition increased, but I'm determined to keep her in Parkview Academy."

"This knowledge will save you money in the long run. We didn't grow up discussing debits, credits, and tax shelters over dinner. Just because I can do hair doesn't mean I know bookkeeping and accounting, and it's probably the same for you."

"I appreciate your advice, but this isn't a good time."

I thought transitioning from manager to owner would be easy, but I was wrong. Our insurance rates doubled because we were considered a new business. The health inspectors came in for their annual visit. Mr. Ben had been grand-fathered into the system, but since ownership had changed, new requirements applied. These were unplanned expenses. Clark and I rotated shifts to lower personnel costs, which meant we spent less time together. But there were bright spots, such as when we received the New Minority Business of the Year award from the Urban League and when my chicken marsala was featured in the Sunday newspaper food section.

The café wasn't the only business to undergo an owner-ship change. Sunshine Foods had been closed for years and was now a Head Start center and Planned Parenthood office. A nail shop and beauty supply store moved into the old hardware store. Only the original owners from Panda Palace, Sam's Shoes, and Yates Sewing Shop remained. Fourth Street was busy, but we weren't seeing it in our cash register. The lunchtime laborers and weekend shopping families were gone. Fourth Street was a quick errand stop rather than a destination.

Because we overestimated our income and underestimated our expenses, we were in a cash crunch. I raised prices and installed a commercial oven in the house so I could do more catering from home. I suggested we begin lunch delivery since we were close to downtown. But Clark said that wasn't reliable enough, and instead found a part-time night job. Another moneymaking idea came from Vanessa.

She came in one afternoon and sat in a booth. When she didn't remove her sunglasses, I knew what had happened. "How are you?" I said as I slid in across from her, even though I knew the answer.

"Not good," she answered. "Me and Harper had another fight."

"From looking at you, I can tell who won. Why do you keep going back to him?" I asked.

"It's different for you," Vanessa said. "I never finished school, so it's harder to find a decent job. And I've gained weight with each pregnancy."

"It looks good on you. I wish I had your boobs. And there's nothing stopping you from getting your GED."

"That's easy for you to say. You've got a good man to help you."

"How can a good man find you if Harper is always around?"

"It's hard doing things on my own. You don't know what it's like to raise small children," Vanessa said and leaned back in the booth. "By the time you got Lana..." Vanessa paused. "Callie, I didn't mean that the way it sounded. I just need a little help. I'm going to get my life together. That's why I came to see you. I'm finally through with Harper. Me and the kids are moving out."

It took all my strength not to say, "I told you so."

Vanessa lived in Imperial Village for two years, then gave up her place and moved in with Harper. They were supposed to be getting married. Then she had another baby, their fighting resumed, same old song.

"I want to help you, but you've got to help yourself," I

said. "The last time you stayed with us was a disaster, I can't—"

"That's not what I want. I could never live with Lana after what she did to Goldie."

"You know Lana would never have intentionally hurt Goldie. I wish you'd stop—"

"That's not even an issue now. It's over," Vanessa said, shaking her head. "But here's my idea. I know you've got those upstairs rooms Mr. Ben used to rent. How about letting me and the kids stay there?"

"Can't you return to Imperial Village?" I asked.

"The waiting list is longer now than it was the first time I moved there. Besides, they got lead pipes. That's not good for kids. I'm not looking for a handout. I'll pay you. I just need to get away from Harper. I can go to Mama's house, but I want to prove that I'm serious this time and make it on my own," she said, as she grabbed a napkin and dabbed the corners of her eyes. "And if you need help around here, I can work some part-time hours. With the kids upstairs, I wouldn't have to worry about a babysitter."

"Uhhhhh, there's not much space up there," I said. "It's been vacant a long time. One of the rooms is unusable because the heat ducts need to be replaced, and—"

"You don't have to make excuses. Can I stay there or not?"

I thought of the days in Price after Daddy died. Me and Mama moved so many times I lost count. She'd tell me not to worry and say, "Jesus will provide." But I wondered, Why did her Jesus let it happen in the first place? At the time, losing my daddy was all I could think about. As I got older, I realized it was just as traumatic for Mama to lose her husband, and how unsettled and defeated she must have felt, and that's what I heard in Vanessa's voice. Even though I knew four people in three hundred square feet would be tight and even though Vanessa already owed me money, I told her she and the kids could move upstairs and I'd hire her part-time.

"I like Vanessa and I know she's your cousin," Clark said when I mentioned it that evening, "but this is business. She's unreliable and always has drama going on."

"Maybe she'd be more reliable and have less drama if she wasn't trying to rely on some man. Living and working at the café a few months can help her do that," I said.

"She's a grown woman. Let her work out her issues on her own time."

"This helps us too. Now we'll be getting rent money for those upstairs rooms."

"It's never a good idea to mix money and family. Let me think about it," Clark said as he answered the ringing phone.

I finished taking clothes out of the dryer and took a basket of clean clothes to Lana's room, then took another to our room. Clark came in as I was folding clothes. "That was Vanessa. She called to thank us for letting her stay over the café and wanted to know when she could get a key. You've already told her it was okay?"

"I couldn't tell her *no*," I said.

"Then why were we having this charade of a conversation about my opinion? You've already made the decision."

"The rooms are vacant. I didn't think you'd mind. If we can help family, shouldn't we?"

"That's not the point. You didn't discuss it with me. Am I a partner or an employee?"

"If we're going to run this business, we need to trust each other's judgment. Even if Vanessa only pays half of what she owes, that's more than we had. I won't apologize for finding a way to make more money. I don't understand—"

"Drop it," Clarke interrupted. "It's done—no need

arguing about it now. But that apartment is for her and her children. I don't want any of her mooching men thinking they got a free place to stay. And deduct the rent from her check before you pay her."

"Thanks for being understanding, honey," I said and gave him a quick peck on the lips. "Vanessa is having a hard time. I couldn't disappoint her."

"So, you disappointed me instead."

CHAPTER 22

Despite Clark's reluctance, Vanessa was a big help. She was good with customers and since she was already on-site, I didn't have to get up before daybreak to open. By the time I arrived, she had coffee brewing and biscuits in the oven.

Vanessa had told me about the good-looking man opening a business in the old flower shop across the street, but this was my first time seeing him. He had a huge Afro and was sweeping the sidewalk when I spotted him. Later that day, he put up a red, black, and green sign that said TIMBUKTU.

"I went over yesterday and spoke to him," Vanessa said. "I saw a bunch of boxes and asked what kind of business it was going to be, and he said he was dropping knowledge. I didn't know what he was talking about, but then he got a phone call, and there were a couple customers over here, so I left."

"I've heard of people dropping acid. Maybe it's one of those hippie sayings," I said.

"There's no one there now. Let's go welcome him," Vanessa said.

"You already went and spoke to him."

"But you haven't. As the owner, it's only right for you to meet him. Let's go."

"And him being super-fine has nothing to do with this outpouring of hospitality and your new miniskirt?"

"Nothing at all," Vanessa said, as she dabbed on some lipstick.

"Hello, my queens," he said when we walked in.

"Hey, neighbor. My name is Vanessa and this is Cal—I mean Margo. She and her husband own the café."

"My name is Salaam. Forgive me for not coming to introduce myself sooner. I've got a lot to do to get ready for the grand opening. Maybe you ladies can help me. I need a caterer."

"What did you have in mind?" Vanessa asked. "We can do Swedish meatballs, or maybe chicken wings."

"Meatless dishes, and no dairy. I'm vegan," he said, while opening a box of books.

"This is going to be a bookstore?" I asked, staring at the stacks of books lining the walls. "I've never seen this many books outside of a library."

"Timbuktu was the center of culture and learning in the fifteenth and sixteenth centuries in the Mali Empire in west Africa. Literacy and books were symbols of wealth, power, and blessings. The earliest universities were in Timbuktu and there were libraries with hundreds of thousands of manuscripts. That's why I named this place Timbuktu."

"You mean Timbuktu was real? I thought it was a made-up word for *jungle*," I said.

"That's why we need a place like this," Salaam said. "We've been brainwashed to believe anything associated with Africa is backward."

"Are all these books from Africa?" I asked.

"They're from across the diaspora."

"I'm not sure where diaspora is," Vanessa said. "Is that where you're from?"

"Most are by black authors in this country," he said with a smile. "We are all part of the diaspora."

"You mean black folks have written this many books?" I asked.

"Sure, this many and more." He told us Nikki Giovanni was coming to his opening and I could come early and meet her. He said it like I should know who she was, so I said okay, even though I'd never heard of her.

"Tell me your name again," Vanessa said.

"Salaam Sangore. It means *peace*."

"That's a lot of syllables to say *peace*," Vanessa said.

"*Salaam* means 'peace.' Sangore is a surname like Smith. I liked the way it sounded."

"It sounds like a drink," Vanessa said.

He laughed like it was the funniest thing he had ever heard. I got the feeling I was the third wheel on a two-person date.

"A couple people just walked up to the café. I'd better get back," I said.

"Good idea," Vanessa said. "Salaam and I can discuss the menu."

His opening was the classiest event I'd ever seen on Fourth Street. There were many college students, black and white. I didn't know there were that many black students at the university. I hadn't spent much time around black college folks. I had always admired them, though. My teachers, the doctor down home, and some of Mama's baking customers had been to college. They were smart and cordial, but seemed elitist, and I didn't feel comfortable around them. This event showed me smart and classy didn't always mean snooty, and this was the world I wanted for Lana.

I browsed the shelves and saw several children's books. I'd never seen books about black children. Something else I discovered—a cookbook section. Nobody I ever knew used a cookbook. Miss Miller had a few in her kitchen, but they were mostly gathering dust, and certainly not by a black author. I was looking through *The Ebony Cookbook: A Date With a Dish* when Ms. Giovanni began her reading and I scurried to the seat Vanessa had saved for me.

"Ego Tripping" was the first poem she read and I was mesmerized. When she finished, I stood clapping and cheering until Vanessa tugged at my elbow and whispered that you don't clap at a poetry reading, you snap your fingers. When she finished, people swarmed her like a movie star. I was working and had to go set up the food, so I didn't get to meet her. After the opening event was over, Salaam said everyone enjoyed the food, especially the sweet potato muffins. He apologized that he hadn't saved a signed copy of her book for me. I didn't know that was a big deal, but thanked him, especially when he asked us to cater three upcoming events.

Timbuktu events were standing room only for people I'd never heard of like Toni Morrison, James Baldwin, Alice Walker, and Chancellor Williams. When Walt Frazier from the New York Knicks came to discuss his biography, even Clark was starstruck. These events brought a lot of customers, but they were sporadic and didn't offset the slow weeks in between. Clark still had his Sears job and holiday catering orders helped make up the deficit, but we were always tired and rushed. With just a few days until Christmas, I finally took time to do my shopping. I went out to the new mall. The mall had been crowded and I barely found a parking spot—such a contrast from Fourth Street.

That evening after dinner, I went to my room to wrap Lana's gifts. She was on the phone past her curfew, but I let her talk to keep her distracted. Clark came in as I was pulling a bag from under the bed. "Quick, close the door," I whispered.

"What's all that?" he asked.

"I'm wrapping Lana's gifts."

"Why does she need all these clothes? She wears uniforms to school. And you bought an Atari?"

"It's called Atari Pong and I was lucky to find it. They've been selling out everywhere."

"This is a lot of stuff, and not cheap either. You know my job situation. We shouldn't be spending hundreds of dollars on toys and clothes."

"Lana gets good grades. She deserves some of the things she wants."

"She's supposed to get good grades."

"I know you're worried about your job, but you'll find something," I said, while cutting silver wrapping paper. "What's the point of working hard if we can't enjoy the holidays?"

"I don't enjoy being broke. And what's the point of spending all this money on stuff she'll just toss in the back of her closet? Next month she'll be on to another fad. If you planned to spend this much money, you should at least have discussed it with me first. But why bother? My opinion doesn't count."

"That's not true. And lower your voice, please. She'll hear us."

"I can do better than that," Clark said, as he put his coat on and left.

We walked around each other for the next few days. Early Christmas morning, Clark handed me a wrapped box. "I thought we weren't exchanging Christmas gifts," I said.

"Then consider it an early birthday present."

"I feel terrible. I didn't buy you anything," I said as I pulled off the silver ribbon. I opened the box and inside were two signed Nikki Giovanni books, and a 1962 first edition of *The Ebony Cookbook: A Date With a Dish.* "Clark, this is so thoughtful. I should've followed my first mind and bought you a gift."

"You can make it up to me later."

"How about right now?" I asked, patting his side of the bed.

"If you insist," Clark said, as he crawled back into bed, and we jingled each other's bells.

"This feels good," I said, as Clark cradled me in his arms the next morning. "It's been a long time since we were both in bed at daybreak at the same time. What would you like for breakfast?"

"You were my breakfast. I've got to get to Mother's. I promised to take her to her sister's house," he said as he hopped out of bed.

"In Chicago?"

"She just asked me yesterday. Since the weather is decent, I agreed to take her."

"But it's Christmas. You'll be gone all day. You should've asked me first."

"Now you know how I felt when you bought that game."

"It isn't the same thing," I said and crossed my arms.

"Yes it is. You wanted to make your daughter happy and I wanted to make my mother happy. We both accomplished our goals."

I fixed Lana's favorites for breakfast and watched her open her gifts. She was thrilled with the Atari, and seeing her smile with the Christmas tree lights twinkling was gift enough for me. After washing dishes and calling my mother and Aunt Lizzie, I planned to finish the dressing I'd started late the night before. But since Clark was gone, I took ground beef out of the freezer. Lana loved my burgers and said they were better than McDonald's. There was no need in fixing a four-course meal just for Lana and me.

Later, we practiced making a vegan chocolate cake, since Vanessa had volunteered me to bring refreshments for Salaam's upcoming Kwanzaa celebration.

She also reminded me to wear red, black, or green. She

and Salaam had become a couple. He helped Kendrick with his English classes and tutored Vanessa for her GED. She said he was working on his doctorate, and they often had study dates at the library. Salaam took Vanessa and her kids to Rockford to meet his family for Christmas. "And you'll never guess what his real name is?" she said. "Melvin Jenkins—how country is that?"

I was happy for her. At least one of us had a thriving relationship.

CHAPTER 23

News reports declared the recession over, but not according to our bank account. Thank goodness, Eva gave us an unexpected lifeline. One of her customers worked for a bridal shop and had mentioned the annual bridal show was coming up. She told me about it and we signed up for a vendor display table. I baked a two-tier cake with gold-and-white scalloped frosting, like my mama taught me. But I also baked a four-tier cake with pillars and strawberries between each tier. It was a replica of the cake in the latest *Redbook* magazine. I called around to see what others charged for similar cakes and priced mine fifteen dollars less. We took so many orders that some days I closed the café and only baked. Those cake sales carried us through the summer, but when wedding season was over, we were back to trying to juggle the bills.

I did have one cake order I was looking forward to, even though we wouldn't make any money on it. Just after Labor Day, Vanessa practically tackled me at the door when I got to the café.

"Do I look different to you?" Vanessa asked, as she spun around, waving her hands.

"Don't tell me you're pregnant," I said, shaking my head.

"I'm not pregnant. But would that be so terrible?"

"I didn't mean it the way it sounded."

"Yes, you did. Mama said the same thing," Vanessa said with her right hand on her hip and her left hand on her forehead. "But my husband and I may want children someday."

I did a double take and noticed a ring on her fourth finger. "Is that what I think it is?"

"Yes," she gushed, wiggling her fingers. "Salaam and I are engaged."

"I'm happy for you," I said and hugged her.

"And none of this would have happened if you and Clark hadn't let me stay over the café. We're getting married Valentine's Day. Isn't it romantic? It seems like a dream."

I went home in a good mood, still excited about Vanessa's news. As soon as I walked in the door, Lana met me, just as Vanessa had earlier.

"Mother, did you complete the Gamma Chi application? It's due this Friday," Lana said.

Lana's friend, Yvette, was going to be a Gamma Chi debutante and Lana wanted to be one too. When she brought me the application, I stuffed it in a drawer, thinking this was another one of those things Lana couldn't live without, like skiing classes, lessons for the flute collecting dust in her closet, and the junior track club membership that she forgot about two weeks later. Besides, it wasn't a good time to be spending money on non-necessities. "Honey, are you sure? I thought you didn't like that type of bougie stuff."

"They do good in the community and raise money for scholarships," she said.

"Since when are you interested in community uplift?"

"Since I found out I get to wear a ball gown and Alexander Harris would be my escort."

"And who is Alexander Harris?"

"He goes to Mount Saint Joseph. He's on their basketball team and looks like one of the Sylvers."

"I have no idea what a Sylver is, but can't you talk to this boy without being a debutante?"

"Please, Mother, can I go? If I don't go, he'll be partnered with another girl. Do you want to talk to Yvette's mom about it?"

I still wasn't used to the idea of my baby liking boys. She'd started having periods, had graduated from training bras, and had her braces removed, but she was still my little girl. I spoke with Yvette's mother, who filled me in on the thirty-year debutante tradition and assured me the evening would be fun and a learning experience for Lana. I put the application and a seventy-five-dollar check in an envelope for Lana to deliver the next day to Yvette at school.

We solidified Lana's debutante plans, then ate the dinner I'd brought from the café. I washed dishes while Lana did her homework at the kitchen table. I had washed a couple loads of clothes and was folding towels when Clark came in.

"Hey babe," he said. "I was rushing to get home before the Flip Wilson show starts."

"And here I thought you were rushing home to see me," I said, poking out my bottom lip.

"Did Mother tell you about the debutante ball?" Lana asked. "Alexander Harris is going to be my escort. And, there's a father-daughter lunch at the Plaza Hotel. I hope you can take me."

"Lana, let the man get in the door before you bombard him with your social appointments."

"Your mother and I will discuss it," Clark said, while looking inside the pots on the stove.

"She's so excited," I said. "It's all she's talked about."

"My sisters were debutantes. I didn't know that was still a thing," Clark said. "As I recall, those dresses aren't cheap."

"None of it is cheap. The application fee was seventy-five dollars," I said.

"Seventy-five dollars? And you already paid it? I thought we agreed to discuss any expenses over fifty dollars."

"I know. It was last-minute and the application is due tomorrow."

"You are determined to spend us into bankruptcy. Sometimes we don't make seventy-five dollars all week at the café. Lana will survive if you tell her 'no' every now and then. And don't you think she's a little boy-crazy?"

"Aren't most fourteen-year-olds? I won't be worried unless she becomes crazy about one boy. I was infatuated with Jesse throughout high school. I'm not saying I regret it, because then Lana wouldn't be here. But I do believe I missed a lot and grew up too fast. I'm glad she's not fixated on one boy."

"That's beside the point," Clark said. "You wrote the check without discussing it with me. As usual, my opinion doesn't matter."

"She's only young once. I want her to enjoy this time in her life and not look back with regret. She's got the rest of her life to worry about bills."

"At this rate, that's how long we'll be paying for this stuff," Clark said.

"Then maybe we should reconsider my plan for a new location. Eva moved and she says her business is much better."

"You want to sell Fourth Street and move?"

"No, but I don't see Fourth Street coming back to the sales it had when I started managing it. If we had another location, our average costs would be lower, and we'd get better discounts."

"I love the café; it's something we've done together. But it takes money to do what you're talking about. Maybe we should quit the business altogether," Clark said.

"Close the café?"

"You were the one who said you never intended to be a cook. You can try something else."

"Like what? I don't want to start over."

"We need to consider cutting our losses."

"There's got to be another way. Vanessa will be moving soon. We can rent those rooms and get more than she's paying," I pointed out.

"Have you been paying attention? No one wants to live on Fourth Street. It's not safe anymore. Anyone who would consider living there isn't going to be able to afford much, unless they're renting by the hour."

For the next several weeks, we were consumed by Vanessa's wedding and Lana's debutante ball preparations. I'd never seen Vanessa so happy. She and Salaam were planning a small ceremony at the tropical exhibit at the Mitchell Conservatory. She found a seamstress to make outfits from a bolt of kente fabric she ordered. Lana was the one who wanted a white gown with gloves and a clutch purse. Her dress cost more than Vanessa's.

On the evening of the debutante ball, Alexander and his parents came to pick Lana up. Mr. Harris was the first black attorney hired by Ross, Gordon, and Stein, and his wife was an English teacher. She and I had spoken on the telephone, but we hadn't met in person. Mrs. Harris was a Gamma Chi member, and she and her husband were formally dressed. "So pleased to finally meet you," she said with an out-stretched, gloved hand.

"Welcome. Lana has been looking forward to this," I said. "I'll go get her."

Eva had been putting the finishing touches on Lana's hair and they'd both kicked me out of the room as she was taking the rollers out.

"Girl, you need a drink. You're going to have the poor

child as jittery as you are. Calm down," Eva said, as she shooed me away earlier.

When I opened the door, I was awestruck. The silver platform shoes that peeked out from beneath Lana's dress, made her look three inches taller. Her skin was flawless and her lips had just the right amount of shine. She wore pearl stud earrings and a single pearl necklace that hit the top of her young, rounded cleavage. Eva had her hair looking like silk, with perfect curls brushing her shoulders. And with the silver tiara, she looked like a princess. The one-hundred-dollar price tag of the white satin and organza dress was worth every penny.

Eva and I followed her into the living room, where Lana and Alexander posed for pictures, looking like the top of a wedding cake. Clark took pictures until he ran out of flash cubes.

"I'm on the greeting committee, so we must be there early," Mrs. Harris said, as she moved toward the door. "We usually take the young people to eat after the ball, so we should have Lana home around midnight. But if we're a little late, don't worry. She's in good hands."

"Okay," I said with a cracked voice, trying to hide tears.

"Not you too," Mr. Harris said. "My wife has been crying all day, saying it reminded her of her debutante ball."

"My baby looks so grown up," I said, while clearing my throat.

"She sure does," Clark said, while quickly blinking so I wouldn't see the tear forming in the corner of his eye.

"You two act like she's going off to Siberia," Eva said. "It's just a dance.

Why don't you all stand outside, and I'll take a group picture."

After more picture taking, they left, then Clark and I went inside. Little did we know, our next interaction with Mr. Harris would be in his professional capacity.

CHAPTER 24

With just weeks to go, we were in the countdown to Vanessa's wedding. I was happy for her, but her marriage also meant she'd be moving out. We were going to miss her rent money and we were losing a trusted employee. Vanessa had become an unexpected, invaluable café addition. She'd passed her GED and Salaam had helped her secure a job as a file clerk with the school district. She was starting in January. Her job wasn't the only new thing starting next year—I was pregnant.

Given my history and age, my pregnancy was considered high-risk. My doctor immediately put me on bed rest. I hadn't been off work longer than three weeks since I graduated from high school. Even when I'd gone back to Price, at least I was baking and delivering cakes. Initially, I was bored, but I developed a routine. I started following the residents of Pine Valley, Llanview, and Genoa City on the soaps, watched talk shows from Mike Douglas to Merv Griffin, and wrote Mama every few days. Salaam sent me stacks of books and I read everything from Iceberg Slim to Gwendolyn Brooks. I tried new recipes and was home when Lana got out of school. I still went to the café, but only a couple days a week for a few hours, and I mostly sat while I was there.

Our pregnancy jubilation was blunted when we discovered we had crappy health insurance. Clark had always had good insurance at the foundry, but his Sears part-time job didn't offer insurance. And since we were self-pay, the hospital required us to prepay half the bill by the end of my second trimester. I went to Planned Parenthood for prenatal care, which charged on a sliding scale, but the doctor told me, the further along I got, I would need to see a specialist. Specialists charged special prices, so instead of enjoying my pregnancy, we were stressing about money.

Clark and I weren't spending any time together. He worked double shifts when he could and was picking up photography jobs on the side. I couldn't tell him to slow down because we needed the money. Whenever we were together, he seemed preoccupied and didn't have much to say.

One day, I was preparing Clark's lunch and watching *General Hospital* when he came in. "Here's the tuition receipt," he said as he took off his coat. "Now we're only two payments behind. I asked the administrator if they would transfer Lana's records if we were still past due, and she didn't know what I was talking about. You haven't told them this will be Lana's last semester?"

"Not yet."

"What are you waiting for? I suppose you haven't told Lana either."

"She's doing so well. I hate to disrupt her routine."

"We've discussed this," Clark said, with a heavy sigh. "I thought we agreed."

"I know we're in a slump, but things may turn around by spring. Her school has a waiting list. If we withdraw her, then change our minds, she might not get back in."

Even as I said it, I knew this was more than a slump. Most area mills and factories had closed. Businesses were either moving or closing altogether, replaced by a boarded-up building or a church. With so much Jesus around, we should've been safe, but crime was getting out of control. *Happy Days* was a hit TV show based in Milwaukee, but that wasn't our reality.

"I want to give Lana the world as much as you do, but we can't afford it right now. She can learn at Brookdale High School as easily as at Stuck-Up Academy. It never made sense to me, anyway. Why pay these high Brookdale property taxes if we're not going to take advantage of the so-called 'good' schools?"

"I'll cut back on a lot of things, but not Lana's education."

"Remember that when we're sitting in the dark eating pork and beans," Clark said, then left the room.

We didn't speak for two days. I finally broke the stalemate to ask if he was coming to my next doctor's appointment.

"No, I don't want to take off work," he said.

"When will you be off? I'll schedule the appointment around your schedule. When you hear the baby's heartbeat, you'll be so excited."

Clark tied his shoes, then put on his cap.

"You're leaving without answering? Honey, what's happening to us? Talk to me."

"Talk about what?" Clark said and grabbed his keys. "I'm too old to be in this situation. This wasn't a good time for you to get pregnant."

"Sounds like you're blaming me."

"I'm not blaming you. But I feel I'm going backward. I should be counting down to my pension, instead of borrowing money from my mama like a junkie. I never had money problems before."

"Before what, before you married me?"

"I didn't know it would be like this. I'm working like a sugar slave, beyond broke, and having a kid I can't afford,"

Clark said. "And I don't even see how that happened. Whenever I try to touch you, you tell me we must be quiet, so Lana won't hear."

"I thought you wanted us to have a baby," I said.

"I never said that. My boys are grown. Lana is in high school. I assumed we were done."

"Then I guess you were relieved when I lost our baby."

"You're putting words in my mouth. That's why I don't talk about it. Things were different then. I was working steady and your health wasn't in jeopardy," Clark said, with his hands stuffed in his pockets. "Forty seemed farther away than it does now. But Lana is almost grown and she'll be gone in a couple years. I thought we'd finally have our time. We could travel, walk around the house naked, go fishing, and sleep until noon whenever we wanted. Especially when we took over the café, I thought we'd have freedom being our own boss. Instead, it's like another anchor holding me down."

"And Lana and I are the other anchors?"

"You said you wanted to know what's going on with us. Well, that's what's going on with us."

"You regret getting married and that I'm pregnant?"

"Of course not. I just need to figure out how to make all this work. Obviously, what I'm doing isn't working."

"But we're supposed to figure it out together," I said. "Once the baby gets here, things will be better."

"You haven't heard a word I said," Clark said, while rubbing the back of his neck. "It's almost three o'clock. I've got to go. I picked up an extra shift. I'll see you in the morning."

Lana came in from school, shortly after Clark left, with her usual burst of energy. Many parents say their teens won't talk to them. Lana was never like that. Since I had been off work, she usually gave me a play-by-play rundown of her day while I finished making dinner. We ate, then she did her homework while I washed dishes. Clark usually called me on his first break, but this time he didn't call. Lana and I popped popcorn, snuggled under my grandmother's old quilt, and watched the Friday night movie. Seeing Lana's carefree disposition always brought me joy. I had sacrificed irreplaceable time with Lana to make this life possible, and she deserved the best. Once Clark heard the baby's heartbeat and felt it kick, he'd be as excited as I was. Until then, I was happy enough for both of us.

CHAPTER 25

On Vanessa's wedding day, Clark had two wedding photography jobs, and I had three bridal cakes to deliver. We knew we were cramming a lot into one day. We thought since Vanessa was having a candlelight evening service, we'd both be finished in plenty of time to get home, then go to the wedding together. That was the plan, until I woke up feeling like my stomach was turning flips, after spending half the night in the bathroom.

"Maybe you should stay home," Clark said, as he brought me toast and a cup of tea. "Vanessa will understand."

"No way I'm missing this wedding," I said, as I struggled to sit up. "It's just indigestion. The baby doesn't like the pizza I ate yesterday."

"Lana and I will deliver the cakes this morning. I'll bring her home, then go set up for my photo jobs."

"But I'm supposed to get my hair done this morning," Lana said.

"Drop her off at the beauty shop after you deliver the cakes," I said. "I should feel better by then and I'll pick her up."

Around one o'clock a sharp stab in my side awakened me. I managed to stand and stagger to the bathroom. The phone rang, but I was moving so slowly, it had stopped by the time I got to it. I figured it was Lana calling for her ride. I called Eva's shop, but she wasn't there and neither was Lana. I made it back to my bed and sat, trying to decide what to do. I had no idea where Clark was. He kept a list of his photo jobs on the refrigerator, but I didn't think I could make it that far. Then the phone rang again. It was in Lana's room. I stood on my wobbly legs and headed toward her room, but it stopped ringing before I got there again. Then I panicked. Lana knew what a busy day this was and that I wasn't feeling well. Maybe something had happened to her. I finally made it to the phone and called Aunt Lizzie, but no one answered. I called Eva, but she had been napping and was incoherent when she answered. I tried Aunt Lizzie again and this time she answered. I could barely talk, but managed to explain that Lana was missing. "I'm so worried," I said.

"I'm sure she's fine. I'm worried about you right now. Max isn't here and my car isn't working, or I would come myself."

I gave her the venues where Clark was working and asked her to track him down.

"I'll try to contact Clark, but I'm calling 911 first," she said. Within minutes, Lana came bouncing in. "Mother, where did this blood come from?" I had unknowingly left a trail of blood from the kitchen to the bedroom. Suddenly the room was swirling and it got very busy. I heard sirens, and Lana's voice.

The last thing I remember is the ambulance door slamming and Lana shrieking. I passed out and when we got to the emergency room, they said my blood pressure was dangerously low. I was in the stroke zone and nothing they were doing was helping. I don't remember any of it. All I know is that morning I was pregnant and when I woke up at the hospital, I wasn't anymore.

They kept me at the hospital two days to stabilize my blood pressure and watch for infection. When we came home,

I went to my room and closed the door. Clark was trying to comfort me, but I wanted to be alone. He slept on the couch and gave me my space.

Two weeks after I got home, Clark came and sat on the edge of the bed. "I don't know if this is a good time to talk, but we've got to make some decisions. The café loan is past due, and we need to tell the employees when or if we're reopening."

"Do what you want," I said.

"All along this has been the Margo Gibson show and now that it's going down the tubes, you tell me to do what I want. I know you're heartbroken, but you're not the only one who lost a child."

"Oh, please. You didn't even want the baby."

"Of course I wanted our baby. I just wasn't—"

"It's done," I said. "And don't worry about me getting pregnant again. I won't put any more anchors in your life."

The next week, Mama came. I was dehydrated because I wasn't drinking or eating enough, and hadn't combed my hair since coming home.

"I know you're hurting," she said, "but you can't change anything by making yourself sick." She gave me a cup with a straw and said, "Drink this, baby," and I did. She ran a bath, washed my hair, then my body, dried me, then walked me back to bed. She parted my hair down the middle, greased my scalp, and braided my hair in two braids.

"You've got to eat." She fed me chicken soup. Either I was really hungry or the soup was delicious, because I asked for seconds. "I'm glad your appetite is coming back," she said.

Lana came into the room and said, "Mother, are you going to be okay? Am I going to have to go back to Mississippi?"

"No, baby," Mama said. "Callie will be fine. She just needs to rest. Go wash the dishes and mop the kitchen."

"Me?"

"Yes, you," Mama said, and closed the door.

I turned to the wall and began crying so hard, I could hardly catch my breath. Then I began to sweat profusely and vomited all over the bed. Mama ran another bath, led me to the tub, then went and made more tea. Again, she washed me, dried me, then walked me back to bed. She'd changed the sheets and raised the shade to let the sun in. "I know you feel bad, but you've got to do what women have done for years: Keep going on."

"I wish you could stay," I said.

"You got your husband. Just pray and lean on each other."

"He doesn't care."

"That's not true. He's showing a strong face, but he's hurting, and Lana is confused and needs her mother. Instead of mourning over what you've lost, live for what you have. Now don't make me get a switch off that tree."

I smiled for the first time in days.

That evening, I joined Mama and Lana at the dinner table. Her smothered chicken, rice, and green peas had always been one of my favorite meals.

"I'm glad you're feeling better," Lana said. "To tell the truth, you're kind of old to be having a baby. That would've been embarrassing, explaining it to my friends."

"News flash—everything isn't about you," I said.

"I was forty when your mother was born. This baby just wasn't God's will," Mama said, as she blew on her coffee.

"If it wasn't God's will, why did He let her get pregnant in the first place?" Lana asked.

Mama put her cup down and asked, "What did you say?"

"I know you're into the God thing, but it seems to me—"

Before Lana finished her sentence, Mama back-handed my daughter. Lana's fork flew across the room and peas scattered across the floor. "Show respect, and don't ever let me hear such blasphemous talk come out of your mouth. We do not question God!"

"What did I do?" Lana shouted, while holding her cheek. "I can't believe—"

Then Mama slapped her again. "Apparently, I didn't make myself clear. When I said show respect, that includes not talking back to me. I cleaned your smelly behind when you couldn't even burp yourself, and I will not tolerate—"

Lana ran to her room and slammed her door.

"Living up here with these white folks, this child done lost her mind. Talking about a 'God thing.' She is out of control."

"Mama, I can't deal with this right now."

"Life doesn't work that way. It's like cooking. It can be messy, but if you don't clean as you go, you'll have a bigger mess in the end."

"She's just going through a phase. All young people rebel against authority. It's part of growing up."

"And part of parenting is to snuff out that rebellious attitude. But you always have been one to avoid unpleasantness," Mama said as she swept up the peas. "I guess I petted you too much after your daddy died. Losing him was such a jolt. Our whole life changed in an instant. I hated that first ramshackle house we moved to. It was just supposed to be until I could get settled. But each place we moved to was worse than the one before."

"Can we talk about this later?" I asked.

"It's not going to go away, but for now, don't stress yourself," Mama said as she fumbled through the junk drawer. "Where's a screwdriver?"

"What do you need that for?"

"I'm taking her bedroom door off the hinges. That child slamming doors like she pay rent or something."

"Just let her calm down."

"Let her calm down? I see Lana's not the one who's lost

her mind, it's you," Mama said, pointing her finger at me. "How can you let her talk to you like that?"

"I just lost a baby."

"You think you're the only woman ever lost a baby? I lost two, and that's why I insisted on having you in the hospital and not at home with a midwife. I never told you because it wasn't anything you needed to know. Me and your daddy were heartbroken, but we licked our wounds, prayed, and kept on going. It's tough, but so are you. You got a daughter to raise and I have a garden to get back to. I'm getting my bus ticket back to Price and you need to get yourself together." Mama removed the door hinges and made Lana join us for dinner. We were sitting at the table like strangers when Clark came in. He looked at our dour expressions and asked, "Who died?"

"The spirit of rebellion," Mama said.

Lana rolled her eyes.

CHAPTER 26

After Mama left, I began dressing every day, cooking, and cleaning. When I cleared the mail from the dining room table, I saw bankruptcy papers from George's law firm. Our debts and assets were listed, and it was sobering seeing the numbers in black-and-white. Clark had found a job making almost as much as he made before he was laid off and he was doing double duty between the café and his new job. But we had fallen so far behind, even with his higher pay we were still struggling. I tore up the papers, then finished dinner. I left Lana a note on the refrigerator, but she was coming in when I was leaving.

"Where are you going?" Lana asked.

"I'm going to the café. Dinner is in the oven. Do your homework and no company."

"Are you supposed to be driving?" she asked.

"I'll be fine."

While my world had stood still for four weeks, the rest of the world had not. The leaves were budding and the days were getting longer. When I turned onto Fourth Street, it seemed dingier than I remembered.

Clark had done his best to keep the café going, and

instead of regular hours, it was open when it was open. I inventoried the freezer to see what was on hand and made a shopping list. But when I called the wholesale market to place my order, I learned our account was cash-and- carry only. A three-inch stack of mail was behind the counter—more bills. A few old-timers came in to welcome me back. It was heartwarming to know I'd been missed, but I couldn't take that to the bank.

Clark came in as I was taking down the curtains. "Lana told me you were here."

"We might as well take advantage of this lull and clean these. When you look at them every day, they don't look dirty."

"I'm afraid it's more than a lull," Clark said.

"We'll do a little more housekeeping, then reopen," I said. "I saw those bankruptcy papers. I tore them up. We're not closing."

"If we don't file bankruptcy, we may lose the house. It's a last resort, but—"

"It's not a last resort. It's not even on the list of alternatives, and I resent you considering bankruptcy without discussing it with me," I said.

"When I tried to bring up the subject, you wouldn't respond. Now you're mad because I did what I thought was best. You can't have it both ways. While you were in bed licking your wounds, I've been trying to find a solution to this hole we're in."

"Bankruptcy is your solution? I don't think so. We'll just have to work harder."

"Speak for yourself. I'm already working hard. I'm not going to keep breaking my back so Lana can wear Jordache jeans and you sit at home and sip tea."

"I needed some time," I said. "I'm better and things will get back on track."

"You're implying I couldn't do it."

"Of course not. I know it's unfair to expect you to do everything."

"So, what's your plan to dig us out of this hole?" Clark asked.

"I don't know yet."

CHAPTER 27

After losing our baby, Clark and I immersed ourselves in the café and Lana's activities. We didn't discuss the baby, nor did we argue. Sex was routine, and neither of us cared enough to try to spice it up. We were the embodiment of the Gladys Knight and the Pips record, "Neither One of Us." I knew things had changed, but I couldn't imagine life without Clark, and figured we were going through one of those marital valleys Mama talked about.

Clark's fortieth birthday was a milestone and an opportunity to focus on a festive occasion. My mother-in-law wanted to throw a big shindig, with formal invitations, a rented hall, and a band. Initially, Clark didn't want a party, a cake, or anything. But as the date drew closer, he agreed to a small gathering at home with a few friends and family. My mother-in-law was surly, but eventually supported the idea and even added several names to the guest list. Eva helped me plan, since I didn't have much time because it was also wedding cake season.

On the day of the party, I was running late and Eva beat me to the house. "It's about time you got here," she said when she saw me. "We only have a few hours. I thought you said Lana would be here to help."

Lana had gone to a track meet that morning, with strict instructions to come straight home when it ended. She had gotten her driver's license and George gave us Eva's old Rambler. He said the dealer was unlikely to give them much for it on a trade-in and he knew I liked station wagons, since they were roomy enough for me to deliver cakes. But it was a gas-guzzler, so I usually let Lana drive it. Even though it didn't cost us anything, Clark had been opposed. But she was in so many school activities, it was more convenient for her to have her own transportation. Her having a car solved our logistical problems, but created others. She never made curfew and we'd even found beer cans in the back seat. Clark wanted to take her keys away, but I said that would be punishing us because we'd have to chauffer her around to all the places she needed to go.

"She should've been home by now. She said her events would be over by noon. Guests are due around five and there's still a lot to do," I said.

"We'll be fine. A five o'clock party," Eva said, shaking her head. "Remember when we didn't start partying until eleven o'clock at night?"

"These days eleven o'clock is way past my bedtime," I said. "We're getting old."

"Speak for yourself. You're the one with the forty-year-old husband."

"I heard that," Clark said as he entered the room and put his arms around my waist. "I'm like a fine wine. I get better with age. Ain't that right, baby?"

"All right, you two. None of that," Eva said.

"For now, I'll take a rain check, Mrs. Gibson. We'll pick this up later," Clark said as he grabbed his keys. I was glad he was feeling upbeat. This party was the thing we needed to lift our spirits and rekindle our romance. His recent promotion helped too. Even though he had less time for the café, the salary increase and his improved mood were worth it.

"Where are you going, honey?" I asked.

"I'm going to get more ice, then pick up the woman who made all this possible. My mother just called and said she's ready."

"How nice. I haven't seen her in ages," Eva said and cut her eyes at me.

When he left, we got busy decorating. Our last tasks were to put streamers across the doors and change a few light bulbs to colored ones. I called the café to check on receipts, but Eva tapped my shoulder. "You'll have to call them later. We don't have much time and this homemade mushroom hairstyle won't do," she said.

"My hair misses having you across the alley," I said.

"I miss being across the alley. But I wasn't making enough to justify staying open. Now I have plenty of parking and air-conditioning."

"I stopped by the new shop a few times when I dropped Lana off for her appointment, but you weren't there."

"Next time, let me know when you're coming. I don't do many heads anymore, but I'll make sure to be there."

Two hours later, Eva said, "Much better," as she handed me a mirror. "I'll start warming up side dishes, while you dress. What you got to drink around here?"

"I think there's orange juice in the fridge. Or would you rather have soda?" I asked.

"Girl, I'm talking about a real drink. I only saw beer in the cooler." Eva got a glass of orange juice and pulled an airplane-sized bottle of vodka out of her purse.

"It's kind of early, isn't it?" I asked, with a raised eyebrow.

"It's the weekend, isn't it? Let's get this party started, especially with your mother-in-law coming. You'll need two drinks to deal with her saditty ass."

After quickly changing clothes, I went to invite the neighbors and warn them about the noise and extra cars that would be parked on the street. We were now a veteran family on the block and the neighborhood was over half black. I usually waved, and other than perfunctory greetings over the years, I hadn't met my newer neighbors. Lana knew the teenagers on the street and Clark never met a stranger. But I was always in a rush. Today, I carried on conversations longer than I'd planned, and saw Lana drive up as I was headed home. With so much left to do, I didn't mention her tardiness. I didn't want to ruin my good mood with Lana drama.

Clark was already home and my mother-in-law was sitting in the living room when I walked in.

One benefit of owning a restaurant is you never have to worry about a party menu. I made a pineapple upside-down cake, one of Clark's favorites. My mother-in-law commented, "You make fancy cakes for strangers, you could have done something as thoughtful for my son. That doesn't even have his name on it." I'd prepared deviled eggs, cheeseballs, meatballs, and vegetable and fruit trays the day before. The main dishes were ham, baked turkey wings, greens, potato salad, macaroni salad, corn, and ambrosia salad. Most people brought a dish, so the kitchen counter and stove were covered.

As I was putting out the napkins, Styrofoam plates, and plastic forks, knives, and spoons, Clark's mother walked in. "Paper plates? The man only turns forty once. I would think this occasion noteworthy enough to warrant real dishes," she said.

"Nobody wants to be stuck washing dishes. Clark doesn't mind," I said.

"He may not say anything, but those nice touches make a man feel special."

I have nice touches planned for later tonight that will make him feel special, I thought. But I just smiled and added napkins to the table, while she tsk-tsked.

Our house was full and it was good seeing folks I hadn't

seen in a while. After a few hours, the women ended up in the living room and most men were downstairs in the rec room, playing pool or watching the ball game. The bid whist players were in the dining room. When the game went off, we gathered downstairs, and Salaam toasted the ancestors before we sang "Happy Birthday" and ate cake.

It had been a long time since I remembered having fun at home. Unfortunately, it was bittersweet. Aunt Lizzie followed me upstairs to get more ice cream and said, "Before you go back downstairs, I need to tell you something. Me and Max are moving home to Price. Vanessa and her family are moving to Atlanta when Salaam finishes his PhD and my boys are in Dallas, so there's nothing keeping us here," she said.

"And I don't count?" I asked, with both hands on my hips.

"You've got your own family. You'll be fine. Milwaukee has changed and me and Max are too old to be scuffling. When we first arrived, jobs were plentiful, but all the factories are gone. And Max says suitcase wheels are the worse invention ever. He used to make our rent in tips. But it's not just the job situation. Young folks got no respect and they don't appreciate what we went through to get them these opportunities. Back then, we weren't afraid to sit on our porch at night, and you didn't need five locks on your door. There was crime, but not like it is now. Maybe it's different out here in Brookdale, but gangs are taking over where we live. And this new thing, crack, is spreading like a contagious disease."

"Price is no picnic either. There are even fewer jobs, and those same racist people you left are still there," I said.

"I know, but at least they're making progress. They even have some black mayors in Mississippi. Milwaukee seems to be going backward. Max's family has land and an old house off Route fifty-four that nobody wants. We're going to pay the back taxes, fix the house, and live rent- and mortgage-free. Max has a job lined up and I'll find something until I can draw my Social Security. They still pay peanuts down there, but we won't have the bills we have here. Plus, this cold, damp weather aggravates my joints. Rich white folks retire to Florida or Arizona. We're going home to Mississippi."

I was disheartened, but I understood. They'd never been able to buy another house after their house was taken for the freeway, and Uncle Max never got a job as good as what he'd had at Modern Metals. "I was trying to convince Mama to move here. She's getting up in age and I worry about her living alone. She'll never move now."

"My sister isn't leaving Mississippi. You'll just need to visit more often. Now let's get this ice cream downstairs before it melts," she said. "I hear party music."

Someone browsed through my stack of 45s and pulled out "Respect," "Soul Man," "Cold Sweat," and "I Heard It Through the Grapevine." We were doing the Temptation Walk, Philly Dog, and boogaloo like it was 1967. Lana and the other young people thought we were hilarious. But unlike 1967, most of us couldn't handle more than three consecutive records before we were huffing and puffing and looking for a chair and water. Then Lana and the other young people took over the record player and were showing us the crazy new dances called the bump and the robot. We played records until about ten o'clock, then everyone started to leave.

"Mother Gibson, George and Eva are the last ones here. I asked George if he would take you home, then Clark won't have to leave the house," I said as Lana and I were clearing ashtrays.

"Clark doesn't mind," she said. "Your friend is going to have a hard enough time getting his wife off that couch and to his car."

"She was here early. She's probably worn out," I said.

"More like passed out," my mother-in-law said. "That woman was loaded before the first guest arrived. Dear, I don't know why you associate with someone like her."

"What's that supposed to mean?" I asked.

"Our friends are a reflection of us. What kind of example is that for your daughter?"

"Don't go putting me in it," Lana said. "I like Miss Eva."

"Young people do not inject themselves in adult conversations. It's called home-training," Clark's mother said.

"Forget that Dear Abby stuff. Miss Eva is cool and my mother is being a loyal and caring friend, that's all. Something you probably know nothing about," Lana tossed back.

"Are you going to let her talk to me like that? Never mind. I shouldn't expect much better. Where is Clark?"

"Oh, hold up," Lana said, in a raised voice. "You're not going to bad-mouth my mother in her own house. For your information—"

"Lana, honey. You don't need to—"

"Oh please," Mrs. Gibson said. "Clark told me you can't control her. Where's my son?"

"My husband is tired—"

"And he wouldn't be so tired if he wasn't working himself to death to take care of you and your unruly daughter."

"Well, since you're so concerned about his well-being, I know you don't want him to drive while he's tired. And since you don't want to ride with our friends, I'll call you a cab."

"I am not taking a cab. I shouldn't have come in the first place."

"Finally—something we agree on," I said.

"No wonder your daughter has no manners. The fruit doesn't fall too far from the tree."

"You have the nerve to talk about manners?" Lana said. "You bring your snobby self in here, looking down your nose at others, and acting like your you-know-what don't stink."

"Lana," Clark said sharply when he entered the room. "What's going on?"

"I'm getting a glimpse of what you endure daily. That's what's going on. Take me home."

"Lana, apologize. Now," Clark said.

"She's the one who needs to apologize—to my mother. All day she's been criticizing her for no reason. She said—"

"Lana, stop," Clark said.

"You cut me off because you're going to take her side, without even hearing my side."

"You are a child and you don't have a side," Clark said.

"Last time I checked, this was still a free country," Lana said.

"Say something to your daughter," Clark demanded, glaring at me.

"How about you saying something to your mother? Lana was defending me, something you never do," I shot back.

"I'm ready to go, son. You may tolerate disrespect, but I will not. Thank God you didn't get saddled with her baby."

My miscarriage was like a sore trying to heal, and she had just torn off the scab. I know it's wrong to hate, but right then, I hated her. And I hated Clark for allowing her to tear off the scab.

"Mother, why would you say that?" Clark asked softly.

"This isn't about me. This is about that child talking to me like she's grown."

"Is that what you told your mother about losing our baby?" I asked. "You were relieved?"

"He's too polite to say it, but Clark is already working from sunup to sundown in that greasy spoon. How were you going to afford a child?"

"*Heyyy*. What's everybody mad about?" Eva slurred. "I thought this was a *parrrrrty*. What happened to the music?"

"Uhhh, we'll be leaving now," George said, and grabbed his wife's hands to help her off the couch.

"Mother and I will walk out with you," Clark said. "We'll talk when I get back," he said, looking at me.

But we both knew there was nothing to discuss and he moved out the next week.

CHAPTER 28

Clark and I had been more like housemates recently rather than husband and wife, but I still missed him when he moved out. Night sounds were magnified, and I woke up every two hours. We didn't tell the employees we were separated, and managed to be civil whenever we were at the café at the same time. He'd been staying with his mother and I refused to call her house. I was thankful when he made the first move. Clark called, said he wanted to talk, and asked if he should come to the house or café. I told him to come to the house. I called Mr. Carter to tell him I'd be late, then did my hair, ironed a skirt, and wore the earrings he'd given me two birthdays earlier. He came over while Lana was at school.

He rang the doorbell, although I hadn't changed the locks. After awkward small talk, Clark said, "I'm getting my own place. I've been promoted and my schedule will conflict with café hours. Also, I've been getting more freelance photo gigs. I'm getting a photographer credit for two pictures in an upcoming issue of *Ebony*. I wanted to tell you in person because the change will impact the café."

His announcement caught me off guard, and I didn't respond right away.

"I'll be paying rent, so I can't supplement café shortfalls anymore. I'll help with the mortgage, but not indefinitely. Both of our names are on the café loans, but we know the café is your baby, and I'm just a glorified assistant."

"Wow. I guess I should congratulate you for the promotion. But I can't help feeling abandoned."

"How long did you expect me to live in this limbo?" Clark asked.

"Just until you cooled off. I didn't expect you'd be gone this long, and I never expected you to move out for good and quit our business."

"Cool off? You expect me to overlook your daughter disrespecting my mother? By disrespecting my mother, she disrespected me, and since you see nothing wrong with what she did, you're also showing me no respect. And this isn't the first time."

"What about—"

Clark raised his hand and said, "I didn't come here to argue. Everything's been said before."

"As bad as things had gotten, I didn't expect this," I said as I sat at the kitchen table. "You say everything has been said before, but something that hasn't been said is that I don't love you and you haven't said you don't love me."

"We're not kids who believe saying 'I love you' magically makes everything okay. I'm too old for drama and too old to be struggling. I feel like I'm carrying this load and it's getting heavier instead of lighter, and instead of you helping me lighten the load, you're adding to it."

"So, we're back to me and Lana as anchors pulling you down?"

"You've got a blind spot when it comes to Lana and I'm tired of fighting it."

"And I'm tired of defending myself. I missed most of her

early years, so I try to make the most of our time together. You should understand how it feels not to have your child—"

"We've been through this. Let's just resolve the café issues and get this over with. I spoke to George, and he said he can still arrange a Chapter 7."

"Bankruptcy? No."

"Be realistic. You'll need at least one more employee, since I won't be there, and we were barely covering the bills as it was. You can't do it by yourself, and I'm not going to keep throwing money at a lost cause. It's time to let it go."

"You're not the first man to tell me what I can't do. Because you want to move on, you think I can't make it?"

"If you want to keep climbing that hill, help yourself. But both of our names are on those documents and we used my VA benefit to finance the house. I'm trying to get my credit together and rebuild my life."

"And part of rebuilding is getting rid of us anchors?"

"You don't want a husband. You want a personal assistant," he said as he took off his wedding ring and placed it on the table. "I'm done."

Lana barely blinked when I told her Clark had moved out. Mama was another story. She came to visit a few weeks after he had moved. When I picked her up from the bus station, I told her Clark and I had broken up. "What happened?" she asked.

"It started when Lana said—"

Mama raised her hand and said, "Say no more. Whatever it is, it started a long time before anything Lana said. I've been warning you about that child for years."

I managed to do something from my teen years—tune Mama out. I wasn't interested in another lecture about Lana.

But despite Mama's nagging, I couldn't have made it without her. She helped my transition to a single parent and a one-woman show at the café. She loved being at the café when she came to visit. She played dominoes with the guys and kept everything spotless. Mama made up her own daily specials. Her crepes and potato pancakes were so popular, I added them to the menu. And I think Mr. Carter was sweet on her. As I was teasing her about him, she interrupted and said, "This will be my third Sunday here and we haven't been to church yet. You've been here all this time and don't have a church home?"

"I prefer to visit churches."

"That's not how I raised you. A lot of folks out here dishonoring the Lord's day don't know better. But you do. We'll go to Lizzie's old church."

"Her church is so long," Lana said. "Me and my friends are meeting tomorrow for cheer practice."

"Sunday is the Lord's day. Only cheering to be done should be cheering for the Lord."

"Let's visit Rev. White's church," I said. "They start earlier, so we'll be out in time for you to meet your friends."

"Thanks, Mother," Lana said and went to her room.

"Lord have mercy, now I done heard it all. Scheduling service to fit some cheerleading."

"It's good for her to take an interest in school activities," I said.

"She got six days to do that. The Bible says 'Train up a child, and when he is old, he will not depart from it.' But you've got to give them that foundation, or they got nothing to return to. You was raised in church, and she was too before she came here."

"Sunday is the one day we can sleep in. Besides, some of the biggest sinners are in church."

"You don't sound like a child I raised," Mama said,

shaking her head. "Anyway, it's not just church. She's running all over you and you should never have given her a car."

"Now you sound like Clark."

"He was right. She's too young to have so much freedom. Callie, that girl—"

"Mama, you worry too much. Lana is fine. Her having a car helps me. I can leave early for the café in the mornings, and she can drive herself to after-school activities. She hasn't given me a moment's trouble."

"That's because you're too busy to notice. You leave her alone too much."

"I have to work and she's too old for a babysitter. We have an understanding. She comes straight home from school and can't use the phone until she does her homework. There's plenty of food and she has a few chores. Don't worry so much. We're a good team."

"That's the problem. You are treating her like you're on the same level. You aren't teammates. She's a child."

"You left me home alone all the time."

"Things were different then and our neighbors tracked your every move. You out here with these white folks, no telling what she's getting into."

"I know how to keep Lana from being alone—move in with us," I said, as I crossed my arms and tilted my head.

"You know I'm not leaving my place. And don't be changing the subject. We're going to church."

We arrived a little before ten o'clock. Since the café was closed, I rarely came to Fourth Street on Sundays and when we were open, I didn't come this early. I was surprised to see the church parking lot full and cars lining the streets. Mama insisted we stand when visitors were acknowledged, and Rev. White told the congregation who I was and encouraged them to stop by the café. After church, several people stopped me to say they remembered coming to the Fourth

Street business district when they were younger. I exchanged pleasantries as we made our way to the car, but it was blocked in. Apparently brunch after church was a regular thing and no one was in a hurry to leave. We joined the congregants in the basement where one of the women's groups was selling chicken dinners. Some ate there and some took plates to-go.

We dropped Lana off after church. As we headed home, I noticed restaurant parking lots, from Red Lobster to Golden Corral, were full. The tradition of big Sunday dinners at home had morphed into Sunday dinners out.

"Rev. White preached a good word today," Mama said as we rode home.

"Did you see that long line? I asked Rev. White if today was a special day, and he said it's like that every Sunday. I'm thinking I'm missing out on big money. I should open on Sundays, but with a buffet of just a few items. I'll do stuffed bell peppers, since they look fancy and I can prepare them the day before. Your potato pancakes and crepes are perfect for a brunch menu, and—"

"Child, do you ever stop thinking about money?" Mama asked. "Instead of worrying about money, you should be thinking about getting your husband home. I know married couples have their spats. After a little while, you usually forget what the fight was about."

"It wasn't one fight. We just had too many issues."

"Lizzie told me Lana was one of those issues. Children are good at pitting one parent against the other so they can get their way. Working is fine, business success is great, but I thought the purpose was to take care of your family. Instead of satisfaction, it seems success just gives you a taste for more. What good is money and a business if you lose your family? You gave up on your marriage too soon. Clark is a good man."

"And I'm not a good woman?"

"That's not what I'm saying, but you done had two husbands. Folks will think—"

"I don't care what people think. You and Daddy taught me to be smart and to take care of myself."

"But we didn't want you to be alone."

"I'll be fine. Anyway, I'm not alone. I have Lana."

"That's what I'm afraid of," she said, with a long sigh.

CHAPTER 29

Mama's visit had been a distraction and once she went home, it was settling in that Clark was gone. Even before he left, I had gotten used to sleeping alone, since we'd been working opposite shifts. But now that it was permanent, the queen-sized bed seemed larger. Seeing his undisturbed side of the bed was a reminder, every morning, that he wasn't coming back. I could've switched sides, or moved to the middle, but I stayed on my side even though both sides were now mine. Clark had kept my gas tank full, even after he left, but now I had to do it myself. Full-service stations were becoming scarce and the ones I found charged almost a quarter more per gallon. And listening to Marvin Gaye was unbearable. The day someone played "Your Precious Love" on the café jukebox, I went into the machine when we closed and removed all Marvin Gaye records.

However, as soon as I thought I had things together, I'd get another reminder. Like the day I drove up to the house and realized my yard was the worst looking one on the block. The grass was high and the tree we planted when we moved in was now taller than the house and shedding leaves. Another simple thing reminding me that Clark was gone. When he first left, he still came by to cut the yard, and when he got the promotion, he hired my neighbor's son to cut the grass. But when the boy went to college, I had to make arrangements myself.

With the start of a new school year, Lana and I established our new normal. Since we rarely ate dinner together, I made sure we ate breakfast together. She left before me and drove herself to school. I didn't hire anyone to replace Clark, so I stayed at the café from open to close. The new Sunday brunch was a success, and I often made more on Sunday than the rest of the week combined.

Mondays were slow, spent usually cleaning up from the busy Sunday brunch. On this day, I had a dull headache, and the rain was keeping the few customers we usually had away, so I closed early. I packed salad fixings to go with the pizza I was picking up for dinner. As I entered the house, the kitchen light was on and the living room TV was blaring. I went to Lana's room, where she was sitting on her bed with a biology book in her lap, album covers spread across the floor, and the newspaper in her hands.

"Why are the lights and TV on in the living room, and lights and record player on in here?" I asked. I believed she was uncomfortable alone in the house, and didn't fuss much. But with a potential disconnection notice coming, she needed to learn utilities weren't free.

Overall, Lana had adjusted and was helping more around the house. I suspected she was trying to curry favor so I'd get her the newer car she kept hinting about. "I found a good deal on a four-year-old Vega. The owners don't live far from here. Can we go look at it?" she asked, waving the classified section.

"I told you we'll have to wait until I get my tax return next spring. Maybe if you curtailed your album purchases and turned off lights when you leave a room, the car fund could grow a little faster," I said. "Besides, a newer car would mean higher insurance."

"But that Rambler is older than me. They don't even make those anymore."

"You don't have to drive it. The bus still runs," I said.

"It's not just for me. It would be better on gas, and I could contribute more to the household."

"I appreciate you thinking of my benefit," I said with a raised eyebrow. "But, I can't worry about that right now. I need to find someone to do the yard." I was no longer the only black person on the block and didn't have to feel like my yard was a representation for the whole race. However, seeing it in such a poor state was a somber reminder that Clark, who had kept the yard manicured, was gone.

"I know someone who will cut the grass and rake leaves. He and his brother do yard work and shovel snow in the winter."

"Ask what he charges. That will be one less thing for me to worry about."

Lana got up the next day, singing another verse of the "I want a new car" blues. I told her what my mother said when I complained about the raggedy 1948 Ford she bought after Daddy's car accident: "A messed-up ride is better than a dressed-up walk." We left the house at the same time and she followed me to the gas station. She knew how to use the new self-service pumps, so she filled up both of our cars and we parted ways—our new normal.

As I pulled into my alley parking spot, I heard several police sirens go by. Unfortunately, that wasn't unusual. But on this day, they stopped down the street. When I came into the café, I saw Mr. Carter standing on the sidewalk.

"We are definitely living in the last days," he said, when I came out to see what was going on. "Folks shooting out here in broad daylight."

There had been a shooting at the liquor store on the

corner. The police put up yellow tape, blocked traffic, and helicopters hovered overhead.

"Let's get back inside. We don't want to take a chance on someone running from the crime scene and coming in here," I said. "With that tape up, we're going to miss our Friday payday crowd."

Fridays were busy days and I had already mailed the mortgage and electric bill payments, in anticipation of depositing Friday's receipts to cover the checks. I'd have to think of a plan to cover the payment, plus the added overdraft fee by Tuesday.

Mr. Carter cleaned the dining room and scrubbed the grill while I pre-seasoned Saturday's chicken wings, prepared stuffed bell peppers, and baked three cakes for the Sunday brunch buffet. I had taken off my wedding rings to batter the wings, but rather than put them back on, I wrapped them in foil and put them in my purse. I would pawn them to cover the electric bill check and retrieve them in a few days as I had done previous times. My hand felt naked, but this time when I retrieved the rings, I planned to put them in the drawer. It was time to get used to a bare left hand.

At two o'clock, the yellow crime scene tape was still blocking the street. "Mr. Carter, let's close. You can take off early."

"Damn shame," he said, shaking his head. "Things just aren't like they used to be."

If I had closed my eyes, I would've thought Mr. Ben was standing there. He used to say the same thing. Since fried fish was one of Lana's favorite foods, I packed a few perch fillets that were supposed to be for the lunch rush, to take home. I closed the curtains and by 3:30, I was out the door.

As I turned into the driveway at home, I could see that my new yard boy had come by since leaf bags were at the curb. I was glad the yard was done, but now I had to figure out how to pay him. When I walked into the kitchen, the radio was blaring, I heard the TV in the living room and lights were on in both rooms, with no Lana to be found.

"Lana, how many times have I told you to turn things off when you leave a room? Electricity isn't free," I said as I scanned the mail on the counter.

I could hear her stereo playing, so I went to her bedroom. "How many times—Lana!" I shouted when I stepped into her room. Album covers were on the floor, along with shoes, jackets, shirts, and underwear. Lana was on her bed, gyrating underneath some boy. "What the hell is going on?"

He fell to the floor and fumbled, crawling around, searching for his clothes. "Hellooo, Miss Ga—ga—ga—Gibson," he stammered.

"You're early. He came to do the yard—" Lana said while covering herself with her pink tie-dyed sheet.

"Shut up. I don't want to hear a word. And boy, you have two seconds to leave my house."

He ran by me like he was trying out for the Olympics.

"Mother, I know you're mad. I'm so embarrassed."

"Embarrassed? You'll be a lot more than embarrassed when I get finished. I'm hustling like a cat on a hot tin roof to take care of you and this is how you act, like you're auditioning for a porno movie. Don't you know you can get pregnant?"

"I'm not worried. I have birth control pills."

"How did you do that? Did you forge my signature?"

"Planned Parenthood doesn't require a parent's signature."

"They say those pills cause cancer. How long—"

"Mother, the government wouldn't allow them to be distributed if they hadn't been tested."

"Well, pills won't keep you from getting no disease. How could you do this? You're barely sixteen."

"You and my father dated throughout high school. Don't tell me you and him didn't—"

"What we did or didn't do is not what we're discussing

right now. If my mama had walked in on what I walked in on, your behind would be raw and that boy would have my hand imprint upside his head."

"Threats of violence don't seem like an effective birth control strategy. Didn't Aunt Lizzie have a baby and drop out of high school? And what about—"

"That has nothing to do with you disrespecting me, my house, and yourself. You barely even know that boy. Put your clothes on, then wash those sheets," I said and left her room.

Another reminder that Clark was gone. His schedule was erratic and he was in and out of the house, indirectly keeping tabs on Lana. I'd been worried about leaving her alone for safety reasons. I wasn't naive about young people, but thought Lana and I had an understanding about boys.

Mama had given me a scary version of sex and its consequences. Girls who got pregnant were put out of school and the boys always left them. Even my request for tampons was cautionary—she said those were for "fast" girls. Mama had me feeling like the devil himself would show up if I let a boy kiss me on the lips. My older sisters gave me a more realistic version.

I wanted a more open relationship with my daughter and I gave Lana my version of "the talk," thinking an adult approach would be more effective. She told me about the boys she liked, and we agreed she'd come to me when she thought she was ready to be sexually active. But obviously, she'd omitted a few details, and the fact that she had pills meant this probably wasn't her first boy.

I went back to the kitchen, pulled Tylenol out of the cabinet, and sat to go through the mail. I didn't need to open the letter from the water company—the pink paper showing in the envelope window told the story. It was a cutoff notice.

Lana came into the kitchen and put her hand on my shoulder, "I'm sorry, Mother. I hate to see you upset," she said.

"You're sorry you got caught and upset me? Not sorry for lying to me, and sneaking boys in my house."

"You know what I meant."

"I thought I knew you, but maybe I don't know you as well as I thought. Sit down," I said, and pulled out a chair. "Honey, you've got your whole life in front of you. These boys won't even remember your name. You're better than this. It's about respect: for me and for yourself. This is my house and certain things are unacceptable. I must be able to trust you. I can either pay an additional café employee, which I can't afford, or you can come to the café after school."

"I don't want to sit around there every afternoon."

"It's not about what you want. I can't work and worry about what's going on here at the same time. Mama warned me you had too much freedom, and I told her you were responsible. I see now, I was wrong."

"I'm sorry, Mother. I won't do it again."

"I still want you to come to the café for a while."

"That's not fair. Instead of fussing, you should be glad I had enough sense to get birth control pills."

"I'm trying to be patient, but you're working my last good nerve. Instead of whining, you should be glad I'm not going upside your head," I said, as I tapped the floor with my arms crossed. "And I need to call his parents."

"Please don't. God, I can't wait to graduate and leave here," she said, and stormed out.

Lana was unfazed by the whole ordeal, but I was ashamed enough for both of us. And it hurt she didn't seem to care that I was struggling to keep us clothed and fed. I thought we had an understanding and this felt like betrayal. But this was just the warm-up. The real betrayal was coming.

PART III

Changing the Recipe

CHAPTER 30

When I confided to Eva about Lana's behavior, she offered me a lifeline. "Since I'm not doing many heads anymore, I'm home when the boys get out of school. I'll pick Lana up and bring her to my house." And a few days later, when Vanessa mentioned that Junior was struggling with fractions, I volunteered Lana to tutor him. Thank goodness, because with Clark gone, I was working more hours and this limited her unsupervised time.

It had already been a trying day, marked by Mr. Carter going home sick and a surprise county restaurant inspection, when Vanessa called and said I needed to get to her house right away. "Did something happen?" I asked, feeling my heart begin to pound. "Is Lana hurt?"

"She will be if you don't get over here."

I closed early and went to Vanessa's house. I couldn't imagine what had happened. As soon as I walked in her living room, I rushed to Lana, who was crying on the couch. "What happened?" I asked.

"She accused Kendrick of stealing, that's what happened," Vanessa said.

"My purse was on the kitchen table and my money is

gone. Junior was in here with me and Kendrick was the only other person in the house."

"I don't know where her money went, but my son didn't take it, and we don't appreciate her accusations."

"Honey, are you sure you didn't spend it or lose it somewhere?" I asked.

"I'm sure," she said, with her arms crossed.

"Kendrick, it's important for you to tell the truth right now," I said. "We won't—"

"Don't say another word," Vanessa said. "You did not just interrogate my son, after I told you he didn't take anything. You and your lying daughter better leave before I forget you're family."

"Let's go," I said.

"I didn't want to come here anyway," Lana said, as we walked to my car. "It's ridiculous that I can't stay home alone. I'll be able to vote next year and you're treating me like a kid."

"If you hadn't proven yourself untrustworthy, this wouldn't have been necessary." We rode in silence back to the café since I still had paperwork to complete. I drove through the alley and saw scattered broken glass near our garbage can and the back door was wide open. I was afraid to go inside, so we went to the gas station to call the police. They took almost an hour to come and after asking a few questions, said they'd file a report. But since no money was taken there would be limited follow-up. They suggested I file a claim with my insurance company, install security cameras, and leave the cash register open when we were closed, so potential thieves could see it was empty.

Two months later, we had another break-in. I bought security bars for the windows, even though they reminded me of Parchman. I filed an insurance claim, then a month later, my insurance increased. They said I'd get a discount if

I installed cameras, but I couldn't afford them. Business was slow and it wasn't wedding cake season yet.

Lana was oblivious to changes in crime, café receipts, or my work hours. That is, until I had to take her out of private school.

"Why don't you get a regular job like other people or marry somebody with money?"

"Money isn't the primary criteria for a husband. A life partner should be your friend. Besides, I'm paying taxes for that public school. It's about time I get the benefit. You're whining because you have to switch schools. Do you realize how fortunate you are?" I asked.

"Yeah, yeah, yeah, I know the story. You went to a segregated, one-room school, walked fifty miles to get there, and had one book for the whole class. It was hard times and—"

"I never said it was hard times. My parents kept a roof over my head, food on the table, and clothes on my back. I had it better than most and I appreciated what they went through to make that happen. Just as you should appreciate what I do for you."

"I appreciate you," she said. "But isn't each generation supposed to do better than the previous one? Isn't this what's supposed to happen?"

"Nothing just happens, honey. We must make it happen."

"Should I get a job or something?"

"Well, you could help out at the café on the weekends."

"I'd rather get a job at the mall. The last thing I want to do is smell like grease and gather quarter tips off the table."

"You do realize that's what I do?" I asked. "Those quarter tips pay for everything you have."

"Don't get all Martin Luther King on me, because I want something better."

"Girl, you have a lot to learn," I said, shaking my head.

Lana could be exasperating, but our conversation triggered something. I decided to follow my own advice and make something happen. I had told Clark years earlier we should open a second café. He said we'd be spreading ourselves too thin, and "if it ain't broke don't fix it."

Well, now it was broke. Fourth Street had a loyal customer base, but they were getting older and their children were leaving Milwaukee or moving farther out, making growth prospects poor. Costs were increasing faster than I could raise prices and the Fourth Street location was slowly dying. I asked Ben Jr. to help me find a second location, since sellers reacted more favorably to a man, especially a white one. We narrowed the choices to two locations, one near the new mall and the other out near the new hospital. "These are both great locations," I told him. "Too bad I can't get them both."

"Why can't you?" he asked.

"I don't have the money and even running two places will be a stretch. No way I can manage three."

"Margo, you're running the café like my father did. You can't keep doing the same old thing, in the same old place. The more locations you have, the bigger discounts you can get and you'll benefit from economies of scale. You shouldn't be in the kitchen frying chicken and baking pies. Write down your recipes and assign someone to manage each location and you're more of a supervisor. Also, you must advertise. You can't rely on word of mouth anymore. I tried to get my father to adapt and expand, but he never would."

"Okay, say I was interested in adding two locations. It would take a while to build up a customer base. How would I afford the lease?"

"I know I've been showing you properties to lease, but in good conscience, I don't believe that's a smart move. It's best to own your building. You'll get more tax write-offs and you'll know your real estate costs. Landlords lowball to get a tenant. Then when they see the business prospering, they increase the rent. You never get ahead."

"Lease or buy, either way I don't have the money."

"How about I cosign and help with the down payment?" Ben Jr. asked.

"Your father was a fair man and I appreciate your family's help, but I couldn't let you do that." I was being polite, but the truth was, I was leery of being in business with anyone. My breakup with Clark had shown me how complicated that could get.

"This isn't a sentimental investment," Ben Jr. said. "Government programs and grants are available for women and minority-owned businesses that I'm ineligible for. You running everything and me as a silent partner, would be the recipe for a successful business partnership."

A counselor at the Small Business Administration office taught me to prepare a business plan and a budget, and said I was eligible for free accounting classes at the community college. The counselor also helped me get a neighborhood revitalization grant available to inner city businesses. I upgraded the electrical wiring, redid the floors, installed central air, and bought a walk-in freezer.

Ben Jr. and I found a building near the new mall that was a pizza restaurant and dry cleaner's. The pizza place was moving, but the dry cleaner's was staying and their rent paid almost half the mortgage. We found an independent drugstore near the hospital that was selling out because a Walgreens was opening across the street. However, the bank wouldn't finance both locations. I tried to use the Fourth Street building as collateral, but the bank proposed a ridiculously low value. When Ben Jr. suggested he buy the locations, I reluctantly agreed. George prepared partnership documents and I made the payments. I promoted Mr. Carter, hired more staff, and floated between locations. We named the new locations Fourth Street Café II and Fourth Street

Café III. Customers that had stopped coming to Fourth Street came to the new locations and sales exceeded my projections.

For the first time since Clark left, I felt a little breathing room. Despite her protests, I put Lana in public school and she was flourishing. She was in advanced placement classes and even got the lead in the annual play. I went on an occasional date, although dating only reminded me how much I missed Clark.

The new locations were doing well, but the original location was still struggling. And thieves had become bolder. Instead of breaking in through the alley, someone broke the window and came in the front door. There was no money in the register, so they bludgeoned the jukebox, obviously looking for money.

Mr. Carter was indispensable, as I tried to pop in on Lana unexpectedly, since she was now home alone in the evenings. He worked when I needed to leave and usually closed with me, even after he was off the clock. "I don't like you being here alone," he'd say.

Mr. Carter and I were getting ready to close when a young man who was the last customer, came to the register to pay his bill. He had ordered a meatloaf sandwich and asked how much the molasses cookies cost. Since there were only two left, I told Mr. Carter to give them to the young man. I was in the storage room, checking how much cake flour and sugar we had, when I heard shouting. I opened the storage room door and saw the young man pushing Mr. Carter to the floor. The young man had asked for change for the bus, then began grabbing money from the register. He was kicking Mr. Carter, who was trying to stop him. I eased behind the counter, grabbed the shotgun, and cocked it. "You'd better give your heart to Jesus, because your butt is mine," I said while aiming the shotgun.

"I'm s-s-s-sorry, Miss Margo," he said with his hands in the air. "I d-d-d-didn't—"

"Boy, you have a half second to get your narrow behind out of here."

He raced out the door and I ran to lock it. "You all right, Mr. Carter?"

"I'm okay," he said, while struggling to stand. "He was fast, or I would've been able to get him with my switchblade. Didn't know you were so handy with a shotgun."

"My daddy took me hunting all the time. Never thought I'd be hunting two-legged skunks."

"He looked like he was on that stuff," Mr. Carter said, as he stood. "Damn shame. Things sho' are changing around here."

The café had been robbed before, but never while we were there. So, I did something Clark had been intending to do: I got an alarm system and bought a handgun, which was easier to carry and conceal than Clark's shotgun. I bought two, one for the café and one for the house, since Mr. Carter said someone might follow me, thinking I had cash at home.

The gun salesman told me to teach any young people in the house about guns. When I got home, I sat down next to Lana and told her about the robbery and the extra protection I was implementing. "I want you to know where the gun is and it's not a toy." She shrugged and returned her attention to J.J. and *Good Times*.

What a blessing to be so carefree, I thought. I stepped in front of her and turned off the TV and asked, "Lana, are you listening to me?"

"Yes, Mother, I heard you. The gun is in the shoebox under your bed. It's not a toy and I'm not to handle it. I got it."

CHAPTER 31

Lana's senior year was busy and expensive. She was voted on the homecoming court for the class of 1976 and that required a showstopping dress. Senior prom required another showstopping dress. My heart skipped a beat when I saw the price tags, but I had missed my prom, so why not? There was also the yearbook, class ring, pictures, cap and gown, commencement invitations, and senior trip to Disney World. Lana was so focused on her trip and picking the right class ring and picture pose, that I couldn't get her to follow through on her college applications.

"Honey, the guidance counselor called and said you've missed the application deadlines. We must hurry if you want to get your first choices."

"I'm tired of school. I want to take a break for a year," she announced.

"Take a break and do what?" I asked.

"Haven't decided. I just know I'm tired of filling my brain with stuff that doesn't matter in the real world."

"Lana, I have indulged you on many things. But college is nonnegotiable. I would have given anything to go to college."

"Mother, please, all you were focused on was my daddy."

"That's because I didn't have the choices you do. It was either get married or work in Miss Miller's kitchen."

"You still ended up in the kitchen."

"But it's *my* kitchen, and you should be thankful I did. If it wasn't for that kitchen on Fourth Street, we wouldn't be having this conversation. You'd be—"

"I know, I know," she said, hugging me, nuzzling her head against my shoulder. "I'm grateful for all you've done."

"Then you need to forget this 'break.' If you don't go to school right out of high school, you lose eligibility for most scholarships. You've got the grades for Spelman. Hopefully you can still get in."

"I'm not interested in an all-girls school. And what was the point of all the integration stuff if you're going to send me to a segregated school?"

"Segregated and selective are not the same. Spelman is highly ranked. You'll be among the best and the brightest, and you'll have a great alumni network. Marquette is another good school. Ben Jr. went there."

"Marquette? No thank you, I want to go away to school."

I completed her college applications for her, hoping once the acceptance letters came in, she'd change her mind. My strategy worked and she received several acceptance letters. Spelman offered a partial tuition scholarship, which didn't include room and board. Southern Illinois University at Carbondale offered Lana a full scholarship and she'd get credit for her advanced high school classes if she passed the placement tests. I had never heard of that university, but it was one of Lana's first choices.

I planned a grand celebration for Lana's graduation. Jesse, who vowed never to set foot this far north, made the trip to see our daughter receive her diploma. Mama even got on an airplane. I didn't hear the valedictorian or the principal's speeches, or the other graduates' names. All I could think about was my baby graduating. *Where had the time gone?*

Lana was accepted into an internship and would be spending the summer in Washington, DC through a program for underserved youth. Rev. White told me about the program and Lana's response was, "I don't want to go to some poor kids' program."

"Income isn't the only criteria. Traditionally underserved zip codes are also eligible. We can use the café address, so that's just a technicality." She reluctantly agreed to go, but the closer the date came, the more excited she became. When she first left, my phone bills were outrageous, because rather than waiting for the cheaper weekend rates, she called and gave me a daily report.

The interns toured the White House, the Washington Monument, and the National Mall. They met and took pictures with Representative Ron Dellums—she thought he was cute, for an older guy, and Representative Shirley Chisholm—her staffer had asked for Lana's phone number. I looked forward to her calls and almost daily postcards. But within two weeks she had settled in and her calls started coming farther apart, usually to ask for money.

I'd never been to DC and Lana invited me to visit for the Fourth of July. The trip was the perfect diversion to take my mind off my recently finalized divorce. We hung out like two girlfriends. She took me to several museums and I was mesmerized by the March on Washington site. We rode the Metro everywhere. I'd never been on a subway, but she was riding it like she had been doing so all of her life. We went shopping at Crystal City, definitely more upscale than any malls in Milwaukee, and we sampled as many restaurants as I could fit in. On my second to last day, we went to the Howard University campus, where Lana announced this was the school she wanted to attend.

"I thought you didn't want to go to a black school," I said.

"That was before I came here. Howard has more black doctorate recipients than any other school. The fine arts program is one of the best. I'm going to major in theater and be an actress. Plus, it has a medical and a law school. What better place to meet my husband?"

"An actress?" I said, shaking my head. "I know you were in school plays, but acting isn't something you can use in the real world. You need to be more practical. This is a major decision and you can't be so impulsive. Besides, we've probably missed the application deadline."

"I met with campus counselors and completed the paperwork. I told them you were a Freedom Rider. They were very impressed."

"Well, there is one more small detail: Money. Howard is a private university. Southern Illinois is public, has reciprocity, and isn't charging out-of-state tuition. Plus they're giving you a full scholarship."

"Are you saying you don't have the money? You've been running the café for over ten years and you just opened new locations."

"I own the business, but the value is in the buildings and goodwill of the business, not cash in the bank. We're talking thousands of dollars for Howard. And you can't hop on the train and come home, like you can in Illinois. All of that adds up."

"That's just great. You had eighteen years to save. You said college was always your plan for me. Now you don't have the money? Forget it. I'll take the year off like I planned, go to New York and go on auditions, work, and save the money myself."

"You can't save that much in a year and New York is expensive," I said.

"Then I'll save for two years."

"I've never seen you this interested in anything. Are you sure this is what you want?"

"More than anything," she replied.

"Let me see what I can do," I said.

"I know you'll find a way. You always do," she said while giving me a bear hug. "And when I'm famous, I'll thank you in my Oscar acceptance speech and buy you whatever you want."

"I'm going to hold you to that," I said.

Because we had missed the financial aid deadlines, I needed to borrow the money for Lana's tuition and her room and board. Interest rates were increasing, and the loan officer told me I could get a lower rate if I got a second mortgage on my house or did a cash-out refinance. Clark and I were divorced, but we had a VA mortgage on the house, and his name was still on the deed. I needed him to quitclaim his interest, so I could get the money for Lana's tuition. I hadn't seen him in over a year and didn't have his phone number.

George tracked him down and relayed my request. Clark told him he wouldn't quitclaim his interest, nor would he sign for a second mortgage. After going back and forth, we arranged to meet. I needed to handle this as quickly as possible, but I didn't want to leave work, so he came to the hospital café.

"Hey, Margo."

I hadn't looked up when I heard the door open, but I knew that voice. "Hello, Clark. Thank you for coming."

"I've never been to this location. It's bigger than Fourth Street. It's nice."

"Thank you. Would you like something to eat? I have hot apple pies."

"You're not fighting fair," he said, pointing his finger at me. "You know I can't resist your fried pies."

"Why are we fighting at all?" I asked. "This doesn't have to be adversarial."

"You know my position. I agreed to meet so you'd give poor George a break. As I told him, I won't sign for a second mortgage or agree to pledge the house."

"Why are you so concerned about the house? If it wasn't for my maneuvering, we wouldn't even have a house to fight over. Let me buy you out. I've got some business I need to take care of and you can get cash in your pocket. This can be a win for both of us."

"I suppose Lana is that business. George told me you had a deadline to pay her tuition. She couldn't find an in-state school? Maybe you should have saved some of that private school tuition for this day."

"Are you still complaining about her attending a private school? I told you then and I'm telling you now, I won't apologize for giving my child every opportunity possible."

"I didn't come here to fight," Clark said with a heavy sigh. "You were right about adding locations. Looks like I was holding you back. I won't quitclaim my interest and lose my equity. I worked hard for that house. I'll give up my interest in the café and you can refinance the SBA loan."

"I already researched financing options, and the appraised values the bank quoted were insulting. Ben Jr. said banks consider the Fourth Street location ghetto property and won't lend down there."

"Then Lana can get student loans or select an in-state school. She needs to learn you don't always get what you want in life," Clark said. "You've got a blind spot when it comes to her. I just hope she doesn't disappoint you."

"My daughter is a smart, beautiful young lady. Lana may be headstrong, but if she were a boy, the adjectives would be 'ambitious and confident.' She didn't get pregnant. She stayed on the honor roll and she's been accepted at Howard University. How could I be disappointed?"

CHAPTER 32

This may not sound very motherly, but with Lana at Howard, I was less stressed. Initially she called almost daily to complain about her roommate. I told her things would improve as they got to know each other, to be patient and work things out. She also had to get used to limited phone time, since the phone was in the dorm hall. Sometimes she'd go to a pay phone and call. But her grades were good and I reminded her that was the reason she was there. At first, the empty, quiet house was spooky. But I quickly came to appreciate my solitude. My phone no longer stayed tied up. There was no loud music, or bass vibration seeping through my bedroom wall, and no waiting for Lana to come in from a date. I even enrolled in an accounting class at the community college. I often worked late, since I didn't have to rush home for dinner prep, or one of Lana's activities.

I'd worked late one evening, and when I locked up and opened the back door, my car was gone. Mr. Carter had told me to stop parking in the alley, but it was so much more convenient than parking on the street. The police found my car two weeks later, without seats, tires, bumpers, tape deck, battery, catalytic converter, or engine. The insurance adjuster declared it totaled and sent me a check for a new car. Clark had always done the car shopping. I hadn't paid attention to the total price, just the monthly payment. As I browsed car lots, I realized the insurance company's definition of replacement cost was significantly less than the dealer's definition. When I went to the Buick dealership, a familiar face emerged from the showroom. "Winston?"

"How're you doing, Margo?"

"I'm okay. Are you car shopping too?"

"No, ma'am. I work at this fine establishment," Winston said, as he lit a cigarette. He was always a snazzy dresser and today was no different. He wore a double-breasted pin-striped black and white suit, pale yellow shirt, and paisley tie. He had a large Afro and sideburns the last time I saw him. Today, his hair was shorter, with a neat goatee and mustache. From a distance, he favored Marvin Gaye.

We walked up and down the rows, doing more reminiscing than car talking. After I admired a brand-new silver Riviera, he encouraged me to test-drive it. It was way above my budget, but I agreed. We cruised downtown, drove by the lake, and swung by one of the cafés so I could sign a check. By the time we returned to the dealership, it was fifteen minutes before closing.

"The car rides so smooth it feels like I'm on my living room couch," I said, as I handed him the keys. "But my money is going to Howard University, so I need to look at your used cars."

"I know I'm talking myself out of a commission, but you shouldn't buy a car here," Winston said. "The markup is obscene. Car rental agencies have reliable fleet cars for sale. They're still under warranty and much cheaper. Tell your husband you'll get a better deal there."

"I'm no longer married, but I still appreciate the tip," I said.

"Then I'll go with you, they know me over there," Winston said, flicking ashes on the ground. "And don't use dealer financing either. That's a rip-off. I have a friend at the bank who will approve your loan."

Winston took me to Hertz car sales and as he promised, I got a deal without the haggling they did at new car dealerships. Within an hour, I held the keys to my almost new Buick LeSabre. "Thank you so much," I said, as Winston showed me how to use the cruise control. "Stop by the café sometime and have lunch on me."

"Not that I wouldn't love some of your cooking, but I know a better way for you to thank me. Let's go out this weekend." And that's how we started dating again.

I had been so wrapped up in the café and Lana that I'd forgotten what it felt like to be pampered by a man. I was approaching forty and figured that type of attention was for young lovers. Winston showed me otherwise. Just as he'd done years before, he wined and dined me. He always managed to get tickets to supposedly sold-out events. We went to plays in Chicago, shows at the Playboy Club in Lake Geneva, and courtside seats at Bucks games—one of the few times I saw him without a suit. He showed me where I could find cheaper restaurant supply options, and he often picked up my orders.

Since there were just a few weeks between Thanksgiving and semester's end, Lana didn't come home for Thanksgiving. Winston asked me to join him in going to his sister's house in Madison. But I was looking forward to some me-time and declined. Since I had been serving versions of turkey all week, I opted for a nontraditional dinner. I planned to prepare a juicy cheeseburger, wear pajamas all day, and go to bed early. The day after Thanksgiving would be a big shopping day, and hopefully shoppers would come by for lunch while they were out.

Around five o'clock that evening the doorbell rang. "I

thought you were going to Madison," I said as I motioned
for Winston to come in.

"I went, but felt bad about you spending the holiday
alone, so I said my hellos, watched the first half of the game,
then headed back."

"As you can see, I wasn't expecting anyone. I'll get
dressed and I hope you ate while at your sister's. I didn't
cook."

"You don't need clothes for what I'm hungry for."

"Well, at least let me comb my hair," I said as I headed to
the bathroom.

"Don't need that either."

The phone rang while I was in the bathroom. I hadn't
spoken to Lana all day, so I yelled for Winston to answer it.
Within minutes, he knocked on the door and said I had a call.
It was my alarm service. Someone had broken into the Fourth
Street location again and the police were on their way.

I quickly dressed and Winston and I headed to Fourth
Street. When we got there, I learned that the alley door had
been jimmied open. The register was empty, so no money
was taken, but the TV was gone. The police came, wrote a
report, and advised me to install cameras.

"Ben Jr. has been encouraging me to close this location.
Receipts are low, insurance is almost unaffordable, and crime
is ridiculous. If I try to sell it, I won't get anything for it. And
if I close, I still have a loan payment to make," I said as
Winston took me home.

"Baby, you're stuck in the past. You can't run that place
like it's Arnold's on Happy Days. There's still money to be
made, but you've got to change with the times. Why don't
you let me help you?"

"No offense, but you've never run a restaurant before."

"Business principles are the same, whether you're selling
numbers, cars, or fried chicken."

"What would you suggest I do differently?"

"I can show you better than I can tell you. Give me sixty days to turn it around."

"What about your job at the dealership?"

"You let me worry about the dealership."

"And what will all this help cost me?"

"Don't worry about that either. We'll work it out."

I should have worried about it.

CHAPTER 33

W inston delivered on his promise. His first suggestion was that I install a roll-up security door across the front façade. "This seems extreme," I said, when the salesman came to the store. "It's a diner, not a bank or jewelry store."

"These junkies out here don't think rationally. They'll sell their mother for five dollars," Winston said.

"I never knew those doors were so expensive. If I do install them, I'm adding a bill I can't afford. If I don't install them, I'm leaving myself vulnerable to theft."

"This is something you can't afford *not* to do. I'll pay for it," Winston said.

"I can't let you do that."

"Why not? You can take Ben Jr.'s money, but not mine?"

"It's not the same. He and I have a business relationship. But I guess I don't have the luxury of worrying about principle right now. I will pay you back."

"I'm not worried. Besides, I know where you live," Winston said with a sly smile.

"I know I need to increase sales. I was considering adding lunchtime delivery as a way to make more money," I said.

"That won't work," Winston said. "Gas and increased

payroll will eat up any profits. The only person that will benefit is the driver because he'll make more in tips. But there are some easy things you can do."

Winston got Mighty Sounds to give me their promotional records, so I didn't have to pay to keep jukebox records current. He also suggested I rent the upstairs rooms. "You're passing up easy money," he said.

"Ever since the riots, finding tenants has been impossible. Clark and I quit trying."

"I'll find tenants, but let me collect the rent. You're too nice and they'll take advantage of you."

I agreed and he found two sweet young ladies to rent the rooms to. They paid on time and kept their rooms neat and clean.

Mr. Carter was almost a casualty of Winston's changes. When he told me he was quitting, he said Winston told the guys who played dominoes every morning that they'd have to spend a two-dollar minimum to occupy the booths for hours at a time.

"I would never have agreed to that if I had known," I said. "I wondered why you guys weren't playing lately. I'll tell Winston—"

"No, Miss Margo. He's right. This is a business and you got to run it like a business. I get a pension check, so I don't need to work here. I just felt like I was helping you. But don't look like you need my help no more."

Winston had another moneymaking idea I'd never considered. "The closest grocery store is way over on Thirty-fifth Street. Folks may only want a loaf of bread or ketchup. I know someone who can get you approved to accept food stamps. Put shelves in the corner where those old guys used to play dominoes, stock them with grocery staples, and hike up the prices. You'll make money and have more foot traffic."

"I was hoping to convince Mr. Carter to come back.

Besides, that's what those foreigners do in the convenience store. They rip off our people."

"Baby, that's basic economics. You squeeze as much revenue out of every square inch of space that you can and charge what the market will bear. You don't need accounting classes to know that."

I followed Winston's advice and slightly undercut convenience store prices. Some days we made more on groceries than on cooked meals. Winston was business savvy, but he wasn't handy. When we got written up during an inspection for using extension cords, I called Mr. Carter. He fixed the fuse box for less than an electrician would've charged and agreed to return to work.

Sales increased and Winston had also managed to lower my expenses. When he purchased supplies, the prices were much cheaper than when I went to the supply stores. "How do you always manage to catch the sale days?" I asked.

"I'm used to negotiating with these cats. If I can't get at least ten percent off the price, I'm gone."

"I didn't know the prices were negotiable. I paid what was on the tag."

"Baby, everything is negotiable," Winston said. "But sometimes I have to walk away from a good deal because I don't have the cash on me. You should add me to the checking account."

"Clark and I had problems with the checking account. It works better with only one signer."

"I told you before, I'm not Clark. I look foolish out here hustling for what I thought was our business, but can't even write a ten-dollar check," he said. "You can't run three restaurants the same way you ran one. Let me handle the bills and paperwork, and you concentrate on the food and employees."

Initially, I was reluctant, but this arrangement was more

manageable and efficient. I didn't feel as overwhelmed and the employees even commented things were running smoother.

Winston still knew musicians from his promoter days and hired a combo for the Sunday brunch. They played gospel with a jazzy feel. We raised the brunch price and had lines out the door. The Fourth Street location was almost breaking even, but it seemed as soon as we'd get in a consistent groove, something would break, or the mail brought news of an increased property assessment. But one day there was a pleasant surprise—a letter from Eva.

She had checked herself into Lakeside Treatment Center, about thirty miles west of town. She said she'd been sober sixty-seven days, her longest sobriety stretch in years. Part of her recovery was to reach out to those she cared about, and I was on that list. She apologized for things I had long forgotten and things I didn't know, like providing beer for Lana and her friends, and drinking up my Marsala cooking wine. Eva also admitted she took the money out of Lana's purse, not Kendrick. She said she was ashamed and didn't blame me if I didn't want to see her again. After I'd read the letter for the tenth time and gotten it wet from my tears, I called George.

"Margo, it's good to hear from you. I presume you've received Eva's letter."

"She's always been a drinker, but I didn't know it had gotten so bad. We're not as close anymore since she cut her hours in the shop."

"She's not in the shop at all. Her hands aren't steady enough and she let her license lapse. We rent it now," George said.

"I feel awful. I've been so wrapped up in my own world, I've neglected my friend."

"There's nothing you could have done. A few months back, she kept saying she felt ill, but I dismissed her complaint and told her it was another hangover. When sleeping it off didn't alleviate the sharp pains, I took her to the emergency room and the doctor discovered an enlarged spleen and early liver disease. The doctor said she was slowly killing herself, and the pain would worsen if she didn't stop drinking. We found a residential program and the cost almost wiped out our savings. I told her, if she came home and drank again, me and the boys were leaving."

"She's my best friend. I should've been able to help her," I said, shaking my head.

"Believe me, I tried. But you can help her now. I know we're asking a lot, but can you hire her in one of your restaurants, until she gets her license reinstated? She can clean tables and sweep, maybe take orders a few hours for a few days a week. She needs to keep busy. If she sits around the house—"

"Say no more. Of course she can work at the café, but do you think she'd want to? I'm not always there, so she'd be reporting to someone else."

"Even more incentive for her to stick to her recovery and be her own boss again."

I was at her house with balloons and a 7UP cake when she came home. Winston wasn't happy about it and hiring Eva was our first major business disagreement.

"I'm not asking. I'm telling you. Eva will be starting at the café next week."

"You aren't running a social service agency," he stated.

"I'm not turning my back on a friend either," I said.

"A real friend wouldn't take advantage of your kindness. If you want a friend—get a dog."

"This discussion is over. Eva is hired."

I wasn't used to explaining myself to anyone. Clark and I had been a good team. We were co-owners, but I ran the café with his input when needed. And Ben Jr. was even more hands-off. Winston was a different type of partner. He wasn't fixing any sinks, or painting, but he knew a guy who would for a reasonable price. He made changes to the menu, something Clark would never have done. He said the liver and veal weren't ordered often enough, and fried pies took too long to cook. He deleted the 7UP cake, saying it required too many eggs, and crossed out pecan pie and German chocolate cake, saying many people, like him, were allergic to nuts. Winston placed ads on the radio and in the black newspaper.

I usually agreed with Winston, but hiring Eva was non-negotiable. She joined us in June and while she couldn't boil water, she was great with customers and acted as my eyes and ears when I wasn't around.

She was an expert at keeping things immaculate and I asked her to help me deep clean on Fourth Street. I picked her up, since her driver's license was still suspended, and as we pulled into the alley, she said, "Fourth Street may look different, but this alley looks the same, except for the over-flowing garbage cans."

The café was closed, so I put the jukebox on free play and even though we were washing, waxing, and scrubbing, time passed quickly. As we were finishing, one of my tenants came downstairs. She tentatively entered the dining room, then said, "Miss Margo, I'll be going out of town and I'm not sure if I'll see Winston before I leave, so here's the rent ahead of time."

"Thank you," I said. "Have a safe trip."

She waved, then got into the passenger side of a Cadillac, waiting in the alley.

"Looks like somebody has a sugar daddy," I said, as I locked the back door.

"You know what's going on up there, don't you?" Eva asked.

"Winston found two students to rent the rooms. I think it's better to be on campus, but I know how expensive college dorms are."

"I love you, girl, but sometimes you are so naive. Those

girls are prostitutes. They work upstairs. They don't live there."

"What? But they seem so nice—"

"You've been reading too many Iceberg Slim novels. I guess you expect them to be foulmouthed streetwalkers in halter tops, tight hot pants, and white go-go boots. Those young ladies cut out the middleman and developed their own form of financial aid. Their customers come late at night and on weekends, by appointment."

"How do you know?" I asked.

"I worked over here a long time. I know people."

"I wonder if Winston knows."

"I assure you Winston knows. He's just trying to have multiple streams of income."

"The only streams I know are for fishing, and I'm not about to have my place associated with prostitutes. Does that make me a madam? What if they get arrested?"

"The police department has more things to be concerned about than the comings and goings in the Fourth Street alley. And it's not like the café business is booming," Eva said. "Just let Winston continue to handle it and you count the money."

I was uneasy about it, but I followed her advice and didn't say anything to Winston. It was good to have a friend to talk to again. Having her around also allowed me to spend more time with Lana during her summer break. Eva designated herself the company designer and updated the Fourth Street décor. She changed the centerpieces and place mats, as the seasons changed.

When I pulled out my garland, tabletop tree, and ten-year-old wreaths, Eva declared those the saddest Christmas decorations she'd ever seen and insisted we go shopping. "Look at that line," Eva said as we passed a Mrs. Fields cookies shop. "Your stuff tastes ten times better than hers. You need to sell something. How about making cookies or your fried pies, and wrapping them in cute boxes near the register?"

"It sounds like something easy to try," I said. "Everyone loves my molasses cookies."

"Wait, here's another idea. Have you ever considered doing a cookbook?"

"Don't take this the wrong way, but have you started drinking again?"

"Girl, I'm serious. There's *Happy Days*, *Laverne and Shirley*, *Grease*; people are into nostalgia. Folks may not come to Fourth Street like they used to, but they remember when they did as the good old days. My Lakeside roommate owns a printing company and with a small investment, you can triple your money. I can arrange a meeting with her."

"I'm just a girl from Mississippi who can cook. I'm no Betty Crocker."

"If a peanut farmer from Georgia can be president, you can write a cookbook. Besides, I don't think Betty Crocker is even real."

"I don't know. I need to talk to Winston."

"For what? He doesn't know any recipes."

"We discuss all investments and—"

"I know he's helping you, but remember, people are coming for *your* food. This is *your* business. Winston is only along for the ride."

Eva's playful decorations and displays near the cash register lifted the mood and sales. I had booked several large catering orders and had extra money in the bank.

The best part—Lana was coming home. I decorated the house with a live Christmas tree and outside lights. I loaded the refrigerator with her favorites and bought a new comforter for her bed. I was disappointed when she told me she'd be home for two weeks, instead of four. Lana had been selected for a part in the campus production of *Purlie Victorious* and had to return for rehearsals.

Since it was snowing and the roads were icy when she arrived, Winston offered to drive me to the airport to pick her up. Lana knew about my relationship with Winston, and we'd talked a little about him, but most of our conversations were about her life at Howard.

Winston circled the airport while I went in to meet her flight. My Lana looked so grown up when she entered the gate area. She had reddish highlights in her feathered Farrah Fawcett hairstyle. She wore a long pecan-colored coat with defined shoulder pads, almost shoulder-length peace sign earrings, and stylish boots not made for Wisconsin winters.

When we got in the car, Winston said, "This can't be the Lana I met at Mighty Sounds. You don't have braces or Afro puffs anymore."

"And you don't have platforms, a 'fro and sideburns," Lana teased. "I still have my signed Jermaine poster and album."

This was the beginning of our brief Christmas holiday. Winston managed to get Lana hard-to-come-by tickets to the Christmas Eve Maze concert. We spent a quiet Christmas Day at home and hit the malls the day after Christmas. Lana planned to leave the day before New Year's Eve.

I didn't feel well when she was ready to go, so Winston drove her to the airport. The next day, I felt worse and couldn't get out of bed. Winston came over that evening and rang the doorbell. When I didn't answer, he came to my bedroom window and knocked. When I saw that it was him, I plodded to the living room to open the front door. Apparently, I had kicked the phone off the hook on one of my desperate trips to the bathroom.

"Wow, you don't look so good," he said.

"I feel even worse," I whispered. I felt too sick to be embarrassed by my musty, unwashed smell, floor full of snotty tissues, and vomit-stained gown. Winston fed me soda and crackers, but it came back up. He sat by my bedside all night, but by morning I wasn't better and had a fever. He dressed me, then took me to the emergency room. I was diagnosed with walking pneumonia and admitted to the hospital, where I slept twenty-six hours. When I awakened, Winston was sitting next to my bed, watching the evening news. "What time is it?" I asked.

"It's five-thirty," Winston said.

"I thought the doctor was coming in today," I said.

"He came in today and yesterday. Happy New Year. The doctor says if your fever stays down, you'll be discharged tomorrow, but you still need to take it easy for a few days."

I was released the next day. Winston had cleaned my house, taken down the Christmas decorations, and handled café business. That's how he got the keys to my house. He still had his place but spent most nights at my house. It was nice having someone to come home to. But I did miss my space. Those nights Winston stayed at his place, I took long bubble baths, didn't worry about dinner prep, caught up on my letter writing, or gossiped on the phone with Vanessa or Eva.

Since we'd implemented Winston's suggestions, my bank account was looking better. Fourth Street was no longer a drag, and brought in more money than the other two locations during the first week of the month. Eva turned out to be a godsend. She was reliable and cleaned so well we scored an "A" on our spring health inspection—our first perfect score.

To commemorate the business turnaround and our perfect score, we closed all locations on a Monday and hosted a thank-you staff luncheon at the Plaza Hotel. It was a chance for our employees to be waited on for a change, and the first time we were together in one space. We played "getting to know you" games, gave away Bucks tickets and Sears gift certificates, and had a fun day.

Winston and I slept in the next morning, then went to the accountant's, an old friend of Winston's, office to sign the tax returns. "I didn't know there'd be so many pages. I wish I'd had more time to review these," I said. "The advertising and supplies expenses seem high. And, I'm unfamiliar with some of these categories. I'd like to compare the returns to my accounting book."

"My man here, is the expert. The book is just theory," Winston said as he lit a cigarette. "The sooner you sign, the sooner we can get this refund."

I didn't like waiting until April 15 to file, but Winston said you were less likely to get audited if the IRS received the return during its deadline rush. There were several more schedules to submit with the return than usual, but I had never gotten such a large refund, so I wasn't complaining.

When we got to the house, Winston said, "This year is rushing by. I can't believe it's almost May."

"And I can't believe my baby is finishing her first year of college. Lana will be home in a few weeks. You should start moving your stuff now."

"What stuff?" Winston asked.

"She can't come home and find you practically living here."

"I *am* practically living here."

"But not when Lana's here," I said.

"Why not?"

"It doesn't look right for—"

"For her mother to have a man? You act like she's six years old."

"It doesn't matter how old she is, I'm not going to have her see a man who's not my husband in my bed."

"I went along with this charade for spring break, but I won't sneak around all summer like some teenager."

"Why is it an issue? It's not like you stay here all the time," I said.

"But that's my choice, not because I don't want to be seen. I'm a grown man."

"You'll have to be grown at your house," I said.

"Looks like I'll have to marry you, then," Winston said as he lit a cigarette.

"Marriage? Are you sure that's just a cigarette you're smoking?"

"I'm okay to mess around with, but not to marry?"

"I didn't say that."

"Then what are you saying? Would you marry me—if I asked?"

"Are you asking?"

"I guess I am," he said with a smile.

"Talk to me when you're not guessing," I said, as I looked through the mail. *Marry Winston? Lord have mercy*, I thought. *Twice was enough for me.*

CHAPTER 34

Wedding season was in full swing and thanks to Winston's advertising, I had so many catering requests, I turned some down. I usually sent one of my employees to cover weddings at Rev. White's church, because those ceremonies reminded me of my wedding day and made me a little weepy. But this wedding was going to be grand and I knew I needed to handle it myself. I stayed downstairs to set up the finger foods and punch, then went to the hall to ensure everything was in place for the reception. As I was checking the chafing dishes, I heard a familiar voice.

"Hey Margo."

"Clark, it's good to see you." He still had that endearing smile, and his gray temples made him look distinguished. I wished I had dressed better.

"Looks like someone finally got Big Jim to the altar. A long way from our little ceremony," he said with a smile.

We talked a few minutes, then he rushed off to take pictures as the bride and groom entered the reception hall. He mingled, taking candid photos, and I focused on the food and the servers. In between, we caught up on each other's lives, reminisced about our own wedding, and laughed about Mr. Ben and his wife's smooth polka moves. "Your business is doing well. I remember when you and I cooked, set up, served, and broke down the catering jobs. Now you have helpers."

"And I remember when you had one camera you wore around your neck. Now you've got bags, and tripods and cords galore." The newlyweds danced to "Your Precious Love" by Marvin Gaye and Tammi Terrell. As Clark took pictures of their first dance, I thought about the times we danced to that song. I turned toward Clark and our eyes met, even though he had his camera directed toward the newlyweds. Stevie Wonder's new song jolted me back to the present and the DJ urged everyone to come to the dance floor for the *Soul Train* line. I lost Clark in the crowd. But since I had another engagement and had already stayed longer than I'd planned, I gave instructions to my staff, then left.

The following Monday, Clark called the café. "Somehow one of your extension cords ended up in my bag," he said. "I dropped it off this morning. Mr. Carter said you were at the mall location, and he'd make sure you got it."

"Thanks for bringing it by," I said.

"I hope I'm not out of order, but I enjoyed talking with you Saturday. Would you like to go out?"

To say I was stunned would be an understatement. I had also enjoyed Saturday and was disappointed to learn I missed his café visit. And it sounded like he felt the same. *But to actually go on a date?*

"Margo? Are you still there?"

"Uhhhhh, yeah, I'm here. How—"

"Look, Milwaukee is just a big small town, and I know you're dating someone. If you guys are serious, forget I asked. I had such a good time with you Saturday, it was almost like old times. I just wanted to see you again."

Talking with him had been so natural and easy, I almost forgot why we broke up. Conflicts over money, miscarriages, and Lana had seemed insurmountable at the time. But Lana was an adult now, and we were all older and wiser.

"It's kind of complicated," I said. "You see—"

"Don't explain. How about this? Mondays are my slow day and if I remember correctly, they're slow at the café too. I'm going fishing at Quarry Lake next Monday morning. I'll say eight o'clock. If you're there, great. If not, I'll know you're not interested."

Winston met with people all the time. I didn't see the harm in meeting with Clark. I told myself that, but I knew this was different. I also knew dormant feelings were being stirred up. *I wonder if he still likes fried pies*, I wondered.

The week crawled by and on Thursday, I only worked a half-day. After I parked in the garage, I checked my fishing gear, which was covered with spiderwebs. Winston came in while I was wiping it down. "Are you planning a garage sale?" he asked.

"No. I'm thinking about going fishing on Monday before class."

"Count me out," he said, as he lit a cigarette.

"It's relaxing. It's a great stress reliever," I said.

"I can think of better things to do to relieve stress. I wish I had more time, because I can show you better than I can tell you. But I just stopped by to get the extra keys to my rent house. They're two months behind and I'm going to evict them."

"Do you know what happened? Maybe someone is sick," I said.

"Not my problem. There's always a sob story. I'll be back later for some stress relief," Winston said. "Here's your mail."

After I wiped down and respooled my fishing reels, I went inside. I fixed a ham sandwich and sat to go through the mail. I saw the letter from Howard and anxiously opened it, thinking it was Lana's grades. Instead, it was a past–due bill for one thousand dollars. Her grades would not be released until it was paid and she could not reenroll. When I called the finance office, I learned that was the balance for Lana's dorm. Without my knowledge or consent, she had moved from her double room, to a single. I called the dorm and left a message for her to call home immediately.

She didn't call until the next morning. "Mom, is everything okay?" she asked.

"Didn't you get my message?" I asked. "I've been worried all night."

"I got in late. We can't use the phone after ten o'clock, and I didn't want to go back out."

"Why are you out so late on a weeknight? Never mind, that's not even why I called. We got a bill from the finance office. Why did you change rooms without consulting me?"

"I told you about my dull, whiny roommate. You said to work it out."

"That didn't mean to change rooms. Your single room cost one thousand dollars more."

"I didn't know it would be that much. But it's easier to study in a single, and me and my scene partners can rehearse our lines. Next semester I'll be able to stay off-campus and that's less expensive."

"All right, Lana," I said with a sigh. "I'll figure something out."

I was making more money, but managing cash flow was still a challenge. Property taxes and insurance were cheaper when paid in a lump sum rather than monthly instalments, so me and my smart self had paid both bills at the same time. With several large weddings scheduled, I expected my cash flow to even out in a few weeks. I hadn't figured on a tuition bill, though. I was sitting at the kitchen table when Winston came in.

"Baby, are you feeling okay?"

"I just got blindsided with another tuition bill. If I don't pay it in ten days, they won't release Lana's grades."

"How much is it?" Winston asked.

"You've given me so much already. I can't ask you to—"

"You aren't asking. I'm volunteering."

"But I still owe you for the security door. I called Ben Jr.'s office to explain and tell him my payments will be late this and next month, but he's out until next week."

"Why was that your first solution? I'm your man, you should've come to me."

"I don't want to mix our personal and professional relationship any more than it is already. I'll figure something out."

I thought Winston's feelings were hurt, since I didn't see him on Friday, and he didn't call or answer my calls. But on Saturday, he was at the house when I came in from the café. His suitcase was in the kitchen and I assumed he was moving his clothes back to his place. When I sat on the couch and took off my shoes, Winston brought me a rolled-up newspaper and a glass of wine. When I unrolled it, an envelope and a small velvet box fell out.

"Winston Dupree, what are you up to?"

When I opened the box, I saw what he was up to. "You were serious about getting married?" I asked.

"You should know by now I don't play. So will you marry me?"

"Wow. This is a big step," I said.

"That's not the right answer."

"It's just that I've been married twice, and I don't want to—"

"But you weren't married to me," he said. "I've packed our bags. We can drive to Indiana tomorrow night, get married Monday morning, and head back home. Eva can handle things here."

"Get married Monday?" I asked. "I have a final exam Monday afternoon."

"That accounting class is just something to pad a resume. I don't understand going to school to learn something you're already doing. Do you want to do this thing or not? Indiana has no waiting period, and you didn't open the envelope."

I opened it and counted fifteen one-hundred-dollar bills.

"I'm not a mushy guy, but you told me a while back that you and Lana were a package deal. So that's the money for our daughter's tuition."

"Winston, I—"

"Depending on traffic, we might even be back before the café closes."

"This is so thoughtful," I said, trying to keep my voice from cracking.

"Is that a yes? Wait! I guess I should get on one knee," he said while kneeling.

I couldn't believe he'd given me the money for Lana's tuition and to call her "our daughter"—even Clark had never said that.

"Yes. I will marry you." I cupped his face in my hands, looked into his hazel eyes, and softly kissed his lips.

"We can do a honeymoon later," Winston said, as he slid the ring on my finger. "We'll be married when Lana gets home, and your reputation will remain intact."

"A honeymoon? Let's go back to Idlewild. I loved that place."

"Since things have opened up for black folks, the place is not as nice and they can't get the big-name entertainment anymore. The golf course is still well-groomed, but I don't want to drive that far to golf. Plus, I plan to be doing a different type of hole in one," Winston said and pinched my behind. "I know you were talking about going fishing. You can go in the morning. We'll leave when you get home."

Winston had never seemed like the marrying kind, but we were compatible, had common goals, and accepted each other. Maybe that was the key to a successful marriage, not all the wide-eyed lust and euphoria I'd felt with Jesse and Clark.

I didn't go fishing. I was a spring bride. By year's end, I would be a widow.

CHAPTER 35

Winston didn't move many of his things to my house. He said he could charge more to rent his place if it was furnished. When we picked Lana up from the airport, she hugged me and said, "I'm happy for you. I hated the idea of you being alone." I was relieved she was happy for me since Mama was not.

"Callie, I know you're grown and I try to support you, but you've gone too far this time. Lord have mercy, men like him are nothing but trouble."

"You haven't even met him."

"Lizzie said he's slick as okra and has hazel eyes. People with hazel eyes are sneaky and born liars. That's all I need to know."

"That's an old wives' tale. You can't judge someone by their eye color. Besides, I think his eyes are cute. I know what I'm doing."

"Ummm-hmmm. I've heard that before."

"You're worrying for nothing. Winston is good to me and good for me."

"I hope you're right. I'll be praying for you. Wouldn't hurt you to pray sometime too."

That summer, the three of us got along as though this arrangement had always been in place, and Winston did something I hadn't been able to do—get Lana to work at one of the cafés.

She said she was changing her major to business and Winston told her if she was going to be a business major, she needed relevant experience on her résumé. Working at the café would be helpful and he gave her the title of procurement assistant.

He also told her the best thing she could do to further a business career was to learn how to golf. That's where the deals were made. This child of mine that I'd had to drag out of bed for school, now willingly rose at dawn, bright-eyed, ready for the golf course. I went with them the first few times, but to me, golfing was long and boring, and the humidity messed up my hair. Since I wasn't trying to be a business tycoon, I stayed home.

Winston and Lana went golfing almost every morning. Winston said she was a fast learner and as it turned out, Lana had an eye for business. She suggested we change our pricing strategy and redesign the menu based on what she'd learned in one of her marketing classes. She said getting microwave ovens for each location would speed up serving times. I was leery about exposing my food to radiation, but she convinced me it was safe. Also, she insisted we lease a Space Invaders arcade game, since kids were out of school. And she nagged me to quit paying employees in cash. She said writing checks was safer and made recordkeeping easier. Her recommendations were helpful. I was also thrilled she was focusing on something more practical than acting, and showing interest in the business.

Winston knew somebody who knew somebody, and we were approved as a Juneteenth parade sponsor. We paid for a booth at Summerfest and the state fair. These off-site events were welcome and helped offset Fourth Street's slow decline. The Schlitz brewery was sold and the twenty-acre site, just three miles from the café, was now a ghost town.

Our days were long and we were working hard, but we were a good team. We hung around the house most evenings. Lana integrated so well into our schedule that when the time came to return to school, she didn't want to go.

"Why should I go to school to learn stuff I'll never use?" she asked, while I was making a salad to go with the leftover spaghetti for dinner.

"College is your passport to a better life," I replied. "A high school diploma isn't enough anymore, especially for a black person."

"Isn't enough for what? More school will only teach me how to get a job and make someone else a lot of money. Neither you nor Winston went to college and you both have businesses. That's what I want—to be my own boss."

"It's not that simple. I'd love for you to take over the café, but even for a business owner, that degree means something," I said.

"Then maybe I'll take a break, get real-world experience," she said. "Berry Gordy, A.G. Gaston, and the McDonald's founder—they never even graduated from high school and they made millions."

"Most people who take a break never go back," I said. "And what about your young man?"

"I'm not interested in him anymore."

"I sure couldn't tell by the long-distance charges on my phone bill this summer."

Just then, Winston entered the room. "I'm glad to see you," I said, while slicing tomatoes. "Maybe you can talk sense into this girl. She's considering taking a break from school."

"You've got a phone call," he said.

"Take a message. I'll call them back after dinner," I replied.

He walked over to me and took the tomatoes out of my hands. "You need to take this call."

It was Aunt Lizzie. Mama had fainted at work, hit her head, and was in Jackson in intensive care. I told her I'd get to Mississippi as soon as I could. Winston found me a flight while I packed.

"I'm not sure what to pack. I don't know how long I'll be gone."

"It doesn't matter," Winston said. "If you need something, I'll send it to you. And don't worry about anything here. I'll handle everything."

"I hope that includes Lana. If she takes a break from school, she probably won't go back."

"Don't worry," Winston said. "I'll handle Lana. You take care of your mother."

Luckily, Mama fainted at work, and not when she was home alone. The doctors said she had a blood clot and put her on blood thinners. They said she should eventually make a full recovery, but her days of eating fried everything and standing all day were over, and someone needed to stay with her for a while. I called Winston and gave him a list of what to send me. He told me there had been an unfortunate incident with Eva and he had to fire her. This was devastating news. I had hoped she would stay sober this time. But I had to focus on my mother. Lana was returning to school and everything else was under control.

I stayed with Mama for two months. It was the first time in years I wasn't rushing from place to place or waking up with an unachievable to-do list. After several calls from the café asking how to make this or that, I realized it would be helpful to record some of my recipes, so Mama and I worked on recipes during the day. We sat on Mama's porch in the evenings and read the newspaper, shelled peas, or listened to the radio. My siblings came home and it was the first time in years that we were all together. And, since Winston wasn't around, I ate peanut butter and jelly sandwiches, made butter-pecan cookies, and ate roasted chestnuts to my heart's delight.

Despite the circumstances that brought me there, I was enjoying my time down home. The Price I'd left had changed. Black people lived on both sides of the railroad tracks and worked everywhere I went. The whites I interacted with were cordial and Main Street seemed quaint and easygoing. I'm sure Jim Crow attitudes still lurked about, but at least it wasn't in your face and the playing field was trying to level. When I left Price, blacks couldn't even get on the field. I didn't regret my decision to leave, but decided to visit more often, and stop bugging Mama about moving to Milwaukee.

Mama got a good report on her six-week follow-up, which meant it was time for me to leave. I stayed two more weeks so I could attend the women's circle program at church with her, and on October 1, I was on the train headed north. When I got back to Milwaukee, the temperature was twenty degrees cooler and trees were already shedding leaves. I had enjoyed my time in Price, but I was happy to be home. My husband was also happy. He met me at the airport with roses and surprised me with our new Buick Electra 225. That man couldn't keep his hands (and other body parts) off me. My first night home, he lit candles, ordered from my favorite Chinese restaurant, and we ate by candlelight. Then he ran me a bubble bath and we went to bed early—not to sleep. The next day, we rode to the café together and worked side by side all day. I made our favorite meal, chicken marsala, to take home for dinner. After we had eaten, Winston called me into the living room. "Have some wine, baby," he said, as he handed me a glass of Lambrusco.

"These past few days have been like a honeymoon," I said. "You've been spoiling me ever since I got home."

"I'm just getting started. Have a seat, Mrs. Dupree, I have a surprise for you. I got a deal on a Betamax. We can record TV shows and watch them at our convenience. And I got some movies." He fumbled with the machine and the movie finally came on. I was sleepy and wasn't up to watching an entire movie, but I didn't want to hurt his feelings. I guess I'd been with Mama too long because I cringed at the thought of possibly spilling red wine on my couch. I was getting up to find coasters, but the three naked people on the screen caught my attention.

"Winston Dupree, where did you get that nasty movie?"

"I thought we could try something different and be a little adventurous," he said and kissed my neck. "Besides, I bet we can do that better than they can."

"Aren't these movies illegal?" I asked, trying to avert my gaze from the well-endowed man on my TV.

"Baby, loosen up," he said. "Didn't you miss me? Don't you want to make love to me?"

"I missed you, but watching this movie is not turning me on...if that's what you're thinking. I just like regular sex," I said and stood.

"I told you a long time ago, the only thing regular about me is my suit jacket size," he said as he emptied his glass, then turned off the Betamax. "I'm going out."

I heard him come in a couple hours later. I got up to try to smooth things over, but before I even got to the living room, I heard him snoring. I left him on the couch and went back to bed. *Maybe I'm just tired. I'll take out one of my rarely-worn negligees and see if Winston wants to be adventurous tomorrow*, I thought.

The next morning, Winston was up and gone by the time the phone awakened me. It was Ben Jr. He wanted to meet with me so we could catch up. "Let me see when Winston is available," I responded.

"I'd rather you come alone," he said.

I went to his office in an area near downtown that was being redeveloped.

"Have a seat. The receptionist is out today," he said when I entered. "It's good to see you."

After a few pleasantries, he got to the nature of his call. "I agreed to be a silent partner because I had full confidence and faith in your ability to run the cafés. My father always said you were more than a cook. So, when I noticed a few changes I didn't agree with, I kept quiet because you're the expert. But now I'm concerned."

"I wish you would've spoken to me earlier," I said.

"I called, but whoever answered said your mother was ill and they didn't know when you'd be back. I left a message for you to call when you could. I came by the café too."

"I never got those messages. What's concerning you?"

"The insurance agent who wrote our policy is retiring. I requested a list of all my policies because I was considering changing companies. Two duplexes were included on the café policy, and I told the agent it was an error. But when they researched it, they said you added them earlier this year."

"I didn't add anything."

"Please call the insurance company as soon as possible to clear this up. Here's the number and a copy of the declarations pages."

"These are Winston's rental houses," I said as I scanned the pages.

"I wonder how that happened," Ben Jr. said. "And when I received my partnership schedule, I saw that a new accounting firm prepared the tax returns," Ben Jr. said.

"Winston recommended them. This new firm got me the biggest tax refund I've ever received."

"I'm pleased with the large tax write-off, but we don't want to risk an audit with questionable deductions. Did you check their references?"

"No, but Winston said he's used them for years."

"There is one other thing. When I couldn't reach you by phone, I stopped by Fourth Street to get a contact number for you. I noticed a line when I came in and it was obvious you guys are exchanging food stamps for cash."

"That's been very lucrative for us."

"I'm not telling you how to run your business, and I'm not a partner with the Fourth Street location, but I can't jeopardize my real estate license by being associated with anything illegal. Food stamp fraud is a felony."

"No need to worry. Everything is in order. Winston helped me complete the paperwork and get the certificate."

"This guy Winston, you've given him a lot of authority. How much do you know about him?"

"I know he's my husband and I've known him for years. He knows what he's doing."

"Oh," Ben Jr. said, tapping his pen on the desk. "I didn't know you'd gotten married."

"It's generally unwise to mix personal and business affairs. But there are exceptions and I hope for your sake, you're an exception."

Ben Jr. had never questioned my business decisions. He was the perfect silent partner. *If he was mentioning these irregularities, maybe his concerns were warranted*, I thought as I drove home.

"We need to talk," I said when Winston came in.

"Let me start. I'm sorry about yesterday. Traveling can be tiring and you've come home and jumped right into work. I should've been more sensitive. Can I help it if I missed my sexy wife?" he said, as he peeked in the pots on the stove.

"Apology accepted, but that's not what I wanted to discuss. Did you add your properties to the café insurance policies?"

"Yeah, earlier this year. I mentioned it to you."

"No, you didn't. And rather than mention it, you should have asked me. Why would you think the café should pay insurance for your rental properties?"

"There's a discount and a cheaper rate if you bundle more properties. How do you think I've been running things while you were gone? I thought we were partners," Winston said.

"That's not the issue," I said as I turned off the stove. "You shouldn't have signed my name."

"Fine. We may miss out on opportunities by not acting right away, but I won't sign your name again. Anything else on your mind?"

"Maybe we should do more research on those opportunities. Acting right away may not be best in the long run."

"What the heck are you talking about?" Winston asked.

"Well, the groceries we sell at the café, for one thing," I said, while stirring the beans.

"What about it? We make good money on those."

"Maybe so, but I didn't know exchanging food stamps for cash was illegal."

"Everybody does it. It's like jaywalking."

"That excuse won't fly if we're ever questioned about it. Ben Jr. said—"

"Okay, now I see where all this is coming from," Winston said, as he began pacing. "Why is that white man all up in our business?"

"Ben Jr. is my partner and he has always been a friend."

"He's a friend while it benefits him. White folks been selling food stamps for years. Now when we enter the game, they got a problem with it. And you do like the good colored folk do. 'Yassir, Mr. Ben, Nosuh, Mr. Ben.'"

"He helped me..."

"And didn't he make money? You think he did that shit out of the goodness of his heart?"

"At least he didn't forge my name and spend my money without telling me," I said.

"*Your* money? If it wasn't for me, that ghetto money pit wouldn't even be open. I put my business interests on hold to help you."

"I never asked you to do that. And like Ben Jr., you've made money too. You've been helping yourself to insurance payments. What else don't I know about?"

"Sounds like you're accusing me of stealing. Either you trust me, or you don't," Winston said as he lit a cigarette.

"Trusting you is difficult when you keep secrets. I know you like shortcuts and using your connections, but I like doing things by the book."

"The book always changes when black folks get ahold of it. We can't let some white man get between us. How about we refinance the mall and hospital locations and pay off Ben Jr.? We should refinance the house too. Then everything will be in our name only."

"Filling out all that paperwork is just a waste of time. Fidelity Bank denied us."

"That's Ben Jr.'s bank. I know someone at Main Street Bank that will make the loan. They don't do title searches and have quick turnarounds if the amount is less than fifty thousand."

"Let's just leave things as they are," I said. "I don't want to deal with yet another bank. Besides, those aren't the only issues. I know you operate on the edges and I've tried to go along with you, but renting to prostitutes—that bothers me."

"We're just their landlord. What they do and how they make money is their business."

"I will not contribute to the downfall of someone's

daughter. I've felt bad ever since Eva and I talked about it. Terminate their lease."

"That one thousand dollars covers several of our bills. How will we make that up?"

"However I was making it before they moved in."

"You weren't making it, remember? You said yourself, you couldn't rent those rooms. You think they're going to stop because you have a stroke of conscience? You're being naive."

"Call it what you want, but I—"

"Look. I apologize about last night and I apologize if I haven't handled things exactly as you would have. I've always worked solo. But we make a great team. We need to get Ben Jr. and drunk-ass Eva and everybody else out of our business. What did I do that's so terrible? All I did was make you money, more than you've ever made, by the way."

When he said it, my concerns sounded petty, and I figured maybe this was how the business world worked.

I should have followed my first mind.

PART IV

Simmer and Stir

CHAPTER 36

Things were running smoothly at the cafés and we decided to plan that honeymoon we had postponed. Winston knew someone with a time-share in Key West we could rent. We usually experienced a lull in dine-in business between Thanksgiving and Christmas, so we scheduled our delayed honeymoon for Christmas week, and Lana was meeting us there. She'd changed her major again and would be cutting her Christmas break short to get back to campus and complete a paper for her independent study class. I was disappointed that she wouldn't be home long, but was glad she was taking college more seriously.

We coordinated our flights, with plans to meet Lana at the Miami airport, drive down, and spend a week in Key West. Then she'd fly home with us for the rest of her semester break. As we were waiting to board, Winston's Ana-Kits fell out when he grabbed a pack of cigarettes from his bag. Security swarmed us and checked our bags for drugs. Winston explained a doctor prescribed the syringes to treat allergic reactions. But by the time they verified his claim, we missed our flight. I was worried about Lana, since we couldn't contact her. But I needn't have worried. She met us at the gate and she wasn't alone.

"Mother, Winston, this is Douglass Townsend, my fiancé," she said, her arm entwined in his, and a sparkling pear-shaped diamond ring on her finger.

"Pleased to meet you, son," Winston said, reaching out to shake his hand.

"Pleased to meet you both," Douglass said. "I've heard a lot about you."

I hadn't heard much of anything about him. I knew there was a young man who called Lana several times when she was home. She told me he was a first-year med student and they met when he tutored her biology class. But she acted like she could take him or leave him, and usually told me to take a message.

We got our bags and made our way to the car rental desk. We rented a car and drove to Key West. The condo smelled new and had breathtaking ocean views. As soon as I could get Lana alone, I asked her, "When did all this occur? And where is he supposed to sleep? You know we only have two bedrooms."

"Oh Mother, don't be so provincial," she said with a dismissive hand wave.

"Call it what you want, but I cannot allow—"

"I knew you'd say that. I told him, he'd have to sleep on the couch. Are you happy now?"

"That solves one issue. Now, let's talk about this engagement. Aren't you rushing things?" I asked.

"I'll be a senior soon. I'm running out of time to snag a husband."

"Lana Denise, I didn't send you to college to snag a husband. The objective is for you to get a degree and not need a husband to take care of you."

"I understand, but why not get my husband too? He's going to be a doctor. I thought you'd be pleased."

"The main criteria is love. If you don't love each other, all the money in the world won't be enough."

"Did you love my daddy?"

"Of course I did."

"Then what happened? Daddy said he didn't want you to go. Why did you leave us?"

"Mississippi was choking the life out of us, and we disagreed on how to break free. I wasn't leaving you. I was trying to save you from living in that choke hold."

"Did you love Clark?"

"I do—I mean, did. He was my first grown-up relationship." I still missed Clark. Marriage to Winston was very different. We were partners, though we weren't a couple like Clark and I had been. But I rarely let my mind go there.

"And now you love Winston. Well, Mrs. Neal-Gibson-Dupree, if love is so critical, why doesn't it last?"

"I'm at a different stage of my life than I was with your father, and with Clark. Winston and I understand each other and want the same things. That's just as important, if not more so, than love."

"I'm not a kid and I don't believe in the fairy-tale romance. I'm skipping the goo-goo eyed, fantasy stage and getting right to the 'understand and want the same thing' stage. I can't imagine meeting anyone more perfect for me than Douglass."

As the week progressed, I could see why she liked him. He doted on her and was very generous. His parents were doctors and he'd completed undergrad in three years. He made it a point to tell me he had a residency lined up with decent pay. He would be able to take care of Lana financially, and would ensure that she finished school.

While he appeared to be a good catch, I noticed things that concerned me. When we went to dinner, he insisted she change, saying her tank top was too revealing. I learned he talked her out of pledging a sorority. I didn't care one way or the other, but the decision should have been hers. When we went to a Cuban restaurant, he chided her for ordering chocolate cake. "You can get that anywhere. She'll have the flan," he told the waiter. The flan was delicious, but if she wanted chocolate cake, let her eat chocolate cake. I was waiting for Lana to tell him so, but she didn't say a word. This wasn't the headstrong daughter I knew, but she seemed happy. Hopefully, it was enough to build a life.

We rented tandem bikes and explored the island. We took a dinner cruise, went on a black history tour, and lounged on the beach. Every restaurant we went to served the freshest seafood I'd ever tasted. A trip highlight was my introduction to key lime pie. I'd never smiled with each bite while eating anything. I went to the kitchen to speak with the chef, much to Lana's embarrassment. I ordered key lime pie with every meal after that.

On a couple of mornings, Winston and Lana went golfing, while Douglass studied and I slept late. We watched holiday movies on Christmas Eve and at midnight, we exchanged gifts before going to bed. We slept in, with not much sleeping—there's something sensual about the ocean breeze. We ordered a four-course room service brunch. Then Winston and I went for a walk down Duval Street in short sleeves, savoring the mild temperature.

"This getaway has been good for us," Winston said as we held hands, something we rarely did. "We work hard, we need to enjoy the fruits of our labor more."

"You're right. Lana announcing her engagement makes me realize I'm not getting any younger. Pretty soon I'll be a grandmother," I said.

"You'll be the sexiest grandmother I ever saw. But you needn't worry. I doubt Lana will be having babies anytime soon," Winston said. "I hope Douglass has a lot of patience. Your daughter can be a handful."

"That's one way to put it," I said.

We stopped for a mimosa—well, maybe two. I got key

lime pie to-go, and we went back to our time-share. When we returned, Douglass was packing and Lana was pacing.

"Can you believe he's leaving me on Christmas Day?" Lana fumed.

"Mrs. Dupree, I apologize. One of the interns' dad passed away, and another one has the flu. They're extremely shorthanded at the hospital and left a message at the front desk for me to please come in."

"It's not his fault, honey," I said. "If you're going to be a doctor's wife, you'll need to get used to interruptions."

"I can't believe no one else is available to fill in. Tell them you can't change your flight. They won't fire you," Lana whined.

"It's my obligation. I may need someone to step in for me one day."

"You're being a little immature, honey. This is what doctors do," I said. "You shouldn't be spending your remaining time together pouting."

"I'm sorry to spoil everyone's holiday," Douglass said. "Getting a flight was difficult. You may want to consider changing your flights. Looks like a big snowstorm is coming your way back in Milwaukee. They've already announced cancellations."

"If there's going to be a snowstorm, I'd rather be here," Lana said with her arms crossed.

"Douglass is right. We need to get home while we can," Winston added.

"And we've got a few New Year's parties coming up, and a big order from the new Timbuktu owner," I agreed.

"Everyone is always against me," Lana said. "Why did we even come?"

"I'll make it up to you, sweetheart," Douglass said as he opened the blinds to look outside. "The shuttle is here."

We hadn't been watching national news and were

unaware of impending bad weather at home. I talked to Mr. Carter, and not only was a winter storm predicted, but the hot water tank was leaking at the Fourth Street location. We'd been closed for the holiday and by the time he went in, the water had done extensive damage in the storage room. The only flight I could find required two connections and a four-hour layover.

"Why are we rushing back to bad weather?" Lana asked. "That flight will take all day. I'm not cutting my vacation short."

"The time-share is paid for," I said. "Winston, why don't you stay with her. It doesn't take both of us to call a plumber. I'll go on ahead."

The last flight was choppy and thankfully the pilot finally announced we were thirty minutes from touch down. He also mentioned the temperature was a balmy fifteen degrees in Milwaukee.

I should be in mild seventy-degree weather with Lana and Winston instead of coming back to this cold place, I thought.

Just like Mr. Ben's children, Lana wasn't interested in the restaurant business. She was marrying well and would have a college degree. I wasn't ready for a rocking chair, but for the first time, I began thinking about an exit strategy. I wasn't going to run the restaurants forever. Visiting Florida reminded me there was more to life than the Fourth Street Café. I made a mental note to ask Ben Jr. if he had any clients interested in buying commercial properties.

We'd left our car at the airport and it took twenty minutes for me to scrape ice off the windshield and for the car to warm up. I stopped by the café to view the damage, grabbed the mail, then went home. The air inside the house was so cold I could see my breath. I turned on the heat and wore my coat to bed.

That morning, I was on the phone for an hour before I found a plumber. My next order of business was to find the insurance policy and call the claims department. The agent told me an adjuster wouldn't come until after the first of the year, but I could start getting repair quotes. She also suggested I notify the second lienholder.

"There's no second lienholder," I corrected.

"Your file says Main Street Bank has a second mortgage," she said. "You should contact them."

"I don't have a loan with them. I wouldn't even know who to ask for," I replied. She gave me the information from her file and told me I could get back to her.

That's why I don't like computers. I don't see why I have to spend time on their bureaucratic error, I thought. But I held my tongue, to avoid alienating the person standing between me and my repairs. However, I did vow to look for another insurance company as soon as this ordeal was over.

A busted tank wasn't the only trouble awaiting me. The health department had inspected the mall location while we were gone. Our score had dropped and we had twenty-one days to implement corrective measures. *This would never have happened while Eva was on staff,* I thought.

After waiting on hold for what seemed like forever, the representative at Main Street Bank told me they granted a line of credit, secured by business furniture and fixtures of all three locations, and also a payment was past due. "This is ridiculous," I said. "I've never set foot in your bank."

"Mrs. Dupree, I can mail you copies of the documents, or you can come to our office."

"There must be someone else I can speak to," I said.

"You can speak to a loan officer. They'll be looking at the same information I'm looking at," she said curtly. "But I'll give you the number."

"Can't you transfer me?" I asked. "I've already been on hold over thirty minutes."

She couldn't transfer me and after she gave me the number, she asked, "When can we expect payment?"

I slammed the phone so hard, my ink pen jumped from the table to the floor. I called the number to speak to the loan officer, but could only leave a message. I tried to call Winston, but there was no answer in the room. I called George, embarrassed I hadn't called since Winston let Eva go, but I didn't have time to waste trying to find another lawyer.

Eva answered the phone. "Eva? I thought I was calling George's office."

"This is his office. I'm his new secretary. George isn't in right now," she said.

"Look, I hate how things ended—"

"Don't worry about it. They told us in rehab getting reestablished wouldn't be easy. I would ask how you are, but if you're calling a lawyer, that usually means trouble," she said. "Hold on. George just walked in."

I gave him the details and he promised to get back to me soon. When we hung up, I made tea and began unpacking. The phone rang and I quickly answered, thinking it was George.

"Hey, babe," Winston said. "Between the weather and the holiday, the price to change our flight was outrageous. We'll arrive tomorrow on our original flight. Can you start my car, since it's been sitting in the garage almost a week?"

"Yeah, sure, I'll start the car. Let me talk to Lana." I spoke briefly to Lana, who was in a better mood than when I left. After unpacking, I called my mother. She thanked me for my Christmas present and said she was looking forward to watch night service tomorrow. I had to rush her off the phone because it was clicking, indicating there was another call. Lana had talked me into getting call-waiting this summer, but I always lost the call when I tried to click over. Usually, I just let the person call back, but I didn't want to miss a call from George, the insurance adjuster, or the plumber.

"Margo, I'm glad I caught you. I was about to hang up. The insurance company is right," George said. "There is a second mortgage on all the properties. You're sure you or Ben Jr. didn't refinance them?"

"Winston said he knew someone at Main Street Bank who could handle the paperwork for us to refinance and buy out Ben Jr. But we never applied."

"These liens were filed in March with a forty-five-thousand-dollar original balance. You'll have to go to the bank and complete a fraud affidavit to get it removed."

"How long will that take?" I asked. "I need to get the insurance process started so I can start repairs and reopen."

"I'll threaten legal action and insist your claim should be a priority. Something else: When there's fraud, perpetrators often open credit cards in the victim's name. I hope you don't mind that I checked your credit reports. There were three new credit cards in the business name, and two in your personal name this year."

"I haven't opened any credit cards. I wonder if they got Winston too."

"I checked his report and I didn't see any activity. He's probably gotten a lot of credit offers after the bankruptcy, but so far—"

"Bankruptcy?"

"Yes, in June. You didn't know?" George asked.

"This is embarrassing to say, but no, I didn't."

"Don't be embarrassed. I know about having a spouse with secrets. I'll do more digging and call you tomorrow."

I was about to get dressed when I remembered Winston had asked me to start his car. I raised the garage door slightly, then turned on his car. But rather than run back in the house, I decided to do some digging of my own. I could hear Mama's words, "When you go looking for trouble, you usually find it." But that was probably a saying invented by a philandering man to keep his woman from discovering his

transgressions. I pulled everything from the glove compartment. There were maps, gum, several key rings, two Ana-
Kits, and miscellaneous receipts. When I grabbed the car
owner's manual, utility bills from his old place fell out. But
they were from this year. Why was he paying utilities for a
place he supposedly had rented out? I also saw bills in my
name. Winston was going to have a lot of explaining to do.
Especially since a six-pack of condoms, less two, also fell out
of the manual.

I went inside, showered, and dressed. My mind was
racing from anger to confusion. *What in the world was Winston
up to now?* I wondered. He always had a scheme or "business
plan," as he called it. That could be, but didn't explain the
condoms. According to Mama, no man was faithful and as
long as he "took care of home" I shouldn't fret. But this
wasn't the old days where women had to take what men
dished out. *I work hard and deserve someone as committed as I am.
Plus, what kind of example would I be setting for Lana if I let a
man disrespect me?* I thought.

I fixed coffee and oatmeal, but picked over my food. I
left the house and went to the hospital and mall locations and
gave them instructions on what to prepare for the catering
orders. I went to Fourth Street last, since I planned to stay
there the longest. Mr. Carter had done a temporary repair on
the tank, so at least we could open a few hours a day. The
dining room was empty and Mr. Carter was playing solitaire
at the counter.

"Has it been this slow all week?" I asked.

"Unfortunately, yes."

"Let's just close," I said. "Enjoy your New Year." As we
were locking up, the phone rang. Mr. Carter answered and
handed it to me.

"Margo, I've been trying to track you down all morning.
I need to talk to you. Come by my office as soon as you can."

★ ★ ★

The first person I saw when I entered George's office was Eva. She met me as soon as I walked in, and we hugged and screamed like schoolgirls. "You look good," I said.

"And you look like crap," Eva said with a laugh.

"I didn't get much sleep last night," I said.

"And what's with those gray roots? We cannot have that."

"Excuse me," George said, after loudly clearing his throat. "I believe she came to see me."

"Of course, boss," Eva said with an exaggerated bow, while stepping aside.

"It's hard to find good help these days," George said with a smile.

It was good to have the old Eva back.

I followed him to his office and had barely sat when George said, "I'm still looking into a few things, but I wanted to let you know what I've already discovered. I went to the county recorder's office. The line was long because folks were trying to get things filed before the year's end. I was one of the last ones to get waited on and this is what they gave me." He handed me a computer printout.

I squinted, trying to decipher the tiny writing, then asked, "Is this what we need to prove the liens were fraudulently filed?"

"This shows that Main Street Bank loaned you forty-five thousand dollars secured by all of your business furniture and fixtures."

"Everyone needs to go back to pen and paper. These computers are unreliable," I said. "The mall and hospital location mortgages are in Ben Jr.'s name and I pay him. There's a small SBA loan left on the Fourth Street location in my and Clark's name, and that's it. I'm trying to pay off debt, not add to it."

"You may not have borrowed money, but it looks like

Winston did. The document has both of your signatures. And the same day, he purchased a duplex on Locust Street and one on Sanders Avenue. Three other properties were refinanced, and the mortgage signed by both of you. All are financed with adjustable-rate, interest-only loans, with higher payments set to kick in next year. There's also a blanket guaranty, which means the bank can foreclose on your house."

"I don't understand why he'd do this."

"I'll do more research, although from my view, it looks very shady," he said. "If this is what I think it is, you could lose everything."

PART V

Boiling Point

CHAPTER 37

When I got home and checked the answering machine, there were two messages for Lana from Douglass. I guess he thought she was able to change her flight. I considered calling Winston to ask him what the heck was going on. But we needed to talk in person. The extra day would give me time to gather my thoughts and calm down. George had been kind when he called Winston's actions shady. It plainly looked like Winston had disregarded my decision not to refinance and buy out Ben Jr.'s loans. *But why?* I tried to work on payroll and other bills, but couldn't concentrate. *How in the world could he explain this and what had he done with the money?* I knew George said he was doing more research, but I decided to do my own.

I gathered the documents George had given me and headed to the addresses on the list. It was already dark and difficult to read house numbers, but there were lights on at the Sanders Avenue address. A lady with three young kids were getting out of a car as I drove up. Two of them ran up the sidewalk, and she was carrying a baby. I sat in the car twenty minutes, then drove off. Their energy and youth seemed so genuine. I didn't have the heart to disturb them.

I drove by the Locust Street address and saw a pizza delivery guy at the door. I was about to drive off when I saw Winston open the door. As he was going through his wallet, I got out of my car and marched up the steps.

"Margo, what are you doing here?" he asked when he looked up.

"I could ask you the same thing," I answered. "I thought you were coming in tomorrow."

"We were—I got on another—"

"Aren't you going to invite me in, since apparently I'm part owner of this place," I said.

"Babe, is the pizza here? It took them long enough," a woman's voice called out. Then, to my shock, Lana came to the door, dressed in Winston's T-shirt and socks.

"What the hell?"

"Now Margo, it's not what you think," Winston stuttered, grabbing my elbow as I knocked the pizza box to the floor and walked past him. He hurriedly paid the delivery man, then slammed the door.

"It's not what I think? Then please explain it to me!"

"Don't bother. I'm glad she's here. I'm tired of sneaking around," Lana said. "I know this is awkward, but you didn't really love him. We didn't want to hurt you."

"And this is how you *not* hurt me? What about Douglass? And how long have you been..."

"What does it matter? Long enough to know we love each other and want to be together. If you weren't wrapped up in money, cakes, and fried chickens, maybe you could be more adventurous and take care of your man."

"Enough, Lana," Winston said as he lit a cigarette.

"That money, cakes, and fried chickens paid for everything from the sass in your mouth to the socks on your feet. How selfish and ungrateful can you be?"

"Margo—"

"What? What can you possibly say to me? I can't believe how blind I've been. Have you been messing with my daughter all along?"

Lana stepped in front of Winston and said, "Mother, let's—"

Before she could finish her sentence, I pushed her and she tumbled to the floor. As I turned to leave, Winston grabbed my arm and said, "Wait, we can work—"

"There is no 'we,'" I said, then spit in his face. "I hope you choke on your pizza."

CHAPTER 38

I was in a daze and had driven twenty blocks before I noticed cars blinking their headlights at me because I hadn't turned mine on. I'd been heartbroken over failed marriages and miscarriages, but this was a new low. I wasn't a perfect mother, or a typical one. Some may have provided more than me, and some may have spent more time with their children, but none loved more or were more devoted than me.

How could she have such little regard for me? And how could this have been going on right under my nose? I thought as I pounded my steering wheel, which was wet from my tears. I hit the steering wheel so hard, my car horn went off, prompting the driver in front of me to raise his middle finger. I had worked hard for years and given Lana everything. How could this be happening? I'd been in a struggle for money every day since my daddy died. My mother struggled after my daddy died because he handled the finances. I vowed not to ever hand over my power to any man. Yet, I had done the same thing. But unlike my daddy, Winston wasn't worthy of my trust, and now I was in danger of losing my business and home. And it wasn't just me. I had a staff depending on those cafés as well. When I got home, I threw Winston's things in garbage bags, put them in the outside garbage can, and poured bleach over them. Then I packed an overnight bag and went to a hotel. I stayed two days and nights and on the third day, I got up at dawn, with empty tear ducts and checked out, leaving Margo the victim behind.

I spent the morning cooking, baking, and delivering orders. Everywhere I went or called, they told me I had just missed Winston's phone call. I went to George's office, then around two o'clock, I called the house and left a message for Winston to meet me at Fourth Street around eight o'clock s. At 7:59, Winston walked in, with roses.

"I'm glad you called," he said. "You don't know how bad I feel and how much I've missed you."

"Save your breath. I wanted to see you because we need to discuss our next steps," I said as I turned off the stove. "Obviously, the marriage is over, so the faster—"

"Let's talk about it," Winston said and sat at the counter. "Whatever that is, it smells great."

"I made chicken marsala for the Urban League brunch. There's plenty left," I said and fixed two plates.

"So let me start by apologizing," Winston said. "I know I was wrong. I hope we can—"

"I told you the other night, there is no more 'we.' I've had a legal separation agreement prepared since a divorce will take a while," I said as I handed him an envelope.

"You've already been to an attorney? I understand you're highly upset—"

"*Upset* doesn't begin to describe how I feel."

"I'm not the only guilty party here," Winston protested after eating two forkfuls of chicken. "Lana isn't the angel you think she is. Do you know how many times she—"

"Stop right there. Do not blame your weak, low-down depravity on my daughter."

"But I need to tell you the whole story," Winston said, then ate two more forkfuls.

"I wouldn't believe a word you said even if your tongue was notarized. I just want you to sign these papers."

Winston coughed, then said, "Can you hand me a soda or a glass of water?"

"No. I can't hand you anything but a pen to sign these papers. You thought wimpy flowers and a few hollow words would erase what you've done? How long have you been screwing my daughter?"

"I know this is bad. But we can find a way through it. Because—" Winston stopped to clear his throat. "Because I'm not going to roll over and walk away with nothing. I've got a lot invested in our partnership."

"This isn't a partnership and I know all about your investments. You've put me in serious debt and have been treating my business like your personal piggy bank. I guess you're trying to drag me into bankruptcy with you."

"If you know all that, then you know I'm not signing anything." Winston took his napkin and wiped sweat beads from his forehead.

"You didn't have any problem signing my name for loans and credit cards."

"I've been having a little cash flow crunch. The state is starting its own lottery, so my guys have been phasing out the numbers," he said, while fanning his face with a menu. "I owe some people some money. I usually cover my shortfalls, but with disco and this new rap stuff, my groups can't get any gigs. I'll replace everything, it's just taking a little longer than I anticipated. Plus, I had a tip the city will be building a new basketball stadium, so I bought a few properties in the area. White folks will be moving back and those prices will skyrocket. You'll be happy we bought them."

"Are you serious? You're a lying, cheating snake, and the

only thing you can do to make me happy is to sign these affidavits admitting you forged my name. I cannot believe—"

"I need water," he whispered, as he grabbed his empty glass.

"Do you need water or one of those Ana-Kits you had in your car?"

Winston's eyes got big and he asked, "What's in that stuff?"

"You mean the chicken marsala? That's one of our favorites. Remember when we went to Idlewild and I had it for the first time? I practiced several versions until I got it just right. I add mushrooms, onions, chicken broth, and make gravy instead of using cream," I said, ignoring his waving hand. "Then I prepare the pasta, but the secret is in the sauce and I'll tell you my secret: I add a teaspoon of vanilla extract. Of course, the main thing is the chicken. I tenderize boneless, skinless chicken breasts. Make sure they're not too thick. Then season them with garlic pepper—hope it wasn't too much pepper for you—then lightly batter in flour and pan-fry in peanut oil. Next, I—"

"You know I'm allergic to nuts!" Winston said as he grabbed his keys and struggled to stand.

"Leaving? So soon? You still haven't signed the papers. And if you're headed to your car, I took those Ana-Kits when I went through the glove compartment. I may have one around here someplace," I said while placing my index finger on my chin.

"Margo, this isn't funny," he whispered.

"Negro, do you see me laughing? Sign these papers."

"You'll never be able to run this business on your own," Winston said, as he scribbled his signature, then slid the papers across the counter. "That will never stand up in court."

"Keep talking and you won't be able to stand at all. And one more thing—you will end your relationship with Lana.

She has her whole life ahead of her and doesn't need you messing it up."

"No problem. She can do that all by herself," he said, "Now, give me my kit."

"No *please*? Where are your manners?"

Winston narrowed his eyes, and wheezed, "*Pulleeeease.*"

"With pleasure," I said. "The sooner you're out of our lives, the better." I went to the storage room and began digging in my purse for the Ana-Kit. I heard the back door open and figured it was Mr. Carter coming in. As I walked toward the dining room, I heard what sounded like a car backfiring, then the jukebox glass shattered.

"Lana, what have you done?" I screamed, as she stood with my gun in her hand.

"Are you crazy?" Winston yelled. "You almost shot me."

"I never should have believed you," Lana cried. She turned to me and said, "He never loved me. He called me a silly slut and laughed in my face. He said—"

"I don't give a damn what he said. What's wrong with you?"

"But Mommy—"

"She's a spoiled, lazy tramp, that's what's wrong with her," Winston said, as he grabbed Lana from behind with one arm around her waist and grabbed the gun with the other.

Lana clawed his face with her nails and drew blood. "You stupid bitch," he said in a raspy voice and wiped his cheek. She squirmed free and began kicking and screaming and hitting him with the gun.

Winston grabbed her wrist and they tussled with the gun. "Let her go," I hollered as I ran and tackled him like a middle linebacker. I tried to grab the gun and pull him off her. We all fell across a table, knocking over stools and sending the napkin holder and sugar dispenser to the floor. The three of us wrestled for control, then the gun went off.

Winston collapsed, then lay sprawled across the floor. It was eerily quiet, and the pungent odor of sulfur and fireworks filled the air.

"Is he dead?" Lana whispered as she struggled to her feet.

I leaned over his motionless body to see if he was breathing. "This is bad. Go home and stay there until you hear from me," I said, pacing, careful not to step on broken glass.

"What should I do when I get there?" Lana asked.

"Now you ask for my advice. Go home, and don't answer the phone or the door. Throw this in the alley," I said breathlessly, tossing her the Ana-Kit. As Lana rushed out the back door, I turned to Winston. His hands were trembling and his hazel eyes seemed double their size as he glared at me. I called 911, then picked up the gun and wiped it. There had been an increased neighborhood police presence since it was New Year's Eve, and it didn't take them long to arrive. "My husband's been shot," I said as I let them in.

"Are there security cameras?" an officer asked me.

"Did you see the shooter?" the other officer asked.

Before I could answer, the ambulance arrived, and two attendants rushed in. One of them kneeled, clasped Winston's hand, and said, "Just hold on, sir. We'll take care of you."

They lifted him onto the stretcher, and I was walking out with them when Winston began coughing. That low-life leech began gasping for breath, then whispered, "She shot me," before slowly closing his eyes.

PART VI

Food for Thought

CHAPTER 39

"That's quite a story, Mrs. Dupree," Attorney Shelton said as she turned off the tape recorder and handed the cassette to George.

"Well, the first thing I'm going to do is destroy this cassette. I knew you'd try to confess," George said, as he stuck his pen in the cassette reel and pulled out tape. "And next, we need to tell the police the 'she' is Lana, not you."

"Absolutely not. She brought the gun in, but I'm not sure who pulled the trigger. I know what she did was terrible, but she's still my child. I must protect her."

"Lana has no problem looking out for herself," George said.

"What if the police question me and give me a lie-detector test? Can I plead the Fifth or something?

"That's TV. They only use lie-detector tests in high profile or unusual circumstances, and I hate to say this, but a dead black man on Fourth Street is not unusual. Plus, you aren't legally obligated to take the test. If they do ask you, we'll object since the tests are notoriously inaccurate."

"How do we know Winston didn't die from the reaction to the peanut oil?" I asked.

"What peanut oil?" George asked. "Oh, you mean the

peanut oil Eva threw out when we got permission to go in to put the food away, so it wouldn't draw rodents and bugs?"

"I appreciate your help, but not if it hurts Lana," I said. "And if you defy me, I'll drop you and get another lawyer or better yet, represent myself."

"That's a surefire way to go to jail," George said with a sigh. "I feel terrible about everything. I should have done something."

"What could you have done?" I asked.

"Eva and I knew about Lana and Winston. Eva kept saying something wasn't right, but I dismissed her concerns. When you were out of town while your mother was sick, Eva took some mail to your house. She said the letter looked important and she wanted to ensure Winston saw it. No one answered the door, so she used the extra key you gave her to let herself in, and she found them on your couch. That's why he fired her. Eva knew you'd be devastated and hoped their affair would pass when Lana returned to school. We knew it wouldn't end well if you found out, but we never imagined anything like this. I'm so sorry."

"I should have known Eva wouldn't let me down. I need to apologize and—"

"Don't worry about Eva. Right now, let's get you home. I'll handle the police and the fraud cases. Refer inquiries to me. Don't answer the phone or the door. If I call, I'll let it ring once, hang up, then call right back."

The neighbors' Christmas decorations illuminated my dark house. I had almost forgotten it was still the holiday season, so much had gone so wrong so quickly. The stench of burnt eggs greeted me when I walked in.

"I am glad you're here," Lana said and wiped her hands on a towel. "Everything is closed and I was trying to fix breakfast. I cooked the eggs too long, but I've got pancakes. You want some?"

"I've just spent the night in jail. Forgive me if your

breakfast isn't my priority," I said. "The police arrested me because Winston said I shot him, but released me because you said you did it."

"I said it was self-defense," Lana said. "My attorney told me to—"

"You have an attorney?"

"You remember my homecoming date, Alexander Harris? His dad is representing me. He told me what to say and he got me out. I wish we had some of that chicken marsala you fixed yesterday. I'm starving."

"A man is dead, and that's all you care about?"

"You want me to act like I'm sorry? I'm not, and you shouldn't be either. He was an evil asshole, unworthy of either of us. He got what he deserved."

"You can't say things like that. They can charge you with murder."

"My attorney said not to worry. I played the grieved and confused stepdaughter and they probably won't even bring charges. I told them he took advantage of me. When they asked when it started, I broke into tears, and Mr. Harris made them stop questioning me."

"When did it start?"

"I just want to forget about it," Lana said with a wave of her hand. "I know some things are unforgivable. You probably hate me."

"I could never hate you. I brought you into this world and you're a part of me."

"I don't know what I was thinking. Winston wasn't even my type. I hope you had insurance on that bastard."

"Lana, I cannot believe you. But this isn't about Winston. I'm your mother. How could you?"

"I wish I could take it back, but I can't," Lana said while grabbing syrup from the cabinet." "Here's the deal. Mr. Harris said the police department won't charge both of us and isn't likely to spend the manpower and resources to determine who's guilty. They won't figure it out because we don't really know who or what killed him. But the truth doesn't even matter, it's what can be proven. Just let the attorneys do their job and this will all go away."

I finally took off my coat, still stunned at what I was hearing. "I guess George should call Attorney Harris. If they can work this out, then you and I can focus on straightening out the cafés," I said.

"I'm leaving. I told Douglass I was pregnant. He reserved a flight for me and we're getting married as soon as we can get a license."

"You're pregnant?" I asked and sat at the table. "Are you sure it's Douglass's?"

"I'm sure he'll be a great father."

"But you don't love him and he seems controlling."

"I'll love being a doctor's wife," Lana said as she poured syrup on her charred pancakes. "You married for love. We see how great that worked out."

"That's because I loved you more, something they couldn't accept. Everything I've done has been for you."

Lana put her fork down and asked, "If you loved me so much, why did you leave me?"

"I left to prepare a better life for you."

"Other people manage to improve their lives without deserting their family."

"I never knew you felt this way," I said. "Is that why you slept with him?"

"That's probably what a therapist would say. My step-mother was awful to me. She'd say my own mother didn't want me, and she got stuck with me."

"I kept trying to have the right home, work schedule, and bank account before bringing you here. You don't know what it's like to know your mother is worried about the rent, to come home and find your belongings piled in the yard or to bounce from relative to relative. I didn't want you to struggle, but maybe I should've brought you with me right away. At least we would have been together. Or maybe I should've listened to Mama and stayed in Price."

"You did what you thought best, despite what your mother said. You made your own way, and I'm making mine. I can handle Douglass. Uggghhh. This is awful," she said as she wrinkled her nose and dumped her food into the garbage. "I need to start packing." She talked of baby names and wedding plans as she packed, while I searched for Tylenol—unsure if my muscles were aching from falling on the café linoleum or from laying on the hard jail cot.

"Don't the police want you to stay in town?" I asked.

"You worry too much. Attorney Harris has it all worked out. By the time I finished crying and slinging snot, they were ready to shoot Winston themselves. And you said acting classes were a waste of time."

CHAPTER 40

Eighteen Months Later

The box arrived today. I peeled back the packing tape and slid out the contents, the final draft of my cookbook, *Fourth Street Favorites*. I'll admit, I dismissed the idea when Eva suggested it. But after almost losing the café, I needed money. I even prayed. I was willing to try anything.

Almost anything. Mama wanted me to come home, but this is my home now. She said she'd keep me in her prayers and ask the women's circle to pray for me. I don't know if my prayers, hers, or all of ours were answered, but things have worked out.

George and Attorney Harris had been right. The police conducted a superficial investigation and ruled Winston's death accidental. Other than two paragraphs on page six of the newspaper, there was no public acknowledgement of the incident. The autopsy concluded the cause of death as a gunshot wound to the chest, with perforation of heart and lungs.

That resolved one problem, but it didn't address my financial mess. George and Ben Jr. tried to help me reorganize and reopen, but we couldn't save the mall and hospital cafés. There were too many transactions to unravel, so Ben Jr. sold the buildings and I was back to just the original location. I haven't reached my previous sales levels, but implementing lunchtime deliveries to downtown offices has almost offset the loss of the hospital and mall locations. I'm making better use of the space I do have and reaching a new customer base.

As Winston's widow, I ended up with two of his duplexes and Mr. Carter helps manage them. Lana stayed in one of them over the summer. I'm not sure what happened between her and Douglass. She called me from the Greyhound station, and I went and loaded her, the baby, boxes and suitcases in my car. She said she didn't want to talk about what happened and I haven't pressed her. I just wanted her to keep moving forward, and she has. She got student loans and returned to Howard. Her baby is staying with me until she finishes her degree, although she might stay longer and attend law school.

I'm having a book release party at Timbuktu and already have several bulk orders. Clark's pictures turned out great. I was hesitant, but called to ask him to refer a photographer. To my surprise, he offered to take the pictures himself. He knew all the tricks, like using light-colored dishes, plating in odd numbers, and garnishing with contrasting colors. I can't wait to show him the draft when we go fishing in the morning.

We don't talk about that awful business with Winston. I've got a café to run and another generation to raise. My granddaughter is so adorable, she should be in commercials. I know everyone thinks their grandkids are cute, but people we don't even know, stop us and comment on how pretty she is, especially her chubby, dimpled cheeks and her smoky hazel eyes.

RECIPES

Fourth Street Favorites

7UP Pound Cake

Cake

1½ cups margarine or butter, softened
3 cups sugar
5 eggs, room temperature
3 cups cake flour
2 teaspoons lemon extract
1 teaspoon vanilla extract
¾ cup 7UP

Glaze

3¼ cups powdered sugar
1 teaspoon vanilla extract
3 tablespoons lemon juice
¼ cup cold 7UP

Using an electric mixer, beat the sugar and butter until creamy, at least 5 minutes. Add in lemon extract and mix. Add eggs, one at a time, mixing after each egg—don't rush this step. Sift flour, then add to mix, one cup at a time, alternating with the 7UP. Mix until just combined. Scrape down the sides of the bowl. Mix for one more minute at low speed.

Pour batter into a well-greased Bundt pan. Bake for one hour at 325° F. Do not preheat oven. Cake is very moist, so it may take an additional 10 to 20 minutes. Bake until a toothpick inserted comes out clean.

While the cake bakes, make glaze. Using an electric mixer, combine the powdered sugar, vanilla, lemon juice, and 7UP. Beat until smooth.

Remove cake from oven and let it stand in the pan for about 15 minutes.

Turn cake over onto a plate or platter, remove pan, and let cake cool completely.

Drizzle with the glaze.

Margo's Tip: If you don't have cake flour, add 2 tablespoons of cornstarch to all-purpose flour.

Best Buttermilk Biscuits

2 cups self-rising flour and more for flouring board
½ cup vegetable shortening, chilled, cut into ½ inch pieces
¾ cup cold buttermilk

Preheat oven to 450° F.

In a large bowl, combine flour and shortening until mixture resembles coarse crumbs. Do not overmix. Make a well in the center. Slowly pour in buttermilk and stir gently until just combined. Dough will be slightly sticky but should come together as a cohesive ball. If dough is too sticky, add a little flour until it is manageable.

Once dough is cohesive, transfer dough to a well-floured surface. Gently pat or roll to about ½ inch thick. Do not use a rolling pin.

Making close cuts, press biscuit cutter or thin-rimmed glass down into the dough. Wiggle gently and extract cutter/glass. Do not twist the cutter or glass (if you use a glass, coat it with flour). Place biscuits on ungreased pan, about ½ inch apart. Gather scraps, roll out and repeat. Make a small dimple with your finger in the center of each biscuit to help the top rise evenly.

Bake for 12 to 15 minutes in preheated oven until golden brown. Remove from oven, and brush with melted butter. Makes about 12 biscuits.

Margo's Tip: Don't give up if they don't turn out at first. Biscuit making takes practice.

Chicken Marsala

3 tablespoons butter
1½ pounds thin-cut chicken breast fillets
1 teaspoon garlic powder
½ teaspoon onion powder
½ teaspoon paprika
½ cup all-purpose flour
1 4-ounce can mushroom pieces or slices
1 can cream of mushroom soup
⅓ cup Marsala cooking wine
¼ cup oil (most prefer olive oil—you can even use peanut
    oil!)
Salt and pepper to taste

Melt butter in the oil over medium heat in large skillet (oil should just barely cover bottom of skillet).

Sprinkle both sides of chicken with paprika, garlic powder, salt and pepper. Dredge each breast in the flour (or put in baggie and shake). Tap off excess flour.

Pan-fry the fillets until lightly browned, about 3 minutes per side. Transfer to a warm platter and set aside.

Sauté mushrooms in skillet. Add wine and half the mushroom soup to skillet and stir. Gradually add more soup until gravy is desired consistency.

Pour sauce over chicken and serve with rice, pasta or potatoes.

Margo's Tip: If you have an Eva who keeps drinking the wine, you can use balsamic or apple cider vinegar with quarter cup white grape juice.

Easy Vegan Chocolate Cake

1½ cups all-purpose flour
1 cup white sugar
¼ cup cocoa powder
1 teaspoon baking soda
½ teaspoon salt
1 cup water
½ cup vegetable oil
1 teaspoon vanilla extract
1 teaspoon distilled white vinegar

Preheat oven to 350° F. Lightly grease 9"x5" loaf pan.

Sift flour, sugar, cocoa, baking soda, and salt together in a large bowl. Add water, oil, vanilla and vinegar, mix until smooth, but don't overmix. Pour mixture into prepared pan.

Bake in preheated oven until a toothpick inserted into center comes out clean, about 45 minutes.Let it cool, then turn onto oval plate. Lightly dust top with powdered sugar.

Margo's Tip: If you don't tell them it's vegan, they'll never know.

Fourth Street Fried Pies

Dough

3 cups all-purpose flour, plus more for work surface
3 tablespoons granulated sugar
½ teaspoon salt
½ cup cold vegetable shortening (chill in refrigerator 10-20
    minutes before using)
1 large egg, lightly beaten
1 cup whole buttermilk (cold)

Filling

3 large apples*, peeled and chopped (about 3 cups)
⅓ cup white granulated sugar
2 tablespoons butter
2 teaspoons cornstarch
1 teaspoon ground cinnamon
1 tablespoon lemon juice
Pinch of salt

Additional Ingredients

Oil for frying
½ cup granulated sugar
½ teaspoon ground cinnamon

   To prepare the dough: Stir together flour, granulated sugar,
and salt in a large bowl until combined. Using your fingers or

*Peaches or pears can be substituted for the apples.

a pastry cutter, cut shortening into flour mixture until it is crumbly. Stir in egg and buttermilk until dough just comes together. Shape into a disk and wrap tightly in plastic wrap. Refrigerate until firm, at least 1 hour or up to 12 hours.

To prepare the filling: Bring apples, sugar, butter, lemon juice, cornstarch, cinnamon, and salt to a boil in a large skillet over medium-high; cook, stirring often, until apples are fork tender and mixture is thickened, 2 to 3 minutes. Different apple types may require more sugar, so taste as you go. Remove from heat and let cool to room temperature.

To make the pies, roll the chilled dough into a large square on a floured surface. Trim the edges to make a rectangle. Cut into 8 to 10 long rectangles, using a butter knife. Spoon a tablespoon or so of filling into the top half of one of the rectangles. Fold the bottom half over the top. Seal the edges, then crimp the edges shut with a fork.

Fill a large Dutch oven or thick pot two-thirds full of oil. Heat oil to hot, but not smoking. Fry pies 2 at a time until golden brown, 4 to 5 minutes per batch. Don't be tempted to fry too many at once—the oil temperature will drop, and the pies won't fry.

Drain on paper towels. Stir together granulated sugar and cinnamon in a large shallow bowl. Toss warm pies in cinnamon sugar to coat. Let cool 2 to 3 minutes and enjoy!

Margo's Tip: Making dough can be time-consuming. They'll taste almost as good with premade pie dough.

German Red Cabbage

2 tablespoons butter
½ large red cabbage, sliced ¼-inch thick
2 tablespoons sugar
¼ cup balsamic vinegar or apple cider vinegar
Salt and pepper to taste

Melt butter in a large pot over medium heat. Add the thinly sliced red cabbage and toss to coat with the butter. Sauté until slightly wilted, about 5 minutes.

Sprinkle sugar over the cabbage and toss to coat evenly. Add the vinegar. Bring to a simmer, then reduce the heat to medium low. Cover and simmer until the cabbage reaches desired tenderness, generally about 20 minutes. Stir often.

Season to taste with salt and pepper.

Margo's Tip: Serve with pan-fried and sliced bratwurst for a quick meal.

Margo's Molasses Cookies

1½ cups white sugar, divided
¾ cup margarine, melted
1 egg
¼ cup unsulphured or dark molasses
2 cups all-purpose flour
2 teaspoons baking soda
1 teaspoon ground cinnamon
1 teaspoon vanilla extract
½ teaspoon salt
½ teaspoon ground cloves
½ teaspoon ground ginger

Mix 1 cup sugar, margarine, vanilla extract, and egg together in bowl until smooth; stir in molasses. Combine flour, baking soda, cinnamon, salt, cloves, and ginger in a separate bowl, then add to the molasses mixture and stir until well combined. Cover and chill dough for 1 hour.

Preheat oven to 375° F.

While the oven is preheating, roll dough into 1-inch diameter balls; roll each ball in remaining ½ cup white sugar before placing 2 inches apart on ungreased cookie sheets. Bake in batches in the preheated oven until tops are cracked, about 8 to 10 minutes. Remove from oven, leaving them on the cookie sheet for 3 to 5 minutes. Then finish cooling on wire racks. They'll stay fresh for about 3 days in an airtight container.

Margo's Tip: If you don't have wire racks, cut open a paper bag, wrinkle it some, then place paper towels on top. Slide cookies onto paper towels.

Mama's Stuffed Bell Peppers

1 pound ground beef
1 teaspoon salt
½ teaspoon black pepper
6 large bell peppers—roughly equal size
3 tablespoons oil
½ cup chopped onion
1 tablespoon garlic powder
1½ teaspoons chili powder
¼ teaspoon dried oregano
1 (8-oz) can tomato sauce
2 tablespoons tomato paste
½ cup diced tomatoes
1 teaspoon Worcestershire sauce
1 teaspoon hot sauce*
1 cup cooked rice (you can also use orzo or any small pasta)
1½ cups shredded Monterey Jack or cheddar Jack cheese

Preheat oven to 425°F.

Precook the rice.

Line a 9x13-inch baking dish with aluminum foil for easy cleanup. Prepare the peppers by washing them, then removing the tops and cores. Red, yellow and orange peppers are sweetest. Green peppers are slightly bitter. The tops of the peppers can be diced and added to the meat mixture or saved for another recipe.

Place the peppers, cut side up, in the baking dish; drizzle with 1 tablespoon of the oil and sprinkle with the remaining

*This will not make the mixture hot. If you want to kick up the heat, add extra hot sauce, a pinch of cayenne, and/or diced tomatoes with green chilies instead of regular diced tomatoes.

¼ teaspoon salt. Sprinkle a pinch of brown sugar if using green bell peppers. Roast the peppers for about 20 minutes, until slightly tender. Some liquid will accumulate in the bottom of the peppers; that's okay, peppers are 90% water.

Heat the remaining 2 tablespoons of oil over medium heat in a large nonstick skillet. Add ground beef and/or sausage and season it with salt and pepper. Cook and crumble until meat is browned, about 3 minutes. Add the onions and cook, stirring frequently until onions are soft and limp. Drain grease. Reduce heat to medium and add garlic powder, chili powder and oregano.

Add the tomato sauce and tomato paste to meat mixture and stir to combine. Add the diced tomatoes, Worcestershire sauce, and hot sauce. Bring to a boil, then reduce to a simmer. Let it bubble gently and reduce/concentrate for 15 minutes or until little excess liquid remains. Stir in the cooked rice, half the cheese and heat through for 1–2 minutes. Remove from heat.

Remove the peppers from the oven and spoon the meat filling evenly into the peppers. Sprinkle top with the remaining cheese and place back in the oven. Bake for 10 more minutes, or until the cheese is melted and bubbling, and the peppers are tender.

Margo's Tip: For a brunch dish, omit chili powder and add a heaping tablespoon of scrambled eggs to each pepper.

Mr. Ben's Booyah Stew

1 tablespoon oil
1 pound beef stew meat
2 pounds chicken breasts and/or thighs, cubed
½ yellow onion, diced
1 green bell pepper, diced
1 carrot, diced
2 celery stalks, diced
8 cups chicken broth
1 medium tomato, chopped
3 medium potatoes, diced
¾ cup corn
¾ cup peas
½ cup chopped green beans
2 cups shredded cabbage
1 tablespoon Worcestershire sauce
1 teaspoon salt
2 teaspoons black pepper

Heat oil in large Dutch oven or heavy bottom pot over medium-high heat until just smoking. Brown beef on all sides, about 10 minutes; transfer to plate. Cook chicken until browned all over, about 10 minutes, transfer to plate. When chicken is cool enough to handle, remove the skin and discard it. Shred chicken into bite-sized pieces.

Pour off all but 1½ teaspoons fat from pot. Add onions and celery and cook over medium heat until softened, about 5 minutes. Stir in broth. Add beef, and chicken, and bring to boil.

Reduce heat to low and simmer, covered, until beef is tender, about 1¼ hours.

Skim off fat, add salt and pepper, then add all vegetables except potatoes, and bring to a boil. Add potatoes, and Worcestershire sauce and simmer another twenty minutes or until potatoes are tender, but not mushy.

Booyah! You're ready to eat.

Margo's Tip: Ladle individual servings in baggies, squeeze out air and freeze. Unthaw for a quick, healthy weeknight meal (only if made with rice, pasta doesn't freeze well).

Wednesday Meatloaf

Meatloaf

2 pounds ground beef
1 medium onion, finely chopped
2 eggs
3 tablespoons ketchup
2 tablespoons butter
⅓ cup green bell peppers
⅓ cup chopped celery
2 tablespoons minced garlic
¾ cup breadcrumbs or crushed saltine crackers
⅓ cup milk
½ teaspoon salt, less if using crackers
1 tablespoon seasoning salt
1 tablespoon Worcestershire sauce
¼ teaspoon ground black pepper
½ teaspoon paprika

Meatloaf Sauce

½ cup ketchup
½ cup barbeque sauce
2 tablespoons brown sugar
½ teaspoon onion powder
black pepper to taste

   Lightly grease a 9"x5" loaf pan and preheat oven to 350°F.
   Melt butter over medium heat, then sauté onions, celery and peppers until soft.
   Mix ground beef and seasoning salt.
   In a large bowl, mix the breadcrumbs and the milk. Add

eggs, sautéed vegetables and remaining ingredients into the breadcrumb mixture.

Gently mix the seasoned ground beef into the other ingredients until all the ingredients are well combined. You can mix by kneading with your hands or stirring by hand. Don't overmix or meatloaf will be dense and dry.

Form a loaf with the ground beef meat mixture. Spread 2 tablespoons of ketchup over top and place in a pre-greased loaf pan. Cover top with foil. Bake for 45 minutes. Make a small slice in the center to see if the meat is brown instead of pink.

While meatloaf is baking, stir barbeque sauce and ketchup together with brown sugar. Add onion powder and pepper to taste.

Spread the sauce over baked meatloaf, then return to oven and bake uncovered an additional 15–20 minutes. Let meatloaf rest at least 15 minutes before slicing.

Margo's Tip: For the sauce, add teaspoon of white vinegar for more tang, or teaspoon of hot sauce for more heat.

A Taste for More—Book Club Discussion Questions

1. How did you feel about the ending? How might you change it?

2. What do you think will happen next to the main characters?

3. During migrations such as the Great Migration of African-Americans from the south, or European immigrants to the United States in the late 19th and early 20th century, many individuals left children and other family members behind. Does economic opportunity outweigh potential feelings of abandonment?

4. Margo had three husbands. Was there a common thread in the demise of each marriage, or did she just have bad luck with men?

5. What is the role of food in the story?

6. Is the pursuit of wealth a sign of materialism and greed or ambition and diligence? What is motivating Margo? What is motivating Lana?

7. Were there times you disagreed with a character's actions? What would you have done differently?

8. Margo did not want Clark to discipline her daughter. How do you feel about stepparents and discipline?

9. Should Eva and George have told Margo what they knew about Lana? Why or why not?

10. How does the evolution of Fourth Street impact the story? What do you think Fourth Street would be like today?

Visit our website at
KensingtonBooks.com
to sign up for our newsletters, read
more from your favorite authors, see
books by series, view reading group
guides, and more!

Become a Part of Our
Between the Chapters Book Club
Community and Join the Conversation

Submit your book review for a chance to win exclusive
Between the Chapters swag you can't get anywhere else!
https://www.kensingtonbooks.com/pages/review/